"WHAT POSSESSED YOU TO DANCE WITH ME WITHOUT ASKING PERMISSION?"

Damara burst out. When he smiled, her new partner became too like the image that haunted her dreams.

"You know, Damara, I think you could use some fresh air," he said while maneuvering them through the French doors that opened onto the garden. His use of her first name was like his manner, presumptuous and far too familiar.

"Now I'll explain why I wanted to dance with you, sweet Damara." His mouth descended to hers, trapping her gasp of surprise.

For a moment an undefinable warmth began to spread through Damara's body. Her sanity returned, however, as his arms tightened around her.

"If you don't free me immediately, I'll be forced to scream for help." Her threat came out in a husky whisper. His lips were moving over the column of her neck.

"I'm afraid no one would think it unlikely that your fiancé wishes to make love to you. . . ."

Jove titles by Sarah Eagle

A REGENCY HOLIDAY
*(with Elizabeth Mansfield, Monette Cummings,
Judith Nelson and Martha Powers)*

THE RELUCTANT SUITOR

The Marriage Gamble

Sarah Eagle

JOVE BOOKS, NEW YORK

THE MARRIAGE GAMBLE

A Jove Book / published by arrangement with
the author

PRINTING HISTORY
Jove edition / February 1992

ISBN: 0-515-10750-6

Jove Books are published by The Berkley Publishing Group,
200 Madison Avenue, New York, New York 10016.
The name "JOVE" and the "J" logo
are trademarks belonging to Jove Publications, Inc.

PRINTED IN THE UNITED STATES OF AMERICA

10 9 8 7 6 5 4 3 2 1

To
Deborah "Sam" Perkins & Linda Varner Palmer
Now you have to read a Regency

— Prologue —

Spanish Peninsula, 1810

The incessant March rains were not noticed by the uniformed men assembled in the dilapidated barn that was a poor substitute for more substantial shelter. Their interest was centered on the pile of currency and vowels that had accumulated steadily during the past twenty-four hours. Only three players remained in the game, but the less fortunate stayed, watching the trio with rabid concentration to see who would be the final victor. The only movement was a mud-spattered boot absentmindedly nudging a clay pitcher to catch the drizzle of a new leak that sprang from amongst the numerous others riddling the roof.

"Sentry!" A strident voice at a distant post carried from the darkness beyond the gaping doorway. The anonymous cry seemed to snap the frozen tableau into renewed life as a sandy-haired Dragoon lieutenant, Albert Featherstone, threw his cards onto the makeshift table that had begun life as the stable door. A self-deprecating smile spread over his freckled face as he exclaimed, "I concede to our Colonial friend's confounded game."

"Featherstone, you nod-cock," called a voice from the back of the group, "you've lasted an entire day at this table. Concede indeed."

"Idiot is more like," another spectator put in disparagingly. "Tremonte is no Colonial. Barely been out of Hertfordshire before last year."

"Then where did he learn this cursed game?" returned the jovial lieutenant, ignoring the insult to his brain's limited capacity.

"M'father," answered the subject of the argument. The Right Honorable Captain Jasper Tarrant, Viscount of Tre-

1

monte raised his smiling emerald gaze from his cards and
ran a careless hand through his already tousled reddish-
brown hair. He tilted back precariously on the crate that he
had commandeered for a chair, his lazy smile matching the
negligent pose of his lean body as he absently surveyed the
assemblage. "The old bloke brought it back from Yorktown
in '81. Said he learned it from some Frog prisoners of war
that called it *Pogue*. 'Course m'sister and I embellished it a
bit with *Maman's* favorite game of *Bouillotte* to add some
excitement."

Still at his ease, his cards fanned against his outstretched
leg, Tremonte lolled his head to the left. His gaze came to
rest on his last, most persistent opponent—a massively
built, dark-haired major with the lacing of an artillery
officer on his blue uniform. "Well, Alton, are you more
determined than our young friend Featherstone?"

Simon Alton allowed a slight smile to grace his angular
face and narrowed his hazel eyes in speculation. He judged
Tremonte to be four and twenty, a mere year or two the
senior of Featherstone. From his own superior age of one
and thirty, both men seemed to be mere halflings. He was
beginning to weary of the endless game, however, as well
as his opponent's extremely genial manner. Weeks of
inactivity in the damp Portuguese winter were almost
making him long for the humid, overcrowded barracks of
his first duty in India.

"My friend," Simon declared in the deep voice used
when ordering his devoted troops, "unless you hold my
person of value, I too must concede."

For the first time Tremonte's green eyes lost their amused
twinkle. Those who knew him well would have shuddered
at the calculated gaze that now measured the large man next
to him. He shifted his weight slowly to bring his arms to rest
on the table before his grin reappeared, even wider than
before, displaying his even white teeth. He flipped his
remaining coins into the kitty. "I call, Major."

He then tossed off the remaining contents of the tin cup
at his elbow, the sour taste of the wine causing him to
grimace slightly as it passed down his dry throat. His
challenge had abruptly stopped the laughter that had erupted

at Alton's words. The silence lengthened as the two men laid down their cards.

"Well, what's the verdict?" queried an impatient spectator, unable to see the cards from the back of the crowd.

"Demmed if I know," said someone else from the opposite side. "Deveraux, who won?"

Lieutenant Henry Deveraux studied the two hands from his perch behind his friend Tremonte, then his delighted laughter rang out in the silence and set off the two adversaries. "Jasper, you sly dog!"

Featherstone could only groan as he stared at the up-turned cards. Tremonte had laid down a pair of tens while Alton had held two eights. "You were both bluffing," he managed finally, burying his face in his hands. "I'd have won with three fives." His horrified moan was met with more laughter as Tremonte gave him a hardy thump on the back.

"Major Alton, sir?" interrupted a guttural voice from out of the soggy darkness. "Gen'ral's compliments, sir, he requests ya attends him at onest."

"It seems, gentlemen, my guardian angel was not quite soon enough." Alton smiled slightly and shrugged his broad shoulders before he scribbled on a dirty scrap of paper which he handed to Tremonte. "Your most obedient servant, sir." He gave a slight bow to his victorious opponent, draped his cloak over his faded uniform, and turned without another word. The men parted automatically to allow his tall, commanding form to pass into the night.

"Jasper, old son, what has the rock-like major done?" Deveraux asked as he slid from his perch to take a seat on the barrel that Alton vacated. Tremonte stared down at the slip of paper with a bemused look on his face. Then he answered in a dazed tone, "He's signed his person over to me."

"T'ain't possible," snapped the same voice that had summoned Alton. All eyes turned to the stocky sergeant major standing in the doorway. "Beggin' yer pardons, sirs," the man murmured uncomfortably under their surprised stares, "but the major, he just becum a marquess. His uncle kicked off."

"Bundy, who was the major's uncle?" asked one of the

officers who recognized the ugly little man who was Alton's constant shadow.

"Marquess o' Emsley, sir," he grunted. Then he seemed to regret his lapse and came to attention, smartly saluting the assemblage before retreating into the drizzle.

"Who's Emsley?" asked an inquisitive Featherstone as the group began to disband now that the game had finally ended.

"Chauncey Fentner-Smythe's sire," someone called in response as the men drifted out of the barn to return to their own bivouacs.

"What became of good old Chauncey?" Tremonte asked abruptly as he came out of the the thoughtful trance that had been caused by Bundy's words, and raised his eyes from Alton's note.

"Stuck his spoon in the wall a few months back," returned an artillery officer who was leaving with the disheartened Featherstone. "Some brawl in the West Indies, I heard. So now the old man's dead, and our major is a marquess. Truly amazing."

With this the last of the men filtered out into the night, only Tremonte and Deveraux remaining near the makeshift gaming table.

"Jasper, what are you scheming in your evil brain?" Deveraux frowned at his friend's expression, the same one that had gotten them sent down from Cambridge during their first term. "You can't hold a fellow peer of the realm in bondage."

"Hal, I've come upon a brilliant idea!" Tremonte exclaimed, slapping his doubtful friend on the back. "Pass me that bottle of despicable wine, and we'll drink a toast to my sister Mara's early birthday present. She deserves a special reward for her troubles in handling the estate since Papa's death. What better gift than our stalwart marquess-major? She'll be a delightful marchioness."

The Honorable Lieutenant Henry Deveraux responded with a muttered expletive before dropping his head to his crossed arms on the table. He did not want to know any more of Jasper's idea; it would only lead to serious trouble for everyone concerned.

— Chapter One —

"Not to worry, Timmons, old friend. I'll announce myself," instructed the petite blonde, rushing past the frowning butler the moment he opened the door.

"Lady Damara is in the library, Miss Townsend."

His chilling tone stopped the hurried visitor's dainty feet in mid-step. She turned back to him swiftly, the flowing skirt of her green riding habit swirling around her ankles. While the gray-haired servant laboriously shut the massive oak door, Evelyn Townsend slowly unbuttoned the single row of brass buttons on her jacket. She continued to count off the passing seconds by tapping one small booted foot on the parquet floor until Timmons's stooped frame turned in her direction.

"So, my man, what has put us into disgrace? I've only just arrived—somewhat early even for country hours, I know—but why not the usual Miss Mara and Miss Evie?" Her sable eyebrows rose in question at the butler's disapproving face. "What *has* Lady Damara done?"

The elderly man looked down his generous nose at the young woman whose head came inches below his bowed shoulders. "Lady Damara is having breakfast in the library, now that the bailiff is gone."

"Oh, ho! Mara hasn't been behaving like the true lady of the manor again. She's not sitting and sewing a fine seam, but dirtying her dainty hands with estate matters."

The butler gave a disgruntled sigh, knowing it was useless trying to intimidate a young woman he had given piggy back rides during her nursery days. She also knew his impervious stare was due to faltering eyesight, rather than the fact that she had neglected to wear a hat. Sir Cedric's oldest daughter was diminutive in size, but she had the stubbornness of a Bodicea when it came to getting her own way.

"Give over, Timmie, what was the final straw? Was it the bailiff, the breakfast on a tray, or was the new footman whistling in the hallway again?" Evelyn asked with a winning grin that displayed an enticing pair of dimples she loathed; however, she never failed to employ them to her advantage.

"She is wearing a *cap*."

Evelyn strove to keep from laughing outright at the man's pained expression. Each new worry since the unexpected death of the sixth earl of Layston, Damara's father, gave the faithful Timmons more wrinkles and additional gray hairs. Now his mistress's self-declaration of spinsterhood at the age of two and twenty had him on the edge of a decline. Of course, the servant still felt guilty over witnessing the codicil to the earl's will that left the management of the estate in Damara's capable hands, while her older brother remained in the army until his twenty-fifth birthday to inherit everything that was rightfully his.

"You have only a few weeks until Jasper returns to set everything right," she said finally in commiseration, "and I have something in my pocket that will certainly take Mara's mind off her accounts. So go down to the kitchen and have Mrs. Breen make you a nice dish of tea while I deal with this wretched cap business."

The subject of the exchange in the entry hall was indeed sitting in the library, wearing a starched lace cap over her auburn hair, which accentuated her very drab, unfashionable—but serviceable—brown dress. Lady Damara Tarrant was frowning down her patrician nose at the household accounts, ignoring the breakfast tray at her elbow on the mahogany desk. Her mind was not on the price of new bed linens, however. She was counting the days until her brother Jasper returned.

For the hundredth time she wondered if Jasper's two years in the military had any effect on her brother's ramshackle personality. That had been their father's purpose in buying his heir a pair of colors. Long before the creation of the Layston title, the Tarrant family had always served their king, but Jasper, Viscount of Tremonte, and soon to assume the duties of the seventh Earl of Layston, managed to embroil himself in one scrape too many and had been sent to have the "nonsense" drilled out of him. The late earl had been shaped into manhood during the rebellion in the American colonies, then returned home to set up his nursery. Jasper was supposed to return to the bosom of his family as the epitome of the respectable son and heir, ready to set to work on insuring the continuation of the Tarrant name.

Reformed or not, she would be glad to have him home, Damara decided with an affectionate smile as she settled her tall, well-formed figure into her father's beloved oversized leather chair. Jasper would take over the estate, and she could return to running an efficient household as she had since the death of their mother eight years before. She would settle happily into a quiet life in the country with her brothers, Jasper and Percy.

Since she reached her majority in Jasper's absence, he could not—would not—insist that she face the horrors of London again to find a husband. It was not just the fact that her coltish, carrot-topped figure had not taken four years ago. She enjoyed the independence she had grown accustomed to in the last two years. Though she missed the companionship of another adult to share any problems, she was more than capable of taking care of herself and determining her fate. And there were no men of her acquaintance who would allow her the freedom of choice that she now had. When Jasper married, her own house and her own way of life would be all she needed.

"Lud, no wonder Timmons is in the glooms. That monstrosity on your head even offends my sensibilities." Evelyn's exclamation from the doorway broke into Damara's pleasant woolgathering.

She sat up and smiled at her friend's militant stance; a kitten in a fine temper. The petite blonde had both hands on her hips, and the expression on her face made her look as if she had caught a whiff of something distasteful. Even with her face scrunched up, Evelyn was still remarkably beautiful. Damara sighed in envy, knowing herself to be only passable, even with her features in repose.

She had thick, reddish-brown hair where Evelyn had saucy golden curls. Damara's complexion was tawny, and her friend's was peaches and cream. While Damara had a long, thin nose and prominent cheekbones, Evelyn had rosy cheeks and dimples. Even Damara's eyes were a nondescript green compared to Evelyn's shimmering blue. Most of all, Damara towered over her closest friend by a good half foot. It really had not taken her dismal season in London to show her that small-boned blondes with ringlets far outshone a red-haired beanpole such as herself.

"Not satisfied that you tower over me so no one sees me, you concoct this," Evelyn complained, crossing the distance to the desk. With a pointed look at her friend's starched adornment, she then dropped into the chair at the side of the desk and covered her eyes with her forearm. The actress Mrs. Siddons never tried for so much pathos as Evelyn arched her back and gave an exaggerated moan. "I'll not have it, you know. That beacon of spinsterhood will warn the neighborhood that *I* have not far to climb onto the old maid's shelf, especially if your addlepated brother doesn't come up to scratch."

"But it isn't *my* forlorn hope for a fiancé that needs discussing," Evelyn continued, sitting up and primly straightening the folds of her skirt. She reached into the side pocket once she was done and pulled out a newspaper, unfolding it to lay it flat on the desk with the print facing her friend. Planting her index finger firmly in the middle of the page, she gave Damara a quelling look. "We need to talk about *your* engagement, which you didn't see fit to tell me about before it was announced to all and sundry in the *Morning Gazette.*"

"My what?!" Damara's well-modulated alto voice squeaked as she gaped at Evelyn's pouting face.

When Damara did not move, the other woman picked up the newspaper with great ceremony and, in perfect imitation of Timmons announcing unwanted guests, read aloud: "The Earl of Layston happily announces the engagement of Lady Damara Tarrant to the fifth Marquess of Emsley—"

"Preposterous," Damara snapped, cutting off the rest of the amazing account. She grabbed the offending paper from her friend, glanced down at the page, and flung the entire newspaper across the room in a shower of newsprint. Springing to her feet, she began pacing the book-lined room. After a few minutes she stopped abruptly, pointing to the discarded paper and demanded, "Who the blazes is Emsley? I don't remember."

"Chauncey Fentner-Smythe's papa until a few months ago," Evelyn answered swiftly in a disgusted tone that was quickly mirrored by Damara's horrified expression.

"Fentner-Smythe! That same toad-faced lout who was responsible for Jasper being sent down from Cambridge?" Damara's voice was filled with loathing as she remembered another unpleasant incident involving the odious Chauncey, whom no one dignified by using his title. He was always Chauncey Fentner-Smythe, since even the title Mister gave him too much dignity.

"I see you're remembering that he abducted my cousin Sophie in one of his many bids to secure money that would support his numerous vices and appease his creditors," Evelyn commented, easily reading her friend's mind.

Damara resumed her pacing, continually muttering under her breath, aiming her pithy comments at the subject of their discussion. Some of her comments—picked up from Jasper and his friends—almost put Evelyn to the blush. "The thing to do is retract this . . . this *insult* immediately."

"That paper is over two weeks old, Mara. The whole town knows by now."

"Good gad. It not only knows, but has dissected it and created a tale totally to my disadvantage, no doubt." Damara was pale as she sank dejectedly into her chair. Memories of sneering dandies and whispering old biddies quickly filled her mind. She remembered endless evenings of standing alone while other young woman danced. Miss Amelia Pettiebone, the toast of the season with twelve proposals of marriage, kept giving her pitying looks.

"There is something strange about this," Evelyn began in a thoughtful voice as she attempted to divert Damara's bad memories of her season in London. For the thousandth time, she wished she had not caught her sister's measles—the worrisome spots had kept her at home while her friend suffered the worst misery of her life at the hands of society's finest. "I heard something important about Chauncey not so long ago. I wish I could remember what it was."

"Whatever it was, I wager it was not pleasant," her furious companion commented. "The first thing I shall do is write to Jasper to let him know he is needed at home as quickly as possible. Then I shall notify our solicitor in London. After that—"

She was not destined to continue her tirade as Timmons shuffled into the room. "Lady Damara, there is a person here who requests to see you. She claims that she's Lady Mathilde Lambert, the widow of your great-uncle, Sir John."

Although his face did not quiver a muscle, his voice clearly showed his disbelief in any such connection. Damara exchanged a puzzled look with Evelyn, who shrugged in confusion. "Please show her into the drawing room, Timmie, and offer her some refreshment."

"Do you know her?" Evelyn asked anxiously the second Timmons left with a disapproving sniff.

"If I remember correctly, she isn't a relation that Father was overly fond of." Damara gave a weary sigh. The morning had begun with such promise. She looked longingly out the multi-paned windows framed in crimson velvet that overlooked her *maman's* rose garden, resplendent in its first bloom. Less than a half hour had passed since she had contemplated a peaceful, bucolic life surrounded by those she loved best.

Now it was all shattered. A mysterious engagement to a nincompoop and a forgotten relation's sudden appearance on her doorstep deflated her daydreams in a fraction of an hour. What could she expect next? She was not sure if her nerves—and especially Timmon's—could stand any more surprises.

Evelyn's expectant cough brought Damara out of her brown study to finish her explanation. "Aunt Mathilde doesn't go out much into society anymore. In fact, I think she refused to sponsor me during my season—although I doubt if anything would have helped."

"Mara, if I hear you speak that way once more, I'll scream," Evelyn returned with vehemence, dismissing Damara's doddering aunt for the moment as she pursued a worn-out argument. "I'm taking you with me on my first trip to London, if I have to drag you there by the hair."

Damara did not rise to the bait as expected, still preoccupied with the morning's interruptions. Absently she waved a hand to signal that Evelyn should follow her to the drawing room. Stepping into the hallway, she noted in mild surprise that the hallway had not somehow been transformed into a carnival tent during the momentous morning. Such a change would be in keeping with the other events that had gone forward since she rose early that morning to the first sunshine the countryside had seen in weeks. She thought it promised a relief from the usual April rains, but instead it was an omen of too many strange happenings.

"I tell you, Damara Renee Tarrant, you will go to London with me at the next opportunity, kicking and screaming if need be!" Evelyn's musical voice, tinged with exasperation, brought Damara to an abrupt halt at the entry to the drawing room. She blinked down at her friend, trying to comprehend what had her in such a taking.

"Really, my gel." The high-pitched voice quickly caused both young women's startled gazes to focus on the peculiar spectacle seated among the delicate yellows and light blues of the late Countess of Layston's superbly decorated drawing room. "I do think, mayhap, that would be a bit drastic."

Neither Damara nor Evelyn moved. Primly seated on the edge of an oval-backed Robert Adam chair was a woman of indeterminate years dressed in the fashion of the last century. She was pitifully thin and pale, except for the bright patches of rouge on her cheeks. The garish red of her face paint was a glaring contrast to the bright purple of her dress and the alarming shade of the pink plumes attached to the broad brim of her frayed satin Gainsborough hat. Neither of the women standing on the threshold regarding this vision knew where to begin.

"Well, my gel, I see you have your mother's looks," the apparition screeched through the embarrassed silence. "No wonder you did not take."

"I beg your pardon?" Evelyn came out of her shock first, quickly coming to her friend's defense. She clutched at Damara's sleeve, dragging her into the room by the coarse material of her gown.

"No need to get huffy, young woman," the purplish wraith returned with a chuckle that sounded like a nail being dragged across a grate. "I meant no offense. 'Tis perfectly understandable that any reminder to the ninnies who lost out to Danielle De Bouvier in the stakes for Layston's heart would be scorned, especially if they had daughters of their own to push forward when her daughter came out. Although you're a bit of a giant, aren't you? Stand away from the blond pixie so I can inspect you properly."

Without hesitation, Damara complied with the woman's order, not sure whether to be amused or indignant. No one had ever spoken of her appearance in resemblance to her beautiful *maman*—except Papa—and she had always dismissed that as parental prejudice. This unbiased interpretation of her failure in London intrigued her, as did the bizarre lady before her.

And what the woman said was logical. Danielle de Bouvier had been sent to England by her foresighted father before the Terror in France began. Of good family, she had been given a season by her father's sister, who had married a minor English peer. One season was all that was needed for the titian-haired, vivacious Danielle to capture the heart of the bluff Sedgewick Tarrant, who quickly made her his countess.

"Hmmm, now that the two of you are apart, I see that you aren't quite so large," Mathilde mused as she inspected her great-niece from head to toe. "You have enough sense to dress plainly, which is a relief. I may be a pattern card of a Bedlamite, but no relative of mine is going to steal my eccentricities. Now then, what's this nonsense about an engagement to Emsley?"

"Is that why you're here?" Damara shot out, not caring if she sounded rude. She sat down rather inelegantly on the powder blue and pale yellow-striped baluster settee. "Then I'm afraid you've come on an empty errand. There is no engagement."

"At least, there won't be," murmured Evelyn, sitting demurely next to her friend and presenting a united front before Damara's martinetish aunt.

"No engagement? This becomes more interesting by the moment. First there's an unknown fiancé, and now no

engagement. Most interesting." Mathilde lapsed into silence, leaving her audience on the edge of their seats,
anticipating her next words. This was a trait of the lady's
which both her companions would become familiar with in
the future, although neither would claim it was her most
endearing habit. To add to their frustration, Timmons
shambled into the room, uncharacteristically bearing a tray
laden for morning tea. Clearly he still did not believe this
disreputable-looking woman could be related to his family
and was on his guard, not trusting the maid to keep a sharp
enough eye on the biddy.

"An unknown fiancé?" Evelyn asked as soon as the
disapproving servant left the room, probably to stand sentry
just outside the door. She could not stand the suspense any
longer while Damara busied herself with dispensing the
refreshments. "We are well acquainted with Chauncey
Fentner-Smythe, unfortunately."

"Not Chauncey. Young fool finally got himself killed in
the West Indies, just a month or so after his father kicked
off, not before time either," Mathilde replied absently,
eyeing the cup and saucer her niece offered her, waiting for
the young woman to add a more liberal portion of milk, then
place three cakes instead of one on her plate. A cat stalking
a hapless canary would look practically inanimate compared
to the avid stare the gaunt woman was giving her serving.

"That is what I was trying to remember. Chauncey is
dead!" Evelyn exclaimed in triumph. She smiled happily at
the news and took a sip of tea flavored with lemon. "Sophie
wrote a few months ago that she had heard he had finally
come to a bad end."

"So, you are a Townsend, are you?" Mathilde's words
were muffled around another generous bite of lemon sponge
cake. "Knew your grandfather years ago. Dear Waldo."

Damara set down the primrose-patterned tea pot with a
decided thump, almost overturning the tray and sending the
remaining crockery rattling. She was fast losing patience
with her newly arrived guest. "If Chauncey is dead, then
who is this unknown fiancé? I wasn't aware of any
engagement until an hour past. I assumed it was another of
Chauncey's cork-brained schemes to pay off his mountain
of bad debts."

"Not exactly unknown." Her aunt stopped to sip her dish of tea noisily as the two waited for her to continue. "The present marquess inherited through his mother, a younger sister of old Emsley. The solicitors have been looking for him for some weeks with little success, since he is a military man and posted in some forsaken part of Portugal. Now this notice appears in the *Gazette*. You have dashed my hopes of a coup over those old harpies of the *ton*."

"You couldn't have come here only to be ahead of the gossips?" Damara asked, surprised that the woman would travel from Northumberland across country to Hertfordshire over such an insignificant matter.

"No, I came to put a stop to this mésalliance," snapped the woman as she licked her fingers to capture the last of her repast, showing her temper for the first time. "I knew that the idiot son was dead, but the Emsley clan have always been a bit loose, a very bad connection. We can soon put things to rights, however, once we reach London."

"London?" Damara and Evelyn said at the same time, finding this piece of news a shock. Neither was prepared for Mathilde's calm pronouncement about a two-day journey that sounded as if she were referring to a brisk walk around the parkland.

"Yes, we have a lot to do before we leave tomorrow," the high-pitched voice droned on as if there had been no interruption. "Naturally, young Townsend, you'll accompany us. I have lost contact with too many valuable connections, even though some of the old witches still correspond with the latest gossip. Before we go anywhere, my young niece, you'll burn that offensive cap of yours. Now that we have that settled, have that old reprobate Timmons show me to my room." With that brusque order, she rose to her feet with a noticeable creaking of brittle bones. Timmons appeared in the doorway without a summons before she was upright and ushered her from the room.

Once the old woman was out of earshot, both young ladies broke into nervous laughter that had been repressed in her presence, helplessly clinging to each other until tears formed in their eyes. Evelyn was the first to regain her composure and spoke weakly while wiping her streaming eyes. "Have you ever seen anything so unbelievable in your life?"

Damara dabbed at her watery eyes with her sleeve as her face became serious. "She is certainly an original, but that woman meant every word she said. Though she is only related by marriage, when it comes to protecting the family name, she won't rest. I recall Papa claiming she attended his wedding in mourning because he was marrying a foreigner and was tainting the family bloodline. *That* was why she refused to sponsor me, because she disapproved of *Maman.*"

"I suppose I had best send a letter by messenger to Mama telling her we shall be in town shortly," Evelyn commented, casually studying her fingernails as she anticipated her friend's explosive response to the suggestion.

But much of her surprise Damara agreed with a resigned sigh. "It would be best if we didn't arrive unannounced. How convenient that your family took Layston Place for Justine's first season, or we would be putting up at a hotel if some strangers were renting the house. I didn't anticipate imposing on your parents' hospitality when we made the arrangements."

"Imposing? You know very well that Mama tried to twist your arm into going with them," Evelyn challenged. "I was planning to leave soon myself for Justine's coming out—"

"Not before the anticipated arrival of a certain relative of mine, I am sure, which has delayed your trip this long," Damara teased gently, watching the color rise in her friend's usually self-possessed face.

"As if Jasper would notice whether or not I was here when he arrived," the embarrassed young lady protested, refusing to look up from the suddenly interesting pattern of blues and whites in the carpet.

"He writes to you more than he does to me," Damara responded cheerfully, glad to have the conversation on a subject other than herself. The long-standing match between Evelyn and her brother was just the diversion she needed after such an unsettling morning.

"Oh, yes, such touching missives. 'Dear, Evie'—followed by a discourse on the weather—'greetings to Lady Kath and Sir Cedric as well as all the little Townies,' then closing with, 'Regards, Jasper.' Very encouraging, I'm sure. You, *my gel*, should concern yourself more with the imminent destruction of that abominable cap, and any more like it."

The resounding bang of the front door and a halted step across the hall to the accompaniment of Cretin's woofled greeting immediately diverted Damara's attention from the demise of her caps. Her younger brother Percy was home from his catechism at the vicarage. What was she going to say to him about this morning's topsy-turvy events? He had become such a difficult child to read since his injury in the same accident that had killed their father. In place of a happy, rosy-cheeked boy, there was a morose adolescent with little interest in anything.

Although the doctor could detect nothing physically wrong with Percy, the boy still limped heavily, favoring his right leg. She could only hope Jasper's return and a little male influence would help Percy snap out of his ennui. He really should be away at school like other young lads of twelve, but she did not have the heart to send him. This sudden trip to London would be even more unsettling for Percy after all the upheaval in their lives.

"Oh, hello, Evie," chirruped Percy in the unreliable voice that had been constantly fluctuating for the past six months. He grimaced in reflex to the sound, then consoled himself by snatching up two lemon cakes and a handful of macaroons. Munching contentedly, he slouched in the chair Mathilde had vacated, feeding crumbs to the curly-haired hound that had followed him into the room. "Mara, who came in the post chaise? When I left the pony cart at the stables, it was all old Ned could talk about."

"Papa's Aunt Mathilde Lambert has come on a legal matter," Damara began cautiously, wishing that after some twenty-odd years the stable master would learn not to gossip with children. "We have to go to London about some family business."

"I see," Percy observed without any show of emotion on his thin face. He did not seem the least put out by the turn of events that would uproot the family. When Cretin had polished off the last macaroon, Percy slid out of his chair and silently headed for the door. He turned back to face his sister when he reached the threshold. "You be careful in the city, Mara. Though I can't say what Jasper will think when he returns with only me to greet him."

He tossed back an errant lock of sandy brown hair that fell over his high forehead and walked with his hesitant step into the hall. From habit the others knew he and Cretin would find a secluded seat in the garden where Percy would read, his faithful oversized mutt at his side.

"Oh, dear." Damara gave Evelyn an imploring look. Since the other woman had siblings of various shapes and sizes in her own family, surely she would have some sage advice that would help Damara tactfully let Percy know he would accompany the three women to London. The prospect of traveling with her great-aunt in a closed coach made her wish she could stay behind in the serenity of her own home.

"You need a restorative after such an amazing morning," Evelyn stated brightly, giving her friend's hand a comforting squeeze. "You run upstairs and change into your habit. A good gallop should blow all the cobwebs away. With a clear head you can deal with your tartar aunt, Percy's sulks, and anything else that crops up."

Evelyn was more than satisfied to see the tiny furrows of worry disappear from her companion's brow before Damara rose and went to change. Evelyn's cheerfulness in suggesting the ride had not been forced. The prospect of actually getting Damara to London was terribly exciting. Mara was a strikingly attractive young lady who was totally unaware of her allure, discounting any compliments from her friends, though kindly meant, as Spanish coin. But once they were in town Evelyn was sure Damara would see that her silly fears of the *ton* were groundless.

Evelyn thought Damara's memories of her failure as a coltish girl of eighteen had been magnified out of proportion. Mature now at the height of her looks, Damara would be a sensation with just a little town bronze. No matter what happened with this mysterious fiancé, there were any number of gentlemen waiting to claim the auburn-haired beauty's hand.

Evelyn jumped up, clapping her hands. Dancing a little jig, she skipped out of the room to request the horses be brought round. Not even Timmon's disapproving look could daunt her spirits. She and Damara were going to London!

Simon Hilliard Alton, newly elevated Marquess of Emsley and late of His Majesty's army, could have used some of Evelyn's cheerful spirits as he surveyed his new domain. His black Arabian shifted its legs under the weight of his rider while Simon's hazel eyes dispassionately studied the crumbling Tudor manor house perched at the top of the rise. This was his mother's childhood home; a home that had once been stately and well kept. He could remember the stories she used to tell of hunting parties and important visitors coming to the house during her early life.

"Well, Bundy, are you reconsidering your decision to come back with me?" Simon asked the stout little man seated precariously on a nondescript hack that they acquired on their arrival in England. Once the news of his cousin's and uncle's deaths had reached them in Portugal, Bundy insisted his major could not take such a momentous step without him.

"It do seem a honenerous task, sir, honenerous," wheezed the little man with a sage nod as he murdered the King's English. The major was just the man for the job, too, by his way of thinking. The man was the devil for hard work and as fearless as they came.

"Ah, Manfred Bundy, one of these days my halo is going to slip, and you'll see before you a mortal man." Simon chuckled and looked down into the faded blue eyes that watched him worshipfully from a perfectly round, wrinkled face. "It will be a *honenerous* task indeed. The house looks as if it hasn't been touched since the day my grandfather died. Uncle Eustace and Cousin Chauncey tended to invest their monies in wine, cards, and women."

"Yessir, there be much talk in the camp 'bout what a loose fish yer cousin were, if ya doan mind me sayin' so."

"Not at all. I only met the creature once when I was still a child, and he was a twit then," Simon remarked without rancor. Once his mother left her home to marry Hilliard Alton, she had only returned to visit her father. After his death she had been content to sever all ties with her wastrel brother and his equally repellant offspring. "Now that we are here, I suppose we should take a closer look and make ourselves known to whoever is here."

"Do ya think these folks'd know about yer affanced?" Bundy's gravelly voice was shaky due to the sudden motion of his horse. He was much more comfortable riding a wagon or a caisson, but he would ride a goat if it was for the major.

"Let us hope someone knows of my fiancée. Just a few weeks ago I was a simple soldier, then I suddenly became a peer of the realm, own a broken down house, and am engaged to a woman I have never heard of, much less laid eyes on," his lordship complained without his usual good humor.

Was money the reason his name was coupled with this unknown woman? One thing he possessed both as a soldier and as a peer was money. He had more than enough funds to repair the damage caused by his relatives' neglect.

The announcement appeared in the papers only three days after he returned to England, but he had other business to attend to before tracking down his impoverished intended. Nothing could be surer than the woman was from a family similar to his own late relatives—a title with no money. A newly inherited peerage was most likely a very attractive lure to an out-of-pocket peer with an anecdote of a daughter to get rid of.

Simon was not an overly modest man. He knew he was passably attractive to the gentler sex. From the Altons he had inherited great height and his wide shoulders, along with a square jaw and straight brows. His mother's family had given him his black-brown hair, hazel eyes, and an aquiline nose as well as the only feature he despaired of—especially as a child—his mouth. Its delicately defined outline was at odds with his otherwise rugged visage. Once he began to attain his towering height and his shoulders filled out, however, there were not as many of his fellow students who chose to tease him.

A few years later Simon discovered that young females were fascinated by what he had thought a detracting feature. He wondered how his desperate fiancée would look upon his person as he dismounted and approached his new home.

His betrothed probably would not care if he was scarred and ugly, as long as his pockets were filled with the ready.

All thoughts of the undoubtedly pinch-faced woman with a squint were forgotten with the appearance of a gaunt, sloped-shouldered figure in the opening of the paneled front door. His fiancée would have to wait a few more days for her comeuppance. First he would discover how much damage his uncle and cousin had done by their debauchery. Once he knew the extent of his task at Emsley Hall, he could return to London and end his entanglement with the conniving Laystons.

"Evie, you're a genius," exclaimed Damara as they slowed their mounts to a mild trot. She grinned at her companion's flushed face and tousled curls, knowing she was in similar dishabille from their hour's ride. "A ride was exactly what I needed. I haven't been out for pure enjoyment in weeks. There's either a field to check or a cottage needing repairs."

"Now you're ready to take on the patronesses of Almack's, I am sure," Evelyn returned with a giggle, wishing a suitable gentleman was there at the moment. Damara was relaxed, her emerald green eyes flashing, and the soft wisps of her auburn hair gleaming with fire beneath the sun's rays. "Your dragon of an aunt and Percy's sulks should be child's play."

"Saint George couldn't have felt as confident meeting his wily opponent." Damara's cheerful reply dwindled off slightly as she spotted a thin funnel of smoke rising to the west of the house near the stables. Without another word she urged her trusted sorrel mare into a canter.

The second she arrived in the stable yard Damara regretted her bravado of a few minutes earlier. A small bonfire was burning in the center of the yard with Mathilde standing next to the abundant blaze, watching the glowing pyre with her hands on her hips and a satisfied smile on her thin lips. She totally ignored Percy, who was standing next to her clutching something in his hand. His piercing shouts rose above Cretin's excited barking as the hound bounded around them, announcing his disapproval as well.

At the sight of his sister's approach, the boy broke off his tirade and hobbled toward Damara. "Mara, where have you been? This woman should be put in Bedlam."

"Percy, settle down and remember we must respect our elders," she chastened him mildly as Ned helped her dismount. She ignored the strange choking sounds coming from Evelyn while she tried to calm her brother.

"But, Mara, you must *do* something—"

"Percy, please calm down and tell me precisely what—" She stopped abruptly as her gaze lighted on the scrap of scarlet and purple in his hand. She snatched the material away from him for closer inspection. The only garment she had seen with that revolting combination was an old robe of Jasper's that she had found extremely comfortable when he had outgrown the garish garment.

A niggling suspicion began to take root, and she turned toward Evelyn, who was trying to muffle the sounds of her laughter so strenuously that there were tears in her eyes, her face beet red. Damara's suspicious became a full-fledged conviction; she knew exactly what her odious aunt was doing.

"By heavens, the old witch is not only burning my caps—*she's burning my clothes as well!*"

— Chapter Two —

"Here, my good man, we'll take this table," Lady Mathilde announced to the sputtering innkeeper, showing little regard for the gentleman already seated in the same spot. "We'll need a screen, of course, since your private parlor was damaged by the fire those persons started while celebrating such a dubious event as a prize fight."

"Yes, m'lady, if the gentleman be willing ta accommodate yer request," the rotund man answered hesitantly, casting a pleading look at the gentleman relaxing at the table near the fire. He was fashionably dressed in a coat of bottle green, buff pantaloons, and highly polished military long boots. The innkeeper had spotted him for Quality when he arrived, but was surprised when the Corinthian—as he dubbed him—simply gave a quiet request for a room and dinner.

"A gentleman is always willing to accommodate a lady."

Damara flinched at her aunt's high-pitched command and was ready to state that another table would be fine, when the gentleman rose to his feet with surprising grace for a man his size. She had to look up to see his smiling face. Somehow ignoring the presence of Mathilde altogether, he bowed to Damara and Evelyn.

"If the ladies would be so kind as to use this table, I'll move to the next," he instructed the harried innkeeper. "It is no problem, especially after your trouble the other day. You were fortunate not to lose your entire establishment to the fire."

With another bow, he stepped aside to allow the poor publican to seat the ladies. Damara gave him a grateful smile before slipping into her chair, the same one he had so graciously vacated. In a matter of minutes, Mathilde's screen was in place; however, by chance Damara noticed it did not block out the sight of the dark-haired gentleman, who now sat facing her at his new table, directly in her line of vision. She did not bother to alert either of her companions to this oversight as Mathilde droned on about the travails of travel on the open road.

Damara's head was already pounding from a day's travel confined in a coach with the woman. She closed her eyes and counted to ten very slowly, knowing as soon as her aunt finished this diatribe, she would renew their argument of the afternoon. Once again she considered a very expedient way to end the disagreement that had originally begun last night at dinner. If she was hauled away to Newgate Prison and charged with murder—no matter how justified—she would neither have to concern herself with her aunt's opinions nor her false engagement ever again.

At least she reached an agreement with her brother, something totally foreign to Lady Mathilde. Percy was contentedly at home under the watchful eye of his tutor, Mr. Ambruster, who agreed to stay at the manor house, and Timmons was keeping an eye on everyone else.

Damara envied the boy his peace and quiet at Tarrant's Mount. He had avoided being cooped up with their harping aunt and Evelyn's maid, who developed motion sickness on her first trip away from home. Damara wished she could be doused with laudanum and tucked into a trundle bed above stairs like the ailing Meg, instead of being barricaded behind a rickety screen in the public room, eating stringy beef.

If Evie mentioned how fortunate it was they remembered to pack clean linens one more time, Damara would scream. They had plenty of room for linens because she had very few clothes to pack that escaped Mathilde's greedy fingers and had not gone up in smoke.

"Damara, are you listening to me?"

The sharp demand broke into her thoughts, and she reluctantly opened her eyes. Fleetingly she glanced at the gentleman at the next table, surprised to find him watching her intently. Embarrassed by his dark regard, she turned her eyes to her aunt's pinched face.

"I repeat, my gel, you can't deny this engagement until

we have contacted this Wilkins person who represents you, and he has completely investigated the matter."

"Aunt Mathilde, this is not the place to discuss—"

"Until then, you'll remain engaged to Emsley," Mathilde finished as if her niece had not spoken. She was totally unconcerned that her voice carried to others in the room, including the dark-haired gentleman who was not disguising the fact he was eavesdropping.

"I still don't see the need to undertake this trip. I was perfectly content to remain at Tarrant's Mount," Damara stated with determination while her aunt was occupied with sipping her wine. Her latent Tarrant temper that was slow to kindle was beginning to smolder; she had been far too docile in letting her aunt have her head. "Mr. Wilkins could take care of retracting the announcement, just as he has handled all our legal matters."

"I'm afraid I have to agree with Mara," Evelyn added with seeming reluctance after delicately hiding a yawn. "How can we face the rigors of the season if Mara can't even identify her fiancé and does not know who is responsible for the announcement? That will give rise to more open speculation than a few discreet inquiries by Mr. Wilkins."

"I don't care if I can't identify Emsley. In fact, I don't much care who he is. I refuse to acknowledge any connection with him," Damara asserted, raising her voice in anger. She had not considered the possibility of facing the taunting faces of the *ton* until that moment. All she wanted was to retract the announcement and return home, not have to primp and preen for countless snobbish strangers.

"Damara, we'll discuss this again when we reach town," Mathilde stated, blithely ignoring any opposition. She stood up majestically, cutting short any further rebuttal. "I suggest we retire now so we will be well rested for the completion of our journey."

Both her companions exchanged agonizing looks, but demurred from further disagreement. Any continued argument would soon escalate to a scene within minutes, and the public room had been steadily filling with other patrons while they ate. Tomorrow, Damara determined, she would regain control of her life for the first time in two days. She rose to follow the others, but hesitated slightly on the threshold to look back over her shoulder at the dark-haired gentleman.

He was leaning back in his chair, watching her every move with his long legs stretched out in front of him. A smile creased his rugged features at her startled expression. He reached for his tankard and raised it in a silent salute. The action released Damara from her frozen stance. She lifted her skirt—unmindful of displaying her ankles in her haste to join her companions—angry that her impulsive action had brought on such a response. The man had no manners after all, or thought his earlier kindness granted him all sorts of liberties from eavesdropping to blatant impertinence. When Damara reached the safety of the other ladies' company, her cheeks were still burning in a mixture of anger and humiliation at being caught behaving like a schoolroom miss.

Troubled by her thoughts, she remained silent when Evelyn gave her an inquiring look. For some unknown reason, Damara had suddenly wondered what Emsley looked like. Was he fair or dark-haired with laughing eyes? Ruthlessly she schooled her wandering thoughts since the man's appearance was of little importance. She was making this journey for one purpose, and that was to retract the engagement announcement. That goal would be easily accomplished without ever meeting the man.

"So, that is my fiancée," Simon murmured, and raised his hand to signal for another round while he considered what he had overheard.

He had been mildly amused when the old scarecrow ordered him from his table, noting how extremely attractive her companions were, especially the tall, auburn-haired lady with the sweet smile. The mention of her name followed closely by his own quickly diverted him from his calculations of refurbishing Emsley Hall.

His first impulse—prompted by his sometimes irreverent sense of humor—had been to step behind the screen to introduce himself before sweeping the loving jade into his arms to complete the farce. Only his mother's gentle schooling in good manners kept him quietly in his seat, although he did blatantly eavesdrop.

He blessed his dear mother's memory when the import of the ladies' heated discussion sank into his tired brain. In addition, he thanked the fates that were responsible for the fact Lady Damara and he broke their journeys to London at the same inn. Now that he had seen his fiancée, he wondered who his benefactor could be in presenting him such a comely betrothed. Or was it a benefactress?

He could not dismiss his first suspicions. As soon as the ladies were seated, the mail coach arrived loaded with hungry travelers. The noise of the other diners frustrated his effort to follow the argument at the next table. What seemed apparent was that the old woman was in charge, but Lady Damara was not pleased with her lot.

He could not deny the lady appeared to be tailor-made for him, not much past marriageable age and more than agreeable to the eyes with a slight touch of temper. He had never cared for the simpering, milksop types he met during his brief visits with his old school friend, Bramwell Dempster. If he were marriage-minded, the prospect of this engagement would be more appealing by the minute—if he felt he could trust his betrothed not to steal him blind to replenish her family's dwindling coffers.

The moment he reached London tomorrow, he would visit the offices of Messrs. Palmer and Perkins to set in motion the needed finances for the repairs to Emsley Hall. Under the guise of needing new servants for the London house, he would call on his godmother, Lady Regina Dempster, Countess of Covering. Aunt Gina would be a font of information about the Layston family, since she would do anything to see either her son Bram or Simon happily shackled with a wife.

No longer overset by the monumental task of practically gutting the inside of his new home to make it habitable, Simon retired for the evening. As he lay in bed hoping the rumbling snores from Bundy on his pallet at the foot of the bed would abate, Simon found himself recalling the look of innocent distress on Lady Damara's face when she left the public room. Was she an unwilling pawn in the marriage stakes or a very convincing actress? He smiled to himself in anticipation of solving the puzzle of his auburn-haired fiancée.

Damara never thought she would be so glad to see the columned facade of Layston Place as when the carriage finally pulled into Cavendish Square the next afternoon. Four years previously she had pledged never to return. Almost two days imprisoned with Mathilde—and poor, suffering Meg—made even the infamous Black Hole of Calcutta seem a haven.

Kathleen Townsend—never one to stand on ceremony—practically flew down the steps to greet them the moment the carriage stopped. She lovingly enfolded her oldest daughter and Damara in her plump arms, patently ignoring her butler's disapproval as she personally ushered her guests into the house from the curb.

"Mara dear, I feel so foolish welcoming you to your own house," she trilled once everyone was settled in the comfort of the gilded Egyptian sitting room. Meg had been turned over to the kindly ministrations of Mrs. Kasey, the housekeeper, and refreshments ordered. "We've been so excited since Evie's message arrived yesterday."

"Aunt Kath, that's nonsense. We agreed I would be treated as a guest as long as you rented this tomb." Damara smiled with genuine affection. Kath Townsend was a constant worrier, but only over trivial matters. With six children, she managed not to be overly concerned with scraped knees or bloodied noses. Instead she fretted over whether the Michaels sisters would have better roses than hers at the annual fete, or if Sir Cedric—who adored all his children—really minded not having a son.

"I think we can compromise and say honorary daughter rather than guest," Evelyn teased, trying to break through her friend's dignified pose. "Mama, what can you tell us about the new marquess of Emsley?"

"Well, you aren't alone in the mystery of his identity," the lady began, perched on the edge of her seat. Here was something she could really worry about, even though there was absolutely nothing she could do. "The only person who can claim any knowledge of him is Regina Dempster. Seems he is her godson, and he attended Winchester with her son Bramwell. Unfortunately, Bram is at sea on active duty, and Regina has not seen Simon Alton since his last leave over a year ago."

"Well, at least now we have a name, even if we don't have a face," remarked Evelyn, noting with interest Damara's sudden flush.

"If you'll excuse me, I think I'll go to my room and pen a letter to Mr. Wilkins," Damara said without meeting Evelyn's curious look. She could not admit her friend's words had conjured up the face of their dark-haired stranger at the inn. The same face that had disturbed her dreams during the night.

"Yes, my gel, you must order him to attend us first thing in the morning," Mathilde commanded to her niece's retreating figure. Then her thoughts were quickly diverted by Mrs. Kasey wheeling in the tea cart.

At an address not too far distant in Hanover Square, another conversation concerning the unforeseen engagement was taking place.

"My dear boy, much as I'm pleased to see you, I'm somewhat disquieted by this turn of events," exclaimed Regina Dempster, Countess of Covering, as she performed the service of pouring her godson a glass of wine with her own hand.

"If you're disquieted, you have no idea what I felt," the gentleman replied with quiet reserve as he accepted the glass from her. He wondered how long the lovely brunette's pretense of exemplary manners would last. She had an unbridled curiosity but refused to ask directly about anything she wanted to know. The more she desired the knowledge, the more she avoided the point. While others fell under her charm and immediately divulged every last ounce of information, there were three who refused to give in—her husband, her son, and her godson.

"Just so, m'lord," the lady answered, clearly torn between exasperation at Emsley's ability to ignore her gambit and amusement at addressing him as a peer. She then gave a huge sigh, signaling her defeat. "You truly have no idea who put the notice in the papers, or know Lady Damara?"

"I had never met the lady until last night," Simon stated,

trying unsuccessfully to repress his triumphant grin. He was not ready to quit his teasing altogether as he stretched his long legs in front of him, inspecting the high gloss of his tasseled Hessians. Nor was he going to divulge all his suspicions to the lady as yet. She would be much more willing to cooperate if she thought she was encouraging a budding romance.

"What? To my knowledge the girl hasn't been in town since her first and only season some four years back. If I remember correctly, she was overly tall and thin, and had the most extraordinary hair." Lady Regina's heart-shaped face was marred by a tiny frown as she tried to recall the details of the less than auspicious event before she realized the full import of Emsley's remark. "Simon, you haven't confronted her already? No, no, you only just arrived in town."

"No, I was simply an impertinent fellow traveler at the Scarlet Lion, overhearing parts of an enlightening conversation. My lady love isn't overly enchanted with the engagement and is set on contacting her solicitor to track me down," Simon explained before pausing to sip his wine. "I must say, it put to rest my theory that Layston had a repulsive daughter he was trying to palm off on an unsuspecting but well-heeled suitor. The lady didn't seem any more informed than I."

"Preposterous. As far as I know, the Layston fortune is as solid as the Bank of England, and the girl was passable even if she did not take. There was something I should remember about the family, but it escapes me for the moment."

"If neither of you knows about the announcement, who is responsible for this comedy of errors?" For a moment she considered the question, giving the gentleman slouching comfortably across from her a speculative look. His expression was much too complacent. "You realize the announcement of this engagement has even taken away the interest in the state of the king's health for the last fortnight. This new puzzle will set everyone on their ears."

"Not is no one knows anything is amiss."

His quietly spoken words caused the lady—renowned for her excellent address—to stare opened-mouthed like a half-wit. "No one will know? You aren't seriously contemplating honoring this fabrication?"

"I confess my immediate reaction was to storm the portals of Layston's home and demand a retraction, but I have reconsidered since then," Simon responded with a smug smile, remembering the tall, nicely curved lady with thick auburn hair. The vision helped him present a suitable expression. If he knew his godmother, she would assume the obvious—that he was infatuated with the lady—and not realize he was playing a waiting game to plan his strategy.

"I'll wager your change of mind occurred within the last twenty-four hours," Regina stated with a knowing look as he had hoped, "and that the lady has changed in appearance over the last four years."

"A most definite change, albeit she is still tall," he explained with care as he measured against his six foot, four-inch frame, encouraging Lady Regina's misconception. "She reaches just below my chin and has filled out very nicely. I think the term Junoesque would be the most apt to describe her figure in polite society."

"Quite a handful," Regina interrupted rather indelicately with an appreciative chuckle, but she had the grace to blush as Simon raised an eyebrow.

"Aunt Gina, I'm shocked. I'm also thankful Bram isn't here to listen to this disgraceful display." He grinned as he teased the unrepentant lady. "I wouldn't call her hair extraordinary. I find auburn rather a relief among the nondescript brunettes and insipid blondes that Bram always complains about."

"Were you able to catch the color of her eyes during this inspection, or count her teeth?" Regina was delighted with the fatuous expression on Simon's face as he listed the young woman's attributes. He displayed the signs of a man on the verge of bowing to the inevitable, though she was not sure he was aware of it.

"You give me too much credit, ma'am. The light was poor." Simon tried to control his features after meeting the lady's triumphantly amused eyes. The delight shining on her face assured him he was grinning like a moonstruck idiot rather than a controlled, mature gentleman of over thirty—just what he planned to achieve. He did feel a twinge of guilt at not fully confiding in one of his dearest friends, but he wanted to know more of the situation before he set his plans before her, so he continued. "I did find her nose to be rather delightful. Yes, I must set to work on the eyes. That was rather remiss of me."

Regina could not continue to restrain herself and burst into laughter. "Is this the same Simon who Bram refers to as the Iron Heart? I can hardly wait to meet this Incomparable."

"Well, my dear lady, I can see no need to retract as yet, but you'll have to wait to make her acquaintance. I'm not quite ready to make my bows in public."

"Oh, really?" She positively beamed at the prospect of more intrigue. Secrets were her favorite pastime, and she had been grilled rather thoroughly already about her knowledge of Emsley, with little success. She only gave out tantalizing tidbits of information.

"I prefer to remain incognito for the time being while you take on the task of gathering a battalion of servants to make that mausoleum fit for the living." All amusement left his face as Simon sat forward, his hazel eyes intent on his godmother's face. "Bundy and I have taken rooms at the Albany, rather than take up residence at Emsley House. If you need to communicate with me, leave a message at the offices of Palmer and Perkins. I give you carte blanche on readying the house."

"I should think your continued absence will make things rather difficult for Lady Damara," she returned in some confusion, totally ignoring the less exciting task of interviewing servants.

"Somewhat, but from what I could hear last night, I have an unexpected ally in her dragon of an aunt, and the engagement won't be renounced before I am ready."

"You'll not find favor with either lady if you delay too long."

"Since sweet Damara can find no fault with me as an unknown, then I don't think there's too much cause of concern. I only plan a week's respite." Simon rose to his feet, signaling he was ready to depart now that his business was settled. He did not want Lady Regina to place too much importance on his next request, so she would think it was an afterthought as he took his leave.

"Then I'll still maintain I haven't seen you in over a year," Regina agreed in a show of reluctance. She would be the pivotal guest at any gathering until Emsley made his official entrance into fashionable society. "And I wish you good fortune if the lady is all you say."

Simon nodded in agreement, knowing his godmother would be on pins and needles until she made her round of calls the next morning to be pestered by questions. "Now remember, not a word. Oh, you might do a little questioning of your own about the formidable aunt and the charming companion who were with Damara, since there weren't any gentlemen escorting them on their journey."

The new marquess was pleased with himself when he left his godmother's house and rode back to his rooms. Life was very good of late, not boring or uninteresting as he had anticipated when selling out. The transformation from soldier to peer was going very smoothly, and he was adapting to his new life very well. Once he settled this little problem of his engagement, he could retire comfortably to the country and enjoy his good fortune. The thought gave him pause as he entered his rooms, wondering why the prospect was not as pleasant as it should be.

The following morning the gathering at Layston Place was not as amicable. Mr. Wilkins found himself placed between two very determined ladies from the moment he was ushered into the study in the midst of a heated discussion, not giving him time to appreciate the rich luster of the bookshelves that were sure to house an impressive collection of literary treasures.

He stood hesitantly behind the imposing figure of the butler, Hasting, peering over his rounded spectacles at the occupants of the room. A rather bizarre old woman clad in a bilious shade of purple scowled across the room at her adversary, who was seated behind an ornately carved desk. This young lady was flushed with emotion, her chin stuck determinedly forward, and remarkably pretty in her anger. Another young woman sat quietly next to the desk, seemingly unconcerned with the ill humor of her companions. Her eyes seemed to twinkle with amusement as she smiled at the bewildered solicitor in welcome.

Once the introductions were complete, Mr. Wilkins determined he would impart his information and make a hasty departure. The late earl had been a bluff, hard-headed individual, but in comparison to these ladies his troubles with the man seemed minimal. Unconsciously Wilkins smoothed back the few remaining hairs at the top of his head as Lady Mathilde regarded him with an icy glare. He cleared his throat against a neck cloth that seemed uncommonly tight.

"I have contacted Messrs. Palmer and Perkins, who are the legal representative for His Lordship," he began uneasily, barely controlling a start of surprise at the old biddy's snort when he mentioned the marquess. "They assure me they would notify me the moment they meet with their client."

"Has there been no word from Emsley?" Damara rushed into speech. Out of the corner of her eye she could see Mathilde filling her lungs to begin her own harangue. How a woman with such a frail frame could have so much lung power, she had no idea.

"No, Lady Damara," Wilkins answered with a grateful smile, eyeing the old woman with trepidation. "They had had no word except a letter from His Lordship when he received news of his uncle and cousin's deaths. This was received over a fortnight ago."

"Just who is this person, my good man?" demanded Mathilde, not to be left out of the discussion.

"His name is Simon Hilliard Alton," supplied Wilkins in a small voice, reading directly from the paper he pulled from his case. "His mother was the late marquess's sister. She married Hilliard Alton, the youngest son of Sir Hubert Alton, who was a military man himself. He enrolled His Lordship at the Royal Military College during its first year at High Wycombe."

"Hmph. I hardly see how this recommends young Alton." Mathilde's pronouncement could have been heard at Whitehall. In spite of her insistence that the engagement continue indefinitely, she never lost an opportunity to slight any member of the Fentner-Smythe family.

"Please continue, Mr. Wilkins," Damara instructed gently, hoping to save the unfortunate man from her aunt's caustic tongue.

"Yes, of course," the small man agreed readily, casting another wary look at his elderly inquisitor. "Lieutenant Alton was sent to India and served there under Sir Arthur Wellesley. He returned to England in '05, then served under Sir John Moore in Spain, earning his captaincy in the field. Last year he was mentioned in despatches, following our victory at Corunna. After Sir John's death, the marquess was awarded a field commission at the rank of major and was appointed to Welles—the Viscount Wellington's staff."

"Ha! A peer on officer's pay."

"Lady Mathilde, I must inform you that though the late marquess and his son were deeply in debt" —Wilkins paused and allowed himself a small grimace of triumph as he anticipated the reception of his next announcement— "both Hilliard and Sir Hubert Alton invested their monies most wisely. The marquess had a substantial inheritance from both gentlemen, with an annual income of fifteen thousand pounds."

"What exactly were these investments?" Mathilde's eyes sparkled at the prospect of anything that had the least hint of trade, ignoring the strange sounds from Evelyn which suspiciously resembled a chuckle.

"Investments on the Exchange and properties in the colonies," the man returned evenly.

"Mr. Wilkins, how soon can this connection be terminated?" Damara did not care a pin for the man's worth, and she was heartily sick of this listing of his life history. She wanted to settle her business and return to the tranquility of Tarrant's Mount.

"Lady Damara, Messrs. Palmer and Perkins and myself agree that no action should be taken until His Lordship returns." As Wilkins spoke, he held back his surprise. Judging her to be past her majority, although attractive, he wondered at her aversion to the marriage. Why insist on denouncing this connection with a titled, wealthy gentleman? "Am I to understand you wish to end your engagement immediately?"

"I can see no point in continuing this farce," Damara

stated through clenched teeth. The man was obviously a fool. She had clearly written in her first letter prior to her arrival and in the missive delivered the day before that the sole purpose of her trip was to deny the news of her engagement.

"In any other circumstances I would readily accede to your wishes," Wilkins replied, watching his client's mounting color with some misgiving. He had no idea what he would do if both ladies lost their tempers. "Due to the peculiarities attached to this notice, I must stand firm with my colleagues."

"Just as I have said, my gel. We'll continue our present course."

Wilkins saw his chance to escape as the old harridan became an unexpected ally. He quickly gathered together his papers, keeping one eye on the old woman lest she begin again. As he bowed himself from the ladies' presence, he murmured he would contact Lady Damara at the earliest opportunity.

With his retreat, Mathilde sat in gloating silence, her arms crossed over her sparse chest. She turned an inquiring eye to her niece, as if challenging her to say one word. When nothing happened, she rose with exaggerated grandeur like royalty leaving the court and processed to the door. The elevation of her chin proclaimed her victory, but unfortunately for her companions, she was overly tempted by her recent accomplishment and pressed her case yet further.

"Remember, my gel, we leave within the half hour for the dressmaker." She left before her niece could begin any lengthy discourse on the reason they needed to make such a trip.

When the highly polished brass lock clicked shut behind Mathilde's still back, Evelyn finally gave vent to the laughter she had contained during the entire interview.

"Well you can laugh, my ungrateful friend," Damara scolded, but had trouble maintaining her own composure. Mr. Wilkins had been as skittish as a newborn colt during his entire visit, all due to her unique relation.

"Oh, that poor man." Evelyn gasped while wiping her

streaming eyes with her handkerchief. "The old dragon certainly put the fear of God into him."

"You give the woman too much honor," Damara returned primly, not wanting to admit Evie was echoing her own thoughts. "As if you were any more help than that mouse of a man. I'm still engaged."

"All you need do is send a retraction and disregard the advice of Messrs. Palmer, Perkins and Wilkins." The assertion held little conviction, since she knew what would be the result.

"Just this morning you heard what that old harpy threatened if I opposed her wishes," Damara exclaimed. Her anger returned as she recalled the argument that preceded Wilkins's visit.

"Yes, I do believe she would put a notice in the paper that you were suffering from brain fever and weren't responsible for your actions." Evelyn's response only confirmed Damara's own bitter thoughts.

"And that I inherited it from *Maman*. Thank heaven I let Percy stay in the country and he can't hear this twaddle."

"All is *not* lost," Evelyn reasoned, always the peace-maker. She was determined to divert her friend's hurt at her aunt's continual slights of her mother. "We now have a knowledge of your intended's background. He is a definite improvement over the odious Chauncey."

"That is small comfort." Damara gave a delicate snort of derision that was remarkably like her aunt's. "At least with Chauncey I would have known what type of vermin I was dealing with."

"Honestly, Mara, you are the most disappointing friend." Evelyn sighed in irritation. "I confess I find all this excitement a bit diverting, but you aren't even interested."

"That's because you're an incurable romantic." Damara smiled as her friend pulled a face at the description. "You picture this Simon Alton as a hero out of a Minerva Press novel, I'm sure. Myself? I feel he is a head shorter than I, fat, and gout-ridden."

"Hardly gout-ridden, my dear. Bram Dempster is barely over thirty. Any school chum of his can't be in his dotage," Evelyn admonished. "I think you're denying your own interest in this affair much too strenuously. Secretly I believe you're every bit as intrigued by this as I am."

"Nonsense. I have much more serious concerns than some man I have never met," Damara returned in haste, but she could not hide the rise of color that accompanied her denial. Just last night she had lain awake again, wondering if Simon Alton had dark hair and laughing eyes that crinkled at the sides when he grinned in an engaging manner. She did not want to admit she was disappointed that Mr. Wilkins said nothing of Emsley's physical appearance. "Right now, I'm more concerned with replenishing my wardrobe, since my determined aunt saw fit to make a funeral pyre of my clothes. I only have three dresses, a riding habit, and one nightdress to my name. That woman even had the nerve to leave me with a single good chemise."

"Then we had best sally forth to the nearest modiste, lest she get itchy fingers once more." Evelyn jumped to her feet and waved her companion toward the door. The day promised to be very enlightening. Damara was suddenly anxious to be properly attired, and Evelyn knew her friend never cared if the members of society gossiped about her clothes. It was possible there was more than one incurable romantic at Layston Place.

— Chapter Three —

"You do know I'm risking my reputation by being seen with a person dressed in faded navy kerseymere?" Evelyn asked dryly an hour later as she stepped down from the carriage in front of the establishment of the Italian modiste that her mother recommended. "If I'm lucky, perhaps they will think you are my maid."

"Don't let the relief of Aunt Mathilde taking to her bed go to your head," Damara returned, trying to suppress her own smile at the prospect of an afternoon free of the irritating woman. The rigors of travel had caught up with the older woman, her aching joints sending her to bed rather than supervising the shipping expedition. "Rest assured her vocal chords are still in good repair. She'll have plenty to say when we return."

"If she hasn't talked herself hoarse ordering poor Meg around while we're gone," Evelyn observed as they stepped into the shop. No further conversation was possible once Madame Lucretia discovered the extent of Lady Damara's needs, and the fact her new customer had also been the subject of the past fortnight's gossip. With an eye on her profit, she brought forward countless bolts of satins, muslins, sarcenet, and poplins accompanied by a towering pile of pattern books.

"Oh, m'lady, this is meant only for you," Madame gushed after an hour's toil. "The blue, she is your color."

"Very well, I'll take the blue, but that is my last purchase." Damara ruthlessly broke into the effusive discourse, knowing the woman would go on for hours. She had been pushed and pinched and tugged through her measuring. The colors and textures she had seen and felt were all a blur. "Four day dresses, a new riding habit, five evening gowns, a pelisse, and a cloak are more than sufficient."

38

"You forgot the spenceret, three shawls, and the sealskin muff," Evelyn supplied from where she sat comfortably on the chaise lounge, sipping wine during her friend's ordeal. "Oh, and of course, those lovely unmentionables."

"But, no, m'lady. I have saved a surprise for the last," cried Madame Lucretia, almost losing her Mediterranean accent in her haste. "It is *bellisima*! Kate, bring the Golden One."

Her order rang out over Damara's further protests, but when the young girl appeared from the back of the shop carrying the bolt of material, she was speechless. The color was pale gold and shot through with delicate golden threads that gave it an ethereal quality. Silently Madame unwrapped the bolt with loving care, draping a length of the shimmering material over Damara's shoulder.

Damara studied the effect in the cheval glass, her resolve weakening by the second as she stared at the entrancing woman in the mirror. The Golden One seemed to spread its magic to her flushed cheeks, making her auburn hair glow with blond highlights. She glanced at Evelyn for her support.

"You really should take it," came a voice from the doorway to the alcove.

All eyes turned to regard the woman who had entered the shop without anyone noticing. She was dressed in a striped poplin walking dress beneath a deep green Spanish vest. She smiled apologetically at their stunned expressions and quickly explained, "I'm sorry to interrupt, but it would be a pity to waste that confection on a mere blonde or a boring brunette, such as myself."

Damara returned the older woman's friendly smile before turning to give Madame her approval. While they were occupied with arrangements for delivery of their orders, they missed the other visitor's quickened interest at the mention of Damara's name.

"Now, Mara, our mission is partially accomplished." Evelyn sighed happily as she thought of her own purchases and the delightful surprise she had planned for her unsuspecting friend. "We still have the glovemaker, bootmaker, and the milliner to visit before your appointment with Mama's coiffeur."

Her companion groaned at the thought of visiting even one more shop without the prospect of some fool attacking her hairstyle. "We'll leave the milliner and bootmaker until tomorrow. Madame has promised me two day dresses by morning—that will also give us another excuse to escape from Aunt Mathilde and your mother's battle plan for Justine's ball."

"Yes, it's such a pity dear Mathilde's rheumatism decided to act up." Evelyn giggled as she pulled on her gloves.

"Pardon me again, ladies," put in the stranger. "I couldn't help overhearing your plans. I'm going to the glovemaker and would be glad to offer you a seat in my carriage."

The invitation was so unexpected that neither woman could respond in her surprise. The lady turned back to Madame Lucretia for a few moments. Given time to recover slightly, Damara and Evelyn conferred in whispers. They had little time for a decision before the lady's return separated them.

"I have been very clumsy altogether. I forgot to introduce myself. I am Regina, Lady Covering."

"This is Lady Damara Tarrant, and I am Miss Evelyn Townsend." Evie rushed into speech the moment she recognized the woman's name. She could not let this incredible opportunity pass, exchanging a secretive look with Lady Regina. "We would be delighted to accompany you, especially after your helpful advice. Our carriage won't be back for another hour."

Once Damara scribbled a note to the coachman, the ladies made their way out of the shop, and Evelyn took time to study their new friend. Lady Regina felt her regard and gave her a reassuring smile with a saucy wink while Damara was being assisted into the carriage. Holding back a giggle, Evelyn wondered how her friend was going to react to the news that their benefactor was Emsley's godmother.

The visit to the glovemaker took little time. The officious clerk measured each lady with practiced skill and helped in the selection of the desired colors. Damara was captivated by her new friend and looking forward to their further acquaintance. She was at ease with the lady and did not feel as if she was under close inspection to see if she would make the wrong move or say the wrong thing.

The older woman was also very pleased with their chance meeting. Although Simon had given a glowing account of his betrothed's appearance, she had been skeptical of his easy acceptance of the situation. Men could be such fools when it came to a pretty face and an alluring figure. It was possible he could be trapped by a scheming fortune hunter, in spite of Layston's good name.

There could still be some financial reverses since the earl's death, and his heir was a well-known scapegrace. A few well-placed questions at dinner the night before had refreshed her memory, but no one could recall seeing Damara's brother in recent months.

The young ladies gladly accepted Lady Regina's invitation to tea, but as they settled into the comfort of Lady Regina's carriage, the lady knew she would have to confess of her relationship to Emsley. She hoped she would not anger the young woman too much and ruin everything for Simon, but she had to discover if Lady Damara was good enough for her godson. "Lady Damara, please allow me to explain my rather impertinent behavior earlier."

"Call me Damara, please," her new friend requested, only adding to the other woman's guilt. "I have never liked formalities, and at home I am simply Miss Mara."

"Thank you, my dear, and I would like you to return the compliment by calling me Gina," she returned before nervously continuing her confession. "Albeit, I'm not sure you'll still call me friend when I'm done."

"You will still have me for a friend," Evelyn put in to ease the older woman's conscience, "and Mara will understand your reasoning."

"Good heavens, what is this mysterious reason?" A confused Damara looked from one lady to the other, narrowing her gaze when Evelyn hastily lowered her eyes. "It certainly can't be all that dreadful."

"I'm Emsley's godmother," Regina stated baldly before there could be any more delay.

"I see." The response was said very quietly. Damara shot a suspicious look at Evelyn squirming uneasily next to her. Her friend's support of Lady Covering before her admission was clear in her mind. "So you knew all along. But I thought the name was Dempster."

"It is the family name," Regina supplied gently. "I attended school with Evelyn's mother as well as Serena Fentner-Smythe, Simon's mother. We all made our bows together, and my husband didn't come into the title until his brother's unexpected death about ten years ago. Kath probably didn't use the title."

"That's why you know so much about Bramwell Dempster."

Evelyn shrugged carelessly at the accusation, giving a small sigh of relief as the carriage stopped at their destination. There was an awkward silence as the three ladies looked at each other, waiting for someone to speak.

Suddenly Damara startled the others with a husky burst of laughter. The subdued expressions on her companions' faces was too much for her composure, much like Percy and Cretin when they were caught in a prank. She gave her hostess an encouraging smile. "I was thinking earlier how much easier this visit was than my season, not having to worry about being judged and measured. Did I pass inspection?"

"Yes, yes, you did most admirably," Gina assured her guest, as if they were discussing the latest fashion instead of narrowly escaping a disaster.

"I'm so glad. It would be very lowering not to be up to snuff."

"Mara!" Evelyn exclaimed, but the others ignored her as they stepped down from the carriage and entered Lady Regina's home.

The trio settled in Lady Regina's rose-hued drawing room, chatting politely about the day's purchases as they waited for tea to be served. Damara was still wary of her hostess's connection to Emsley. She could not just come right out and admit she had an aversion to meeting Lady Regina's godson, or that she did not know who was responsible for the notice in the newspaper. Judging by her reluctance to say who she was, the older woman knew something was not right about the announcement. Could it be because Emsley was responsible? And if he was, why?

Contrarily Damara wanted to discuss the matter directly

with Emsley, thoroughly weary of debating over her supposed engagement with everyone else to no end.

"Have you heard from Emsley recently?" Evelyn could not resist asking after a lengthy discussion on the possibility of rain the next day. If they were going the learn anything further about the man, she would have to take the initiative since Damara was purposely avoiding the subject.

"I received a short letter last week," Regina lied in order to keep part of her promise to Simon, knowing she was in for a stern lecture when he learned of today's exploit. "He plans to visit me when he arrives in town, but I've learned nothing more. It was so strange that he never mentioned a word about your engagement. I was terribly surprised when I saw the notice."

Damara took a deep breath and let the words rush out before she stopped to consider how strange—and possibly rude—her words would be. "Lad—Gina, I propose we don't discuss Emsley at all. Then we shall have nothing to trouble us."

Both her companions stared at her with identical expressions of amazement and frustration. They moved as one, both taking great care to place their cups in their saucers. While Regina nodded silently, Evelyn gave her friend an agonized look and could not contain her thoughts. "But, Mara, this is a perfect opportunity to—"

"Evie, you know we have to wait until Jasper decides on the matter," Damara broke in, keeping the laughter in her voice in check with great effort. She raised her eyebrows to signal that Evelyn must follow her lead, and—hopefully—not arouse Lady Regina's suspicions any more than necessary. Damara knew she had to take charge, since she already let the situation get out of hand by allowing Mathilde too much freedom of opinion.

"Yes, I expect Jasper will have something to say about it when he returns," Evelyn murmured with a disheartened sigh. She was more than slightly miffed that Damara chose to take charge at this moment, leaving no chance to ask what Emsley looked like.

"Jasper will only treat it as a huge joke and be of no earthly help," Damara remarked disparagingly as only a sister could manage. "He'll then proceed to tell me it is high

time I did settle down, even though he couldn't care a whit
one way or the other."

"Now, Evie, Gina must think we're rag-mannered to go
on this way."

"Not at all, my dear." Regina fixed her best social smile
on her face and began to think of a successful career on the
stage. Simon would have her head for this, but how could
she anticipate that Damara would not want to talk about the
engagement? She had to salvage something from the mare's
nest that she created. Simon wanted to know about his
betrothed's companions and family. The Townsends were
above reproach, but what about the Tarrants? From Damara's tone, Jasper must be a relative. She decided to hazard
a guess at his identity, thinking purely of Simon's interest.
"Will your brother be away long?"

"I'm waiting to hear from him any day. He is with the
army in Portugal." Damara was relieved to discuss anything
that would keep the conversation away from the Marquess
of Emsley.

"I'm surprised he hasn't returned before this." Regina
rapidly tried to calculate when Layston had died. It must be
well over a year since he was laid to rest, and the heir was
still gone. She could not remember any talk, other than
some boyish pranks, so there must be a very interesting
reason for his continued absence. A reason Simon would
certainly want to know.

"Father requested Jasper remain in the army until his
twenty-fifth birthday, which is now just a week and a half
away." The ease of her explanation surprised Damara. In
recent years she had become accustomed to keeping her
own counsel, and here she was about to confide in someone
she met only a few hours before. "Jasper must—"

The rest of her words were forgotten as a shriek sounded
from across the hallway, followed by a loud clattering of
metal striking against metal and the barking of a dog. Lady
Covering was on her feet immediately; however, before she
could move, a large canine with reddish-brown fur trotted
into the room, unconcerned with the havoc left behind in his
wake. At the sight of Lady Regina's startled form the dog
came to a sudden stop, settling long enough for Damara to
realize the newest guest was an Irish setter.

"Ajax, who let you into the house?" Regina demanded. Her words were colored with her barely suppressed laughter and exasperation, which Ajax immediately sensed. Cocking his head to the side, he seemed to smile before looking with interest at the other two occupants of the room. His attention was caught by Damara's smile, and he crossed the room to make her acquaintance. He sat directly at her feet and prettily offered his paw.

"Hello, Ajax," she said solemnly, and gravely shook his proffered paw. "You're a handsome beast."

"Well, beast is very accurate." Regina dropped back into her seat and grimaced in apology. "I really must apologize. Ajax is our foster child while Bram is at sea. Unfortunately the animal wants to be a house dog and always manages to escape his gaolers, sooner or later."

"I understand completely. Our canine child is even larger than this, and is in the not-so-diligent care of my younger brother Percy." Damara thought wistfully of the pair, missing them both more than she could have imagined, though they would undoubtedly be constantly shattering her nerves if they were in London. "Percy is twelve and barely bigger than his faithful hound, who is neither as handsome as Ajax nor as nicely behaved."

"Thank you for your patience." Regina gave the younger woman a genuine smile of gratitude, since any number of society dames would have created a scene by either going off into a dead faint or screaming the house down. The wretched animal did deserve some kind of punishment even so, for interrupting them when Regina was beginning to make progress. She was anxious to pursue this promising subject of Damara's older brother, but she knew she had to step carefully. It would not be due to her careless intervention that Simon lost his accidental, and very agreeable, fiancée. The young woman seemed ideal for her proud godson, so whatever the mystery attached to the engagement announcement, it could not be lain at Damara's door.

The clock on the mantel chimed the hour, taking all three ladies by surprise. Damara gathered up her bonnet and gloves, giving her hostess a regretful smile. "We really must be going. I'm sure Aunt Mathilde is driving Lady Kath to distraction."

"Tell Kath I'll call at the earliest opportunity," Regina instructed as she rose with her guests, frowning over the other name Damara mentioned. Was this who Simon called the dragon aunt? "Good heavens, your Aunt Mathilde can't be Mathilde Lambert. She hasn't been to town in ages. In fact, I thought she was de—"

"No, she's still among us." Evelyn saved the lady from making a social blunder. "Mother will be pleased to see you again. She hasn't made her usual calls while preparing for Justine's ball." She wanted to encourage this connection as much as possible. In fact, she was becoming rather enamored with Emsley. A life of spinsterhood for her friend did not suit Evelyn. This fiancé was beginning to shape up into a prime candidate.

The trio discussed their various engagements for the coming week as they awaited the arrival of Lady Regina's carriage. The ladies of Layston Place were somewhat preoccupied with Justine's upcoming presentation, but another shopping trip was being planned as the sound of carriage wheels were heard in the street.

Entering the carriage, both young women discussed what they would tell Mathilde on their return. Dallying with a connection of Emsley's—no matter how highly placed in society—would hardly be an excuse for their lengthy absence. Neither lady noticed the gentleman approaching astride a black Arabian stallion.

Their departure was observed with interest by the rider, however. He pulled in his mount a short distance away, his eyes narrowing in recognition and a slight smile appearing on his tanned face. Shaking his head ruefully, he waited for the carriage to depart. When it had proceeded to the end of the square, he urged his mount forward to the residence the ladies had just left.

The gentleman was admitted by Lady Regina's austere butler, who allowed him the freedom to announce himself. The major domo had more than enough to occupy him between the hysterical maid cleaning up the scattered silver in the dining room and Ajax locked in the cupboard under the stairs while he answered the door. The caller found the lady of the house seated at her Sheraton secretary, penning a letter.

"Well, what color are they?" Simon demanded as he struck a pose of apparent dissatisfaction, his arms crossed over his chest.

"Simon, what a delightful surprise." Regina turned to smile weakly at her caller. With great care she laid down her pen before moving across the room in a bid to collect her wits. "What was it you asked?"

"Aunt Gina," Simon chided gently, attempting to maintain his grim countenance in the face of her dissembling. "I had a most interesting view of your recent visitors as I rode up. To repeat, what color are her eyes?"

"You'll have to discover that for yourself," she replied, and gave his determined chin a flick with her slender finger. Her confidence returned as she recognized the gleam of amusement in his hazel eyes, and she *had* discovered some interesting facts about Lady Damara.

"After all that conniving and not one ounce of cooperation," he grumbled, lounging back on the settee. He stretched one arm along the back, then grimaced slightly at the pain the movement caused, quickly shifting to a more comfortable position.

"Aha! You don't approve and yet—Simon, what's wrong?"

"It's just a trifle. Merely the girth giving out finally when I was mounting Nemesis earlier and tumbling onto my shoulder." Emsley dismissed the incident without disclosing the finer details while she fussed over him, rearranging the cushions.

He did not want her to worry over the fact the saddle had been purchased only a few weeks before, or that the break in the leather had been too clean—as smooth as a knife cut. Nor did he tell her of Bundy's discovery when he took Nemesis back to the stable. A nail had been pushed through the stallion's blanket. If Simon had been able to mount successfully, the horse would have bolted and undoubtedly thrown his rider. Simon knew a few pulled muscles were a small price to pay, and until he knew more about the incident, he would keep his own counsel. No one at the stable saw anyone but Bundy near the animal.

He continued his teasing banter to divert his godmother. "I should have known better than to confide in you and expect you to stay uninvolved, especially with Uncle Kendall still away."

She began to make a sharp retort but was forstalled by the maid's appearance. "Wine or tea, Simon?"

"Tea will be fine."

"Just freshen the pot, Mary," Regina instructed as she settled herself next to her guest in a confident pose. "Although you believe the worst, I met Lady Damara purely by accident. We seem to share the same modiste."

"And naturally you couldn't resist such a golden opportunity."

"Exactly, you infuriating man," she returned in defeat under his stern look. She knew she would have her revenge when Simon saw Damara in her golden dress; yet another wicked idea took form under his persistent teasing. She did not deserve such scorn after her hard work. "I pity poor Damara. She is going to have quite a time controlling you, if you succeed."

"So, you *do* approve?" Simon asked with keen interest. Despite all the teasing he, like Bram and Kendall Dempster, respected Regina's intellect. Then he became suspicious of her last comment in that oh-so-innocent tone. "What do you mean, if?"

"You could do much worse, my dear." She paused to prolong his suffering, determined she would not tell him just how much she approved of his finacée, with only a few qualms that were probably of no import. "There is a gentleman named Jasper who may have some say in the matter."

"Indeed." Simon's voice was dangerously quiet as he wondered if this Jasper had a jealous nature. Perhaps he was a penniless suitor who wanted revenge because his lady love was promised, albeit falsely, to another. He watched his godmother closely, waiting for her to explain further.

"Now, if you wish to enter the lists, you had best order proper evening dress from Weston by next week," she instructed, blithely ignoring his searching look, running her eyes appreciatively over his coat of blue superfine. Damara would be hardpressed to dismiss this man so lightly once she met him in person and in formal attire. As for Simon, he would find out soon enough that Jasper would be the man to ask permission to pay his addresses, not a rival.

"Well, you can't be taking me to Astley's Amphitheater again," he considered carefully while naming his and Bram's favorite adolescent entertainment, knowing from long experience not to pressure the lady. She would tell him in good time what she learned from her cose with his betrothed. "What is my treat that needs fancy dress, Madame Tussaud's traveling exhibit?"

"Fool. Justine Townsend is to have her coming out ball next week."

"Now that certainly clarifies my need for fancy togs."

"The Townsend family is staying at Layston Place this season, along with Damara and her ancient fossil of an aunt, Lady Mathilde Lambert," she explained with a great show of patience, enunciating each word carefully, then waiting in anticipation for his response.

"And the Marquess of Emsley will make his debut into polite society during the evening," Simon answered promptly, not able to keep from smiling in anticipation. Now he would be able to judge for himself if Damara Tarrant was an innocent dupe or the mastermind of this engagement. Perhaps then she would not constantly be on his mind, day and night, while he tried to solve the puzzle of her personality. "The Townsends may be sponsoring the event of the season."

Lady Regina and her guest both broke into delighted laughter at the prospect. She, because she knew intuitively Damara would be wearing the golden dress for the occasion to wipe that smug smile off her fiancé's face. He, because he would be able to turn to a more important matter—such as repairs of the tenants' cottages and clearing the drains— once he put Lady Damara in her place. The maid, returning with the freshened tea, wondered at the foolishness of her betters as the two continued to act like giggling children.

A serving wench at a distant inn near the docks would have gladly traded places with Lady Regina's Mary as she served the three men seated in the darkest corner of the room. Jem and Squeeze were regular customers and did not frighten her, though they looked as if they had been spawned at the bottom of the Thames and crawled ashore. They did not have brains enough to be threatening. It was the third man with a face like a weasel that she did not like. She thumped their tankards down on the grimy table to interrupt their whispered conversation and make sure she got her payment.

"Show yer blunt, or I takes it back," she announced in definace, wiping her scraggly hair out of her face with the back of her hand. She gave the unknown man, sitting in the middle, a hard look.

"Here, my lovely. Don't go wasting it all on gin," the man sneered. He flipped the coins into the air, his eyes gleaming in amusement as he watched the scrawny girl scramble to catch the money before it fell on the filth at her feet. Once she bit the coins to see if they were real and shuffled away, he turned back to his companions.

"Wot 'bout our pay, gov?" asked the man called Jem as the spokesman for the pair.

"You'll get your money when and if you succeed. Emsley wasn't even hurt this morning, only a little dusty from his tumble," growled the man. "I don't pay for uninspired gymnastics. I'm paying for a corpse, so I suggest you redouble your efforts."

"I tolds ya it'd take a bigger nail, Jem," Squeeze stated with a sage nod. "That's wot we needs."

"Gentlemen," their employer said through clenched teeth, "don't tamper with his saddle again. This is to look like an accident, remember? I'll leave you to your planning, since I have an appointment with a charming little Opera dancer after her performance tonight." He rose to his feet and flipped another coin onto the table. "That's the last you get until you accomplish your task. I'm not made of money."

He walked off without a backward look, leaving two disgruntled henchmen behind him. Jem clamped his hand over the single coin, glaring at his companion and daring him to make a move. "We best do ther job kerrect, or the squirrely cove'll see us curlin' up our toes. So, best order anuther round while we cogitat ther next plan."

Squeeze nodded, shaking his head, shoulders, and torso in his enthusiasm. When Jem looked at him expectantly, he realized he was supposed to attract the barmaid's attention. After a glance across the noisy, smoke-filled room, he gave his companion a worried look. A burly giant of a man was standing in the middle of the room bellowing out a challenge to all comers. Looking back at Jem, Squeeze knew he was going to be bruised and battered for the sake of a pint of ale.

The lady's maid at Layston Place was wondering if she would be able to leave the room unscathed the next afternoon. She was observing a heated discussion between Lady Damara and Miss Evelyn. They had retired to Lady Damara's room after lunch to forage among the boxes from Madame Lucretia, who made her newest customer's order her first priority to make a favorable impression.

"Evie, you're the one who will be declared mentally unstable if you think I'll wear this scrap of material. It's bad enough you allowed that man to scalp me yesterday afternoon." Damara ran a distracted hand over her shorn mane. Etienne had hemmed and hawed for a full half hour before he even touched her hair, just walking around and around until she became dizzy. Finally he began to cut but refused to let her even have a hand mirror until he was done. In the end he allowed her to see her new style; a fringe of curls at her forehead and the thinned and trimmed, formerly unruly, mop gathered at the top of her head, cascading from the securing ribbon in her curls. She was now *à la Sappho*, so Etienne proclaimed.

Evelyn was becoming as infuriated as her friend, and she knew the worst was still to come. "This scrap of material is the latest fashion. And I'll remind you that the nightdress and negligee are gifts."

"I couldn't even look at myself in the mirror if I wore *that*," Damara snapped, tossing aside the sheer peach-colored material she had been clutching in her hand. "I'll stay with my muslin nightdress, thank you very much. At least with that I won't be in danger of catching influenza."

A distressed sound from Meg, who had remained out of the way near the dressing table, caught Damara's attention. As she looked at the girl's troubled face, a gnawing suspicion entered her mind, the same as it had the day of the great clothing fire at Tarrant's Mount. The assumed innocence of Evelyn's expression only served to confirm her fears. Swiftly she moved to the clothes press at the end of the room. She thoroughly searched each drawer, knowing she would find no trace of her old gown.

"Evelyn Danielle Townsend, you traitor," she shrieked, sending the already nervous Meg scurrying from the room.

"You have to become used to less moderate styles," Evelyn stated firmly, and remained surprisingly calm under the renewed attack. "You can't remain enclosed from neck to toe day and night."

"I don't have to go around half naked either," she returned as she paced the room to dissipate her ire. The past two days had been one trial after another; one stranger after another telling her what to wear and how she should look, all because of a man she strongly suspected was not honorable. It seemed more than likely Emsley was the one responsible for the false announcement. Of course, wild horses charging toward her at breakneck speed would never make her admit she was enchanted with her new clothes, the exception being Evelyn's diaphanous present, or that she found her new hairstyle comfortable and attractive. Now she had springy curls that rivaled Evie's ringlets. Unfortunately it was all the result of the odious Emsley's cruel joke.

"You'll feel half naked when you wear any of your new evening gowns for the first time," Evelyn continued the fight with real conviction. "I spent half of my first ball trying to hide behind a very large plant and the other half attempting to pull up the neckline of my dress. And I'm not so well endowed as you. You're also beyond the age where a chemisette tucked in your bodice is necessary."

"So the continued destruction of my clothes has become a mission of mercy?" Damara inquired, clearly skeptical of her friend's motives. She dismissed the troublesome Emsley from her mind to focus all her energies on the determined blonde in front of her.

"Consider what Mathilde would supply as a replacement. She ordered Meg to confiscate your remaining undergarments and nightdress as soon as the packages began to arrive, though how she remembered between writing notes to everyone she knows in London, I'll never know. I merely anticipated her commands and thought you might prefer this to purple."

Damara stood regarding her friend without uttering a word. Her lips began to twitch involuntarily. "I wouldn't have been too upset if I didn't have to wear an ostrich feather with it," she managed to say before succumbing to her laughter. In apology for her short tirade, she gave a relieved Evelyn a generous hug, vowing that Emsley would have a great deal to pay for when he finally appeared.

They settled themselves in front of the fire for a companionable chat. "You know, Evie, I don't remember laughing this much in a long time."

"You've been running a household since you were fourteen and have not been away from Tarrant's Mount in four years," Evelyn observed, "and have forgotten how to relax."

"Old and careworn at two and twenty." Damara chuckled at her friend's earnest tone.

"Precisely. As much as I care for your brother, I would as soon strangle him as kiss him when he finally shows his face."

"Evie, it was never his wish to neglect his family." Damara defended her brother readily, in spite of her anxiety over his delayed return. "Papa was most emphatic that Jasper remain in the army, and what would Percy and I have lived on if all the money went to charity?"

"Uncle Sedge didn't foresee Percy's accident or the need to raise rents on the estate when he wrote that silly codicil. And he certainly wouldn't have allowed you to continue to hide in the country."

"We've been over this too many times in the past and still have reached the same impasse, my friend," Damara said sadly. She did not want to discuss what her father would have done about her avoidance of London. If he was still alive, he most probably would have had her married to Emsley by now, by proxy if necessary, no matter what the scoundrel's motives.

"Yes, but this time we're actually in London," came Evelyn's smug answer, " and that brings us to a new topic of dissension."

Damara stiffened, positive that Evelyn was going to begin dissecting the wonderful Emsley once more. She was heartily sick of the subject herself, while Evelyn seemed to revel in spinning fantasies about the man. He was all *anyone* seemed to talk about. Even Sir Cedric had a few words to say about the gossip at White's over dinner last evening. Well, she was going to put a stop to it now.

Evelyn forestalled her. "We shall now argue over what dresses we shall wear to Justine's ball."

— Chapter Four —

"Mara, will you please stop that pacing? It makes me dizzy simply watching you," Evelyn exclaimed from her dressing table. She could not turn her head since Meg was twining a blue satin ribbon through her blond curls. "You need to conserve your energies for dancing at Justine's ball tonight."

"I've been conserving my energy all afternoon," Damara returned, giving her friend a speaking look and tightened the sash of her wrapper without losing step. "Why I let Meg apply the noxious potion you call a skin restorative, I'll never know. I would have refused, if you had told me it would keep me in my room most of the afternoon with only one of Justine's novels from the lending library for entertainment. Confess, Evie, that slime really came from the flower beds at the back of the house."

"Not true. Mama has sworn by it for years. She has it specially mixed at the apothecary." Evelyn chuckled as Meg put the finishing touches on her coiffure. Turning away from the mirror, she studied her friend, now wandering aimlessly around the room—first picking up a figurine, then sorting the silks in Evelyn's embroidery box. "I thought you received a note from Mr. Wilkins this afternoon."

"He could have saved the expense of the paper," Damara said with a snort of derision. "There's still no news from Messrs. Palmer and Perkins, and our timorous Mr. Wilkins repeated his position on waiting for His Lordship's return, not clarifying whether he meant Jasper or Emsley. So I've come to a decision."

"What do you plan to do?" Evelyn sounded cautious, almost hesitant, watching Damara pick up a china music box from the mantle. "You're not thinking of returning home, are you? I thought you were enjoying yourself."

"I'm enjoying myself, much to my surprise. I think I've finally laid the ghost of my disastrous season to rest, thanks to you and your family," she answered, almost surprised at the admission. During the past week, she had gone to various entertainments and had made the acquaintance of a number of friendly, charming people. The shy gangling girl who had fled society four years ago was now a mature young woman. She no longer worried about saying the wrong thing or making an inappropriate move; she had confidence in herself.

"Fortunately the news of the Baron Gigglewick's daughter running off with her groom—or was it her coachman—has already supplanted the gossip about my engagement," Damara continued with a small twist of a smile at how easily the *ton* was distracted. "So I've decided to forget about my non-existent fiancé as well and enjoy my visit to town, since I don't think I'll return in the near future."

"Come and let Meg tidy your hair. We don't have much time before dinner," Evelyn said, ignoring Damara's pronouncement, and rose from her seat. Lady Kath planned for the household to dine *en famille* before the evening's festivities. "Mama is already in such a nervous state I don't think she will survive tardiness in her family."

" 'Tis such a lot of bother," Damara said, giving a sigh of exasperation but taking her place in front of the mirror. "That is why I like living in the country. There's never all this fuss and bother for only a few hours. I really don't have the patience for it. Lucky Percy to be home at Tarrant's Mount. I hope he is behaving himself."

"Is that what has you in such a pucker? Worrying over Percy?" Evelyn asked from her perch on the bed as she adjusted her stockings.

"Just a little," Damara admitted as she surrendered to Meg's ministrations. "I really should have brought him to London, instead of abandoning him to the servants."

"He is much happier where he is," Evelyn returned easily. "If he were here, he would simply close himself up in the library every day."

"Probably," his sister agreed, stoically allowing Meg to powder her neck and shoulders. "I think I had too much time to think this afternoon. I've been wondering why I haven't heard from Jasper."

"You forget that he is the world's worst correspondent, and you know Papa would have heard something from Whitehall if anything had happened to him," Evelyn returned, her pixieish face marred by a momentary frown before she dismissed her dark thoughts. "Your main worry should be Lady Mathilde conveniently recovering in time for the ball. Though I wonder that she didn't exhaust herself from writing so many messages and directing every servant in the house to do her bidding. Poor Meg will need a new pair of slippers after the running about town she had to do in the past week."

"Meg, if Evelyn is agreeable, I think you deserve an extra afternoon off for extraordinary service," Damara told the girl, who blushed prettily at the sudden attention.

"You may have the whole day off tomorrow with my compliments," her mistress instructed as she snared a crystal perfume bottle from the dressing table. She studied Damara's new curls critically as she dabbed perfume behind her ears. "I think we're ready to dress now, Meg."

Within a matter of minutes both ladies were ready for the evening's entertainment. Damara studied herself in the cheval glass, amazed at her tall shapely reflection. Madame Lucretia had surpassed herself. The shimmering gold material fell in a molten shower from the gathers beneath her bosom, the white satin underskirt adding to its luster. Every movement she made allowed the golden threads to capture the candlelight.

"Now you see why I insisted on your new nightdress," Evelyn stated from behind her, the blue of her satin gown reflected in her laughing eyes.

"You always have to be right," Damara stated, wrinkling her nose at her friend's smug reflection. Without thinking she placed her hand over her *maman's* pear-shaped topaz necklace framed by her low, square-cut decolletage. If she had worn this gown when she first arrived, she would have wrapped herself in bed sheets to cover the alarming amount of flesh that rose above her dress.

"Now, shall we make our grand entrance?" Evelyn asked and linked her arm through her friend's. "Poor Justine will be under everyone's scrutiny tonight, while we're free to enjoy ourselves. Thank heaven, we shall never be eighteen again."

"Here, here," Damara chimed in as they descended the stairs. A shiver of anticipation skated down her spine. For some reason she was looking forward to the evening, almost like a child anticipating Christmas.

"Well, my gel, you should be prepared for this gathering after all your gadding about this past week," Mathilde snapped an hour later as they stood at the entrance to the ballroom. The old woman's ailment had not sweetened her disposition.

"Yes, Aunt," Damara replied while scanning the newest arrivals for known faces as the Townsends greeted their guests in the receiving line. She was determined not to let Mathilde's disagreeable humor destroy her newfound poise.

"Is your friend Lady Covering going to put in an appearance?" Mathilde did not try to hide her sneer, which was present whenever she spoke of any connection of Emsley's.

"I believe so."

"And what of her precious godson. Has she mentioned him lately?" She allowed herself a slight smile as Damara stiffened at the mention of her betrothed.

"There is no further word," Damara answered, her voice stilted, giving her aunt a quelling look. "Now, excuse me, but I see Evelyn signaling me." She calmly walked away before the old crone could form another barb.

"How is the old ogre?"

Damara chuckled, her good humor quickly restored by Evelyn's laughing question. "She is in rare form. After her enforced confinement, she was merely sharpening her claws on me in anticipation of seeing any old acquaintances."

"From what Meg told me, the old biddy has not had much luck finding any of her cronies in residence, but she has plenty of new material to alienate in this crush." Evelyn giggled behind her fan once more. "I never thought we knew so many people. Mathilde will need days to recuperate after this, especially since she isn't using her cane tonight."

"Let us see if we can enjoy ourselves equally as well," Damara murmured the moment Justine entered the ballroom on her father's arm. A number of gentlemen were heading toward Damara and her friend. "I believe we're about to be overcome with requests to dance. This may be the first ball I've attended with a dance card that will be completely filled by the end of the evening. Oh, for the sunrise tomorrow."

"Hopefully by sunrise I will be dreaming, not dancing." Evelyn's jest was the last time they were able to exchange a word for the next few hours. Their respective partners seemed to be conspiring to keep them apart.

As each set formed, Damara would see her friend further down the room. Even at the interval for refreshments Damara found herself seated amongst strangers with her garrulous partner informing her of his endless, and somewhat colorless, life history. As her escort's friend and his companion simpered together over yet another inane remark, she longed for escape. She was beginning to doubt her reason. Surely she had not been intimidated by these people during her season? She must have been very green to allow them to frighten her.

As the musicians began to play once more, she was hard pressed not to laugh hysterically at the posturing gentlemen seeking her attention. She could not remember any of their names; they all seemed to be a reflection of each other. Of the half dozen men surrounding her, only two could meet her height, and if she remembered correctly, three were several years younger. During the last set she had stared down at her partner's bald spot, which was not as discreetly covered as he thought.

Across the room she met Evelyn's inquiring blue gaze and sent her a desperate look. As her friend moved toward her and her group of admirers, Damara rose from her chair in hopes of making a speedy escape. She excused herself gracefully from the gentlemen as the music changed for a new set. As each gentleman pleaded for the honor of the dance, she began to feel the panic rising in her. If she continued in the present company, she could not be responsible for her actions.

At the touch of a hand at her elbow she turned expect-

antly to greet Evelyn. Instead she found herself staring into
the intricate folds of a gentleman's neckcloth tied faultlessly
in a *Trône d'Amour*. Before she could recover her surprise,
a firm hand clasped her hand. Automatically her feet moved
as she was propelled onto the dance floor. For the first time
that evening she had to tilt her head back to see her partner's
face—a face she had seen before at the Scarlet Lion, she
realized as she met his unfathomable expression. She knew
the face from her dreams.

His dark brown, almost black hair was styled *au coup de
vent*, but slightly shorter than the current fashion as it
framed his face, though he did sport side-whiskers that had
recently become popular. His skin was tanned and weath-
ered from the elements, a sharp contrast to the pale-
complected men she had danced with earlier. He was not
conventionally handsome, but his hazel eyes and aquiline
nose gave him a certain attraction. His mouth intrigued her;
so delicate and perfectly sculpted, totally out of character
for a man of his height and the impressive breadth of
shoulder that filled out his black tail-coat without a crease.

Damara realized she was staring rudely and looked away
in confusion as she tried to think of something to say. In
desperation she lifted her face to his again and burst out,
"Where did you come from?"

Her partner threw back his head in laughter, deepening
the character lines around his eyes. She felt her cheeks start
to burn. When he smiled, he became too like the image that
had haunted her dreams.

"That really isn't important right now," he answered in
the deep timbre she remembered, laughter still lurking in
the depths of his sherry-colored eyes.

She felt uncomfortable and gauche under his amused
regard, too much like the gawky eighteen-year-old who had
been a wallflower four years previously. It would be
impossible to move away from him in the middle of the
dancers without creating a spectacle of herself. She was
becoming angry at herself for her own discomfiture, and at
him for causing it. So she vented her frustration verbally.

"What in the blaz—I mean, what possessed to you to
dance with me without asking permission?" As soon as she
finished, she realized how silly she sounded. Looking

around the ballroom, she tried to discover a means of escape and noticed a number of people were staring intently in their direction. The dowager set were busily whispering behind their fans. Most of their sharp gazes were focused solely on her partner and herself.

"Damara, is something wrong?"

She turned back to her partner, amazed at his easy use of her given name. "Have you noticed we're being watched rather closely?"

"More than likely they are pleased to see you have a partner tall enough that you don't need to look over the top of him," he reasoned smoothly as he executed an intricate turn, separating them momentarily, "or perhaps they are admiring our prowess. You know, Damara, I think you look a little flushed and could use some fresh air."

"Really, sir, I find this all highly irregular," she finally managed, horrified that she sounded like some stiff-rumped dowager as her partner maneuvered them to the French doors that opened onto the garden. Once outside she expected him to release her and allow her to withdraw from his disturbing hold. Instead he continued to dance across the expanse of the terrace to the shadows beyond the noise from inside.

"Now I'll explain why I wanted to dance with you, sweet Damara." His voice deepened to a very quiet, dangerous level. She raised her head to reprimand his familiarity only to discover his face was barely an inch from her own. His mouth descended to hers, trapping her gasp of surprise.

She froze in astonishment. This was beyond the realm of her experience; no man had ever kissed her. For a moment she gave in to the desire to continue the novel experience as an undefinable warmth began to spread through her body. It was very pleasurable to be clasped within the embrace of this large man. Her sanity returned, however, as his arms tightened around her, drawing her more firmly against him.

Stunned by his boldness and her own stupidity, Damara pushed against his broad chest. The man obviously thought she shared the same lack of morals with a number of the ladies of the *ton*. Unfortunately, due to his superior strength, she was helpless. Her arms were trapped between their bodies, and the kid leather of her evening slippers were highly ineffectual against his sturdy legs. With no other course, she bit into his lower lip.

Although her lips were released, her body seemed to be crushed more tightly against the hard muscles of her assailant.

"If you don't free me immediately, I'll be forced to scream for help." Her threat came out in a husky whisper that ended in a gasp. His lips were moving over the column of her neck along her jawline.

He spoke directly into her ear, his voice clear and low. "I'm afraid no one would think it unlikely that your fiancé wishes to make love to you."

She jerked her head back, away from the disturbing touch of his lips. Just as she was about to demand an explanation for his words, someone called across the terrace.

Simon turned his head at the sound of his name, frowning when he recognized the woman approaching them. He knew he was behaving improperly, but the temptation had been too great. After a week of thinking and dreaming about Damara, he could not resist, but now he was more perplexed than before. She seemed to respond one minute, then abruptly began to resist. Her face held all the innocence of a young girl barely out of the schoolroom, as if she had never been kissed.

"Really, Simon, I would have expected this from some of the younger idiots attending. You're a peer now, not a rough and tumble offic—" Regina broke off as Emsley's companion turned her face toward the light. "Oh, I didn't realize you were with your fiancée."

"Aunt Gina, what a rotten thing to say in front of Damara. Who else would I be with?" Then he chuckled as a taunting smile broke across the older woman's face. She was taking her matchmaking seriously.

"Yes, well, don't be too long at it, my dears," she returned, "or at least find a more discreet place. I'm pleased to see this irregular engagement has proven so amicable, but others might not be so understanding."

"She's right, you know," Emsley whispered into Damara's hair, his breath disturbing her carefully arranged curls and distracting her from seeing Lady Regina's withdrawal.

"I wouldn't consider going back inside with you, much

less finding a more secluded place," she snapped, still unable to release herself from his arms. Whatever dignity she tried to emulate was lost as she addressed her heated statement to his neckcloth.

"My dear girl, I merely meant we should continue a rational discussion about our betrothal at another time." His voice was still laced with amusement as he clearly read her conflicting emotions in her expressive face. Instead of being able to see through her dissembling, she was even more of an enigma to him.

With determination Damara straightened to her full height; unfortunately this only allowed her to gaze at her companion's chin. Undaunted by this, she spoke evenly, as if engaging in a commonplace conversation about her appointments for the next week. "If you are indeed the man who is my supposed fiancé, my solicitor will contact you for the time and place of our next meeting. He has been trying to locate you for more than a week and will be most anxious to make your acquaintance."

"I've no doubt he will," Emsley returned without giving any sign he meant to release her. "I've been away settling some matters on my estate. Perhaps he can inform me who is responsible for the fortuitous—if somewhat premature—announcement of our engagement? I would like to know the name of my benefactor."

"Demmit! Will you let go of me?" Damara's reserve finally broke, and she stamped her foot in vexation as he patently ignored her struggles throughout his calm discourse.

"Such language from a lady," he admonished, and relaxed his hold.

Damara found she was only allowed to move back a few inches while he retained a firm grip on her elbows. Tilting her chin up, she found his warm hazel eyes watching her intently. "This is ridiculous," she muttered through clenched teeth. "Someone else will be coming out at any moment, and I don't relish being discovered on intimate terms with you."

"If I know my godmama, that door is now either locked or she is standing just inside, turning away all comers," Emsley explained, still holding her in place. "But in deference to your scruples, I'll allow you to go inside momentarily."

Before Damara could guess his intent, she found herself swept into his arms once more. This final kiss was swift but equally as devastating as his first. By the time her tumultuous thoughts could be gathered, she found herself propelled toward the door with a gentle push. She found little satisfaction in discovering Lady Regina was indeed guarding the door. The other woman gave her a conspiratorial wink, which Damara answered with a weak smile before turning and walking away. She searched the crush of people for Evelyn, rather bemused by the entire incident.

"Mara dear, are you feeling unwell?" a male voice broke through her nervous state a few minutes later.

"Oh, Uncle Cedric," she gasped in relief. The gray-haired man gave her a searching look, his blue eyes filled with concern.

"You're very pale. Is something wrong? No sudden news from Japser, or is it Percy?"

"Oh, no, Uncle Cedric. I think I'm a little overtired from my new social life," she answered, trying to give him a brilliant smile of assurance. She discovered that she was not prevaricating; she was feeling weary. "Would you please make my excuses to Aunt Kath and Justine? I think I'll retire now."

"Yes, certainly, dear," he answered promptly, still watching her closely. "Shall I escort you upstairs?"

"No, don't bother. Really, I can manage perfectly well on my own," she exclaimed in a rush as she caught the movement of a large figure at the door she had recently entered. Emsley had returned and was ambling over to stand next to Lady Regina, who was watching the other guests on the dance floor. Over the heads of the dancers, Damara met his intent look before he bent to listen to his godmother. While his attention was distracted, she fled with a rushed excuse to her bewildered host. If she had overheard the couple's conversation, she would have considered running all the way to Tarrant's Mount that night rather than her bedroom.

"Well, my boy, what about her eyes?" inquired Lady Regina as she smiled stiffly to an acquaintance.

"They are emerald green, m'lady—quite striking," he returned with an equal lack of expression since the lady already knew the answer. "And you're right, she is quite a handful."

His observation was rewarded with a sharp rap from Lady Regina's fan before she gave a delighted laugh. A few heads turned in their direction at the musical sound. When a number of whispered conversations began, Lady Regina spoke tersely to her companion. "Unless you're prepared to be bombarded with questions, 'tis time for a strategic retreat."

"I believe you're right," Emsley agreed, eyeing a clutch of giggling debutantes who were casting none-too-subtle glances in his direction. He swiftly bowed to his godmother and promised to call on her the next day.

"And Simon," Regina said when he was about to depart, giving him a stern look, "remember, you're not a soldier assaulting an objective, and Damara is still an inexperienced young woman. Go gently."

He took his leave in a thoughtful frame of mind. Innocent or accomplished actress, he still was not sure. Damara's response to his kiss had seemed so tentative and untutored, making him actually wonder if she had ever been kissed before this evening. Although Lady Regina was convinced, it seemed impossible to him. He needed to know more about the Tarrant family and their finances, no matter how sweet the taste of Damara's lips.

Unconsciously he rubbed his sore shoulder. This engagement business was not his only trouble. Apparently being a peer required more responsible thinking than he anticipated. The anonymous announcement in the newspaper and the equally mysterious attempt to injure him both occurred in less than a month. Were they connected somehow, and if so, why? In the army he would have lined up his men and grilled them until he had some answers, but he could hardly order the cream of society to stand at attention while he interrogated them.

Subtlety was what was called for in this situation, and Lady Damara Tarrant was the key to solving the mystery. He was a patient man and could work slowly to that end. He would discover if she was as truly innocent as she would

have him believe; sooner or later her guard would have to
falter. Simon signaled a passing hack to take him back to his
rooms. Now he knew why Bram complained so strenuously
about the dictates of polite society, especially when it came
to young ladies.

Damara felt that she had barely closed her eyes when a
hand shook her awake. She had lain awake until dawn,
trying to erase the disturbing scene on the terrace from her
thoughts. Opening her eyes to mere slits, she discovered
brilliant light pouring into the room from the garden, telling
her the hour was well advanced. Focusing her eyes a few
minutes later, she found Evelyn pouring her morning
chocolate at the Pembroke table in front of the sitting room
fire.

"It's about time you became conscious, my friend,"
Evelyn chided as Damara stretched her still tired body. She
moaned as she discovered a few tender spots on her sides.
With a self-conscious flush, she remembered the cause of
her discomfort—the arms of Lord Emsley.

"You look as if you could use some more sleep."

"What time is it?" She ignored Evelyn's pointed look and
donned her much discussed negligee.

"Nearly noon. You have been abed for nearly ten hours.
Papa reported that you escaped the festivities around one
o'clock. I thought you were over your nonsensical fears."

"I was feeling a little lightheaded and decided to retire
early." She seated herself and took a sip of chocolate,
ignoring her friend's audible sniff of disbelief. There was no
need to admit she was still awake when Evelyn had tapped
on her door on her way to bed, or that she had written a
letter to her solicitor soon after.

"Was that before or after you danced with that rather
large specimen of the British male?" A probing look
accompanied the question, causing Damara to squirm uneasily.

"You were very observant last night," she responded
after a moment's consideration whether or not to continue
her evasion.

"Naturally if it is a male, over six feet, very nice to look
at, *and* whisks my closest friend out from under my nose."

Evelyn paused, clearly waiting for an interruption, but none was forthcoming. "*And* who disappears for quite some time on the terrace with said friend."

"Perhaps you would like to tell me who this gentleman was? We don't even have to have a conversation. You can merely continue with your enlightening monologue."

"Unfortunately that's all the information I have," Evelyn admitted with a frustrated sigh. "No one knows who he was. The only people he was seen talking to were you and Lady Covering, then he left. Speculation is running high that it was Emsley. Was it?"

Damara studied the entreating expression on her friend's face. A smile suddenly replaced her own frown as she anticipated Evelyn's response to her answer. "Yes."

Evelyn tried to make her voice work, but nothing would come out. She had only teased to discover the man's identity because last night was the only time Damara had shown any animation toward a male outside her family. Emsley had been a hopeful guess, and she still could not think why the gentleman looked familiar. Another thought quickly brought back her speech with a delighted laugh. "I was right."

"What?" Damara spilled some of her chocolate as she tried to comprehend what could cause Evelyn's glee.

"You said he would be short, balding, and gout-ridden," Evelyn challenged, pointing an accusing finger, "not a hero conjured out of a novel. I would say he stepped directly from the pages, although he is a bit large.

"I don't think so," Damara murmured, surprising herself and forgetting her companion's acute hearing.

"Now that is most interesting."

"Hardly more than an observation, my small friend." Damara pulled a face at the other woman to hide her embarrassment over the admission. What did his height matter, since he was rude and obnoxious? "It was simply nice getting a crick in my neck from looking up at my partner rather than down."

"There were any number of tall gentlemen present last evening," Evelyn replied tartly, defending her lack of inches.

"Apparently they were dancing with someone with de-

cidedly fewer inches than I possess." She hoped this
disagreement would keep Evie from questioning her more
closely about Emsley. There were too many questions she
could not answer herself.

"If you found him that agreeable," Evelyn began with
heat, rising to her full five feet, one inches of height, "then
why not just have done and marry the man."

"Evie, you can't be such a widgeon," Damara called
above the sound of stomping feet and the slamming door
that signaled the departure of her friend. "Well, Lord
Emsley, now look what you've done. I'm arguing with my
closest friend over you, and you aren't worth the bother."

She would not have been quite so put out with the
gentleman if she could have seen her friend skipping down
the hallway, stifling her laughter. Evelyn hurried toward her
room, busily composing a note to Lady Covering.

Evelyn's challenge repeated itself in Damara's mind an
hour later as she watched Emsley enter the library. During
their previous meeting, she had been preoccupied with his
face; now she had time to assess the rest of his person as he
introduced his solicitors.

He was indeed large, towering over both his companions
who were of average height. His dress was faultless, from
the broad shoulders of his corbeau-colored superfine coat to
the gleam of his boots. The unadorned waistcoat he had
chosen for the day accentuated his lean waist above buff
pantaloons that graced his muscular legs like a second skin.
She was pleased she had chosen to wear her antique
lace-trimmed cornflower blue cambric, as she raised her
eyes to the fine lawn of Emsley's shirt. Then she realized
the introductions were completed, and the others were
waiting for her to begin the proceedings.

With as much dignity as she could muster under the intent
hazel eyes of Emsley, she graciously acknowledged the
presence of Messrs. Perkins and Palmer, who could only be
told apart by Mr. Palmer's constant nodding. "Gentlemen,
please be seated. I feel we must get to the bottom of this
rather strange situation."

"Lady Damara, I understand from correspondence with

Mr. Wilkins that you're also mystified by the sudden announcement of your engagement."

"Yes, Mr. Perkins," she agreed with a grateful smile, noting that Mr. Palmer seemed to find her answer agreeable by the vigorous nodding of his head. "I only met His Lordship last evening."

"Oh, dear," Mr. Perkins replied, looking to his client since that lady's tone clearly implied she was not pleased with making his acquaintance, recently or otherwise.

"We seem to be blessed with a fairy godmother," His Lordship remarked dryly, his eyes firmly fixed on Damara's face.

"As I informed Mr. Wilkins and His Lordship, there seems to be no one who can identify the source of the news," Mr. Perkins continued, treading carefully. "I contacted the *Gazette* as instructed, but could find no one on the staff who remembered where the notice came from. Regrettably the other newspapers simply printed the item as gossip."

"Surely the publisher of the *Gazette* wouldn't print an official announcement without some authority," Damara exclaimed.

"The publisher remembers receiving a letter with an authentic-looking seal," Mr. Wilkins put in to claim his client's attention. "But since he had no idea it was a hoax, the missive was discarded as soon as the notice was printed."

"This is preposterous," Damara sputtered as the gentleman next to her remained silent. "I demand that the engagement be retracted as soon as possible."

As she jumped to her feet in agitation, she did not see the signal that passed between Emsley and Mr. Perkins. The solicitor had been given explicit instructions on how his client expected this interview to be resolved.

"Lady Damara, it wouldn't be in the best interests of His Lordship or yourself to deny the engagement at this time," Perkins began uneasily as the lady's face became more thunderous. Mr. Palmer sat at his side bobbing his head in agreement.

"My dear, Lady Damara," Mr. Wilkins intervened as he also read the warning signs, "if you'll be seated, we'll explain the necessity of continuing this . . . er, arrangement for the present."

"Here, my dear, perhaps a touch of wine will help settle your nerves."

Damara found a glass thrust into her hand. Her first impulse was to fling the red liquid in Emsley's face. How dare he offer her her own wine without her consent? The man was a mannerless oaf, and she wanted no part of him. Unfortunately her good breeding did not permit her impulse, or telling him exactly what she thought of his high-handedness in front of their solicitors.

She tried to make her feelings apparent by glaring at him. For a moment there seemed to be an almost entreating look lurking in the back of his eyes. Before she could be sure, the amused tolerance she was becoming all too familiar with from the man was back in place. It was the same look she had seen parents give a not very bright child.

"My dear, you can't find this situation any more uncomfortable than I," Emsley said in a low tone. "I was given the news the moment I stepped ashore. Added to this, I had recently inherited a title and property. You'll excuse me for saying that at first I questioned your own motives in this announcement."

She sat down abruptly as she digested his accusation, disguising her confusion by taking a healthy swallow of wine. The man was insane as well as rude and overbearing. How could he possibly think that she would want to marry him, by fair means or foul? Marriage, even to a suitable party, was not what she wanted, and she was going to let his high-and-mighty Marquess of Emsley know that in no uncertain terms.

She was not destined to do so as the library door was flung open. Lady Mathilde stood in the opening, resplendent in a red-violent concoction. As she stood surveying the startled group, Damara thought she heard Emsley murmur, "Enter the helpful dragon."

"Damara, why wasn't I informed of this meeting?" her aunt demanded, stalking into the room, her cane thumping against the wooden floor.

"Lord Emsley, may I present my aunt, Lady Mathilde Lambert." Damara made the introduction with relish, biting back a smile as she realized for the first time in weeks that she was glad to see her aunt. Emsley and his minions had had the upper hand for far too long, in her opinion, and Mathilde would take on the House of Lords single-handedly without batting an eye. One domineering solider-turned-peer should be child's play.

Emsley came forward to assist the older woman as she was hindered by her stiff joints. He was quickly disabused of his charitable thoughts. The onyx head of her stick rapped across his hand as it came out to take her arm. "Young man, I'm not in my grave as yet," she snapped before stomping across the room to take the seat he had vacated. "Now, we shall see how these gentlemen plan to conclude this nasty business."

Damara waited expectantly for any of the gentlemen to contradict her aunt's assumption that the matter was settled. She stifled a groan as the mousy Mr. Wilkins fiddled with his spectacles and Mr. Palmer sat nodding his head. Fortunately Mr. Perkins did not share his colleagues' timorous characteristics, but he glanced at the marquess for permission to speak.

"Lady Mathilde, we have decided not to terminate the engagement until we have investigated further." He looked straight into her deadly gaze, his eyes never wavering. "Since there's no apparent connection between His Lordship and your niece, we must know the motives of the perpetrator before taking action."

"You gentlemen have had almost a month to discover more than enough to conceal ten engagements," the old woman taunted in an angry voice that rose to a piercing shriek. "You've allowed my niece's continued involvement in a most embarrassing situation."

"Yes, m'lady, it is a most perplexing problem," Mr. Perkins agreed without hesitation. "There would too much speculation if we ended the engagement too soon. We're simply thinking of our client's best interests."

"Yes, we must think of the family reputation." Mathilde gave her niece a piercing look. "You'd best listen to these fools after all, my gel. The Tarrant family has a proud heritage to consider. This brief link with Emsley can be simply blamed on your mother's French blood."

"But, Aunt, I really—"

"Really, my gel, if you insist on a course of action that will only drag the family name through the mud, I'll wash my hands of the entire family," the old woman stated in an imperious command, ignoring the fact that those same words had been uttered over the past years with little results, to her relatives' regrets. "When Jasper returns we shall discuss this again. So, gentlemen, we're satisfied for now."

The three solicitors gave a joint sigh of relief that they had come through the interview without·a mark from the old woman. They quickly began gathering their papers. Mr. Wilkins seemed to find his voice finally as the group began to disperse. "Lady Mathilde, I assure you we'll leave no stone unturned." Her disdainful sniff sent him back to inspecting his spectacles as she swept from the room.

Damara watched in dumbfounded fascination as Messrs. Perkins and Palmer took their leave. She could not believe this was happening. Her aunt's sudden reversal on the engagement had taken her completely by surprise after all her badgering to break all connections with Emsley. Though she had joked about it before, Damara had not realized how strongly her aunt felt about preserving the family name.

Mr. Wilkins quickly scurried out the door after one angry look from his client. Damara watched his departing back, thinking of finding a new solicitor, one who would listen to *her*. In her distraction, she forgot Emsley until his hand closed over hers, which were clenched together in her lap.

He pulled her to her feet, watching the play of emotions over her expressive face, her green eyes clouded with confusion. He was experiencing some confusion himself, wondering why he was feeling sorry for her. The meeting with the solicitors had gone almost the way he had planned it, but he was somehow dissatisfied. Her aunt was the one who agreed to continue the engagement, not Damara. His betrothed was the innocent dupe once again, or was it a carefully staged act? He was beginning to doubt his own name.

"M'lord?" She said the single word in a tentative tone at his continued silence.

"Simon," he prompted gently before bringing her hands

to his lips, one at a time. He would continue with his plan. An innocent would not know how to deal with an amorous fiancé.

"M'lord," she stated again with determination, though her fingers trembled slightly as his lips brushed over the backs of her hands. "I believe our meeting is over. So if you'll excuse me—"

"Not without extracting some penance for your formality," he interrupted softly as he dropped her hands and gently grasped her shoulders. He bent his head before she could protest. Damara remained stiff under his hands. "Now perhaps my name will come more easily to your lips," he murmured against her mouth, "for I'll require a forfeit when it does not."

With that he was gone. Damara stood bemused, gazing at the empty doorway. She had reached the age of two and twenty without encountering the advances of a gentleman; now a man she had known less than a day had kissed her several times. He was the most infuriating man, never giving her time to voice her objections. Did he think a lady had no say in the matter? She shook her head in bewilderment at the curious turn of events.

First she had a fiancé whom no one knew. Now she had met the man, and he seemed bent on making the engagement real—or was he simply taking advantage of the circumstances? Damara caught her breath. Emsley must be responsible for the circumstances. He sent the notice to the newspaper, though she could not fathom his reasoning in selecting her. The working of the male mind utterly defeated her.

She would consider the matter until she found a suitable answer, she decided, and went in search of Evelyn to make up their squabble as well as give her friend an edited account of the recent meeting.

— Chapter Five —

The Marquess of Emsley was amused, standing in the entry hall of the famed "Great House" under the quelling stare of the steward who could not be any more imposing than the original White from where the club took its name. The little man, however, was not intimidating to a former officer who had served both Sir John Moore and the Viscount Wellington. The servant was watching him closely as if he were a cut-purse, or was waiting to snare one of the candlesticks and run.

Simon knew he could make the little man happy by telling him he was the guest of Sir Cedric Townsend, a member in good standing, but his sense of fun made him prefer the role of interloper. The evening would turn serious enough once Sir Cedric arrived and began grilling him about his intentions toward the fair Damara. Although the lady—and haughty steward—found him wanting, Simon was sure he could pass muster with Townsend. He led a simple, straightforward life. He did play cards, drink, occasionally indulged in a good cigar, and only visited the better quality ladies of the *demi-monde*, believing in moderation in all things.

His faults—which some would not find adverse—were the single-minded pursuit of a goal, a disregard for the rigid, hypocritical dictates of polite society, and a sense of humor that came to the fore at the most inappropriate times. Lady Damara Tarrant would undoubtedly call them faults, since all these qualities were at work to break through her reserve. His secret weapon was his patience, which he had employed in the past two days by not seeing his auburn-haired temptress of a fiancée, except in his dreams.

Damara had not seen him, but she had been aware of him, as had the florist and dozens of shopkeepers. As an engaged woman, she was allowed to accept gifts from a gentleman. That gentleman knew better than to be available when the gifts were presented and have them thrown in his face. Although he had only known Damara a short time, he sensed she would not vent her anger on an innocent delivery boy.

"Emsley?"

Simon turned to face the middle-aged, gray-haired man who had just entered from St. James Street. Although his gray thatch was arranged in a fashionable Brutus crop, Sir Cedric still wore the traditional evening dress of knee breeches with his coat of black kerseymere. Simon wondered if his own black pantaloons were what the pretentious steward had disapproved of as the older man rid himself of his cloak and *chapeau bras*.

Within minutes the two gentlemen were regally escorted to a quiet table, in sight but out of earshot of two boisterous games of chance. Simon began to raise his estimation of the revered establishment when he took his first sip of their tolerable claret. By inches he was finding his elevation to the peerage very agreeable, rather than the trial he had anticipated.

"As you know, I have taken it upon myself to act in loco parentis," Sir Cedric began after clearing his throat repeatedly, "due to our family's long association with the Tarrants. Damara is very dear to me and my wife, who by the by does not know of this meeting."

"We think alike, sir, since I only want what is best for Damara." Simon liked this cautious, self-imposed guardian of Damara's. Sir Cedric was direct and did not shilly-shally, but he could not confide his suspicions about the engagement as yet. His godmother vouched for the Townsends, and he did not want to disillusion them about his fiancée without proof. The older man's kindly blue eyes showed real concern for a friend in an awkward situation, as well as understanding for the man he was prepared to interrogate. "Our first duty is to find the person who sent the notice. Myself, I find this a delightful dilemma, an attitude that the lady doesn't seem to share."

Sir Cedric studied the younger man across from him in the soft glow of the wall sconce above their table. Emsley met his eyes steadily. What the older man saw confirmed what his friends at Whitehall had said. This was a rock-solid, dedicated soldier. For the first time since he had sent Emsley the invitation for dinner, Cedric relaxed. With a silent nod, he gave his approval.

"You're going to need some help, Emsley." The statement was said decisively as the waiter appeared with two platters that would satisfy the hardiest trencherman.

"How so? Is the lady so unwilling?" Simon hoped he sounded offhand, though his heart had skipped a beat. Finally he was going to learn the answer to the question that had been plaguing him since he had first set eyes on Lady Damara Tarrant. Was she an innocent or an accomplished actress? He kept his eyes directed at his knife and fork, deftly cutting into his fowl.

"Damara's greatest desire has been to stay quietly in the country taking care of her family," Cedric continued, aware of his companion's unease. He remembered too well his own painful interview with his Kath's papa. "She didn't like her first season, and though she seems to be adapting well during her recent sojourn, life at Tarrant's Mount with young Tremonte and Percy still has a nice, safe appeal."

"Tremonte? I know that name," Simon said abruptly, trying to place where he had heard it in the not so distant past. This was the first common link to Damara; someone they were both acquainted with.

"Actually, I should get accustomed to calling him Lay-ston with old Sedge meeting his maker. Tremonte is Damara's older brother and—I shudder to think—probably my future son-in-law."

"Ahhh. Is Tremonte by any chance in Portugal with the army?" A boisterous shout from the card players across the room helped jog Simon's memory. In his mind he returned to a rundown bard outside Lisbon and saw a cocky young captain with reddish hair and green eyes; there was a family resemblance.

"Yes, the Fourteenth Dragoons. His father felt the young idiot needed some discipline to bring him around," Cedric explained, not able to conceal a rather satisfied smile of his own. He had an affection for Jasper but felt the boy wanted for sense on occasion. "He should be home soon, and you can formally request Damara's hand."

"Actually, I believe I'm already in his debt," the younger man stated while wondering just how much in Tremonte's debt he was. He needed to find out more about this older brother. Was he enough of a scapegrace to shackle his sister to a stranger? "For tonight, however, I need a strong ally to help me win over the fair Damara. It's always best to know one's adversary's strengths and weaknesses. Tell me all you can."

"With pleasure, although this could take some time," Cedric returned, all but rubbing his hands together in anticipation of playing matchmaker. "We'll need another bottle or two to sustain us. Damn shame we can't blow a cloud as well, but we haven't been able to get a majority over the old fussbudgets to allow tobacco."

"We'll have to suffice with the grape, and I don't want you to miss the most insignificant detail." Simon poured the last of their first bottle into the older man's glass. This might prove to be an evening he would curse in the early morning light, but having a valuable ally in breaking through the gentle and innocent Damara's reserve was worth a thundering headache and even having to swallow one of Bundy's noxious cures. Now that he was fairly sure of the answer to the engagement notice, Simon needed to win the lady's trust.

"In turn, Emsley, you must give me your views on this business with Mrs. Clark last year and the Duke of York's resignation."

"Simon, my dear boy, you're sure you want to walk?" Cedric questioned when the two men walked none too steadily out of White's a few hours—and several bottles of wine—later. "Have some sense and join me in the hackney."

"I'm not mad, merely a bit well to live. The walk will clear my head," his companion assured him, although he was swaying slightly as he spoke. He looked up and down the deserted thoroughfare, its brick surface wet from a recent shower that had dissipated the nightly fog. "Besides, hardly anyone, either friend or foe, would be out on a night like this."

"Even so, have a care. We don't want to lose Damara's suitor so soon after finding him," Cedric returned, giving him a hearty slap on the shoulder of his caped greatcoat. The friendly gesture caused Simon to stagger, although the older man's touch would not normally have moved him.

Simon tipped his curled beaver to his drinking companion, who had some difficulty mounting the steps of the hired coach. Once the task was accomplished, he began his solitary walk, carefully placing one foot in front of the other on the slick bricks of the footpath. He focused on the wooden posts that marked the beginning of the carriage way until the damp night air cleared his head enough for him to see exactly where he was going. He hummed under his breath while he recalled the tales of Damara's childhood that Sir Cedric had related. She was a little girl who had climbed trees, refused to let her older brother bully her, and hid a litter of puppies in her bed so the stable master would not destroy the mongrels.

A strange scuffling noise drew his attention back to the present. As he predicted, the evening air had worked on his wine-soaked brain, and he was alert to the movement of shadowy figures between him and Piccadilly, which was in sight. He slowed his pace, trying to discern what lay ahead in the dim, moonlit street. Fleetingly he wished St. James rather than Pall Mall had been one of the areas where the new gas lamps had been tried.

Two shapes materialized from a doorway on the right. Simon still moved in an awkward, staggering pattern to give the impression he was most decidedly under the influence of the grape. The shapes were two men, both a head shorter than he, which he was pleased to note as he drew level with them. "Dismal evening, gentlemen, dismal."

The slurred statement seemed to necessitate a discussion between the pair. "Jem, this be the bloke?"

"Nub it, Squeeze," his friend answered in a guttural voice. "We tain't paid ta jabber."

"And what exactly were you paid to do, my good man?" asked Simon in an unmistakably sober tone, straightening to his full height.

The pair panicked and both rushed their prepared victim at the same time. Simon's fist connected with Jem's jaw at the same time Squeeze landed a blow to the shoulder Simon had wrenched during his fall from Nemesis. Only finely honed reflexes enabled Simon to plant a solid blow to the man's stomach in time to parry Jem's renewed attack. Thanks to both assailants' inept skill at fisticuffs and Simon's superior strength, the odds were about even. Then Jem pulled a knife from his boot.

Simon knew he had to eliminate his other opponent to defend himself successfully. With a right uppercut, he sent Squeeze to the pavement. He was not, however, in time to deflect Jem's first swipe with his knife before it grazed his cheek. In spite of the sharp pain of the cut, Simon grabbed the man's wrist, exerting pressure until the weapon clattered to the ground. But he underestimated Jem who struck out with his other fist, slamming it into his victim's eye. Simon was caught off balance and joined Squeeze on the damp bricks.

"Oy, what's 'appenin' 'ere?" came a shout from down the street. The clatter of boots against brick sounded, telling Simon that someone was running toward him. Out of his uninjured eye he saw Jem haul up his groaning partner in crime by the scruff of his neck. The pair stumbled off into the darkness before Simon's rescuer arrived.

"Ay, gov'ner, ya be all ri't?"

Simon rolled over onto his back to find a stocky man dressed in a top hat with a scarlet vest under his black suit of clothes that announced he was a member of the Bow Street foot patrol. "Ya shouldna be out alone, sir."

"How true," Simon muttered as he sat up, every bone in his body aching. He did not need the runner to tell him he had done something foolish. The fact he was sitting in a wet gutter was proof positive that he had been foolhardy to walk and equally foolish to take on two footpads when he had been drinking. He knew, however, he would have met Jem and Squeeze at another time from their earlier comments. Had the same person who hired the scum been responsible for his cut girth, he wondered as he took his rescuer's proffered hand and got to his feet.

"My friend, besides a reward for this night's work, I have

a commission for you," Simon offered and leaned heavily against the runner as they began the rest of the walk to his chambers. The journey to the Albany was not long as Simon gave his new acquaintance, Oliver Peal, a review of the past few weeks.

The sound of the brass knocker echoed ominously through the house, or so Damara thought as she sat alone in the drawing room the next afternoon. For the past three days, morning and afternoon, yet another reminder of her persistent fiancé had arrived, but always by messenger. In the morning an extravagant floral tribute arrived and later something more personal. First he had sent a delicate woolen shawl that she recognized as a product of the East that was all the rage. Yesterday came a silk, hand-painted fan depicting a charming woodland scene that was delivered by the same messenger.

Each time the boy asked if there was a reply. Damara knew Emsley purposely sent his gifts through an intermediary, knowing she would not vent her frustration on an innocent party. The man was diabolical in unwittingly choosing a boy who looked so much like Percy. How could he know she had enough trouble disciplining her brother, and she would not take her anger out on another young boy? Men!

Nervously she picked at the jaconet overskirt to her flowered sprig muslin dress while she tried to hear the low-voiced conversation as Hastings challenged the caller. What was Emsley sending today? Perhaps a delicately carved bouquet holder or possibly fine linen handkerchiefs trimmed in Irish lace? She had to acknowledge that Emsley had excellent taste. Then she chided herself for being distracted. The marquess deserved a stern lecture, no matter how lovely his gifts were. She could not allow herself to soften towards the man in any way.

Hastings appeared in the doorway with his perpetual frown in place. Damara jumped as he announced the last name she expected to hear. "The Marquess of Emsley."

There was no time to deny she was not at home, for the aggravating man was two steps behind the butler. As much as she railed against dictates of polite behavior, she wished just once Emsley would behave properly.

Then his appearance erased every other thought from her mind. He was impeccably dressed in a coat of chocolate brown kerseymere over fawn-colored breeches and tasseled Hessians, with one surprising addition: a black sling supporting his left arm. His face had not escaped whatever catastrophe had befallen him; a jagged cut ran down his right cheek, and the skin under his left eye was badly discolored. He seemed unconcerned with his injuries under her startled gaze.

"Di . . . did you have an argument with your tailor, my . . . Simon?" Damara attempted lightly, not willing to admit her distress over his marred appearance. Suddenly she realized how her stumbling words sounded and she felt the color staining her cheeks. Emsley's twinkling sherry-colored eyes only increased her discomfort, telling her he enjoyed being called "my Simon," even if she had intended to say "m'lord" at the start.

"No, apparently two gentlemen—at least they were of the male gender—took some objection to my sojourn home last evening," he explained glibly and ignored the chair she indicated, sitting close to her on the settee. "I managed to convince them there was no need for their rather curious attentions."

"But, Simon—" Damara began uncertainly, but stopped as he casually pulled out his watch to check the time. Clearly he did not want to discuss the incident, although she thought it unwise to dismiss the incident. Such attacks did happen frequently in the city, but she had never seen anyone so offhand. Men were enough of an enigma to her, and apparently Emsley's army life made this seem a mere scrape. Besides, she cautioned silently, if she made an issue of it, he would only misconstrue her interest, and of course she felt only mild distress for a fellow human being.

"I believe if you can change in fifteen minutes, we can manage to arrive in the park within the dictated hour," he speculated, studying the tips of his boots while he replaced his watch in his waistcoat pocket. He seemed to be inspecting the glossy surface of the boot leather for scratches, unaware of the sudden intake of breath from his companion.

When he received no reply, he raised his head, giving Damara an inquiring look.

She returned his innocent gaze through narrowed green eyes. Since their first meeting at Justine's ball, he had studiously avoided her company. Yet here he sat calmly announcing they would join the afternoon promenade in Hyde Park as if it were an everyday occurrence. On a perverse whim, she decided to play along with his plan; however, he would be dancing to her tune.

"Horses or carriage?" she asked demurely, noting with satisfaction his start of surprise at her easy acquiescence.

"Horses for the present," Simon responded after masking his initial astonishment, since he had been prepared for her opposition. Perhaps his gifts had softened the lady, but he doubted that was the cause. Sir Cedric said she would do what was least expected if it suited her purpose. "I would have difficulty handling the ribbons with only one good arm."

"Fifteen minutes, I believe you said?" Damara inquired with a tilt to her chin that the untutored could mistake for flirtatiousness. She rose majestically to her feet and graced her fiancé with a fleeting smile. "I'll have Hastings fetch you something to quench your thirst to wile away the time."

Although she sauntered leisurely from the room, Damara's demeanor changed the moment she sent Hastings into the drawing room. With lifted skirts, she took the stairs two at a time. As she entered her room, she called breathlessly for Meg to assist her with the tiny row of buttons down the back of her dress. By the time she struggled out of her gown, both she and the lady's maid were in a nervous state.

Meg was eyeing her strangely as Damara kept muttering under her breath. "Can I be ready in fifteen minutes? Of course I can. 'Tis silly males who stand preening like peacocks in front of the mirror for hours, admiring a single neckcloth. And how long did it take you to dress this morning, Your Aggravating Lordship?"

Ruthlessly Damara pulled on the brown velvet riding habit that had been delivered the day before. There was little time to admire how the military cut complemented her her statuesque figure after a glance at the ormolu clock on the mantel. With four minutes to spare, she placed a matching felt shako at a daring angle atop her auburn curls. Satisfied with her apparel, Damara walked sedately into the sitting room with half a minute to spare, the expression on Emsley's face a suitable reward for her haste.

Within a matter of minutes they were moving their mounts out of the square and onto Oxford Street. Damara bowed graciously to Emsley's escort, determined he would need to initiate any conversation. She needed some time to assess his character. He had already proven himself a worthy antagonist, and she would need time to prepare her defenses. Under lowered lashes, she studied him.

She could not deny he had a fine seat. Atop his black stallion, his military bearing was unmistakable. He was in perfect control with the use of one hand. By the time they entered the park, Damara was moving restlessly in her saddle—from more than a desire to gallop instead of the forced sedate walk—because she could find not one flaw in her temporary fiancé, except that he was persistent and bossy. He blithely ignored her continued silence as he discussed the weather and the latest gossip as if she had responded to every word. To add to her irritation, the progress of the afternoon traffic was slower than usual.

In spite of his outwardly placid appearance, Simon was equally unsettled. Damara was riding beside him, but she was as responsive as a stick of furniture. His cautious elation at her acceptance had completely dissolved. He felt like a general whose right flank had come under surprise attack, and he had no reinforcements. Time was too short for him to make so little progress. He must have some sign of progress with Damara before her chuckle-headed brother returned to announce himself the author of their engagement. Of that fact he was sure, after a sleepless night of pondering who was trying to injure him, and if Damara's brother was calling in his debt. He did not like not knowing his course or the possible outcome.

The sound of angry voices directly ahead of them over the usual hubbub took his thoughts from his immediate problems. In their path was a curricle whose young driver was having difficulty controlling his horses, forcing others to go around him. His outspoken female companion was no more agreeable than his team of high-spirited grays. Her shrill, accusing voice rose above everything as she berated her escort, who was at least ten years her junior. Simon quickly summed up the pair's relationship, but before he could suggest to Damara that they move along, his attention was drawn to a woeful figure at the side of the disturbance. A muddy and disheveled youth stood clutching a quivering oversized bundle of brown, curly fur in his thin arms.

"Dear Lord, it's Percy and Cretin," Damara exclaimed from beside him, impetuously jumping from her saddle without any assistance. She pushed through the curious spectators, giving no thought to anyone except the boy. She was unaware of Simon dismounting and taking her reins before following a few steps behind. He kept his face impassive under the raised eyebrows of the crowd, although he was as perplexed as they over her interest in the cowering ragamuffin.

A collective gasp came from those standing close enough to see when Damara clasped the disreputable boy in her arms. Simon smiled as the name Percy finally struck a responsive chord in his brain. This was Damara's younger brother.

"Oh, Mara, I've found you!" The weary exclamation was punctuated by a bark coming from the wiggling mass of curls in the boy's arms.

"Percy, my dear, what a mess you are," his sister returned with a laughing scold, matching the grin on his face as she relieved him of his large, squirming companion. "What are you doing here?"

"He be settin' that fee-roshus beasty on lovey's 'orses, that's wot he be doin'," a shrill voice announced from above them.

"Maudy, hush. It wasn't the boy's fault," reprimanded the young man next to the harridan without much conviction. He flushed deep red as he met Simon's bland stare over Damara's shoulder. Hastily he gathered his reins together and awkwardly moved his vehicle through the laughing crowd. The spectators' sympathy was all for the boy, especially since his sister was quality. Simon, however, knew the climate could change in the blink of an eye.

"We have to get you home at once," Damara ordered her exhausted and quite damp brother, echoing Simon's sentiments but oblivious to the possibility of gossip springing from this tiny incident. "Emsley, you take Percy in front of you while I quiet Cretin."

"Do you plan to mount with that unruly hound in your arms?" Simon inquired with a slight smile after assisting Percy onto Nemesis's back. He gave his fiancée credit for many talents, but mounting side-saddle with a wiggling dog just might be beyond her.

"No, you'll hold him," she snapped and thrust the muddy dog at his chest with little regard for his injured arm. If there was one thing she hated, it was being laughed at, especially by this man who always seemed to regard her with an amused twinkle in his brown eyes. Her anger allowed her to accomplish a creditable seat in one fluid motion without even requesting a leg up. She took Cretin from Emsley with a smug smile that wavered only when her gaze lowered to his soiled sling.

Their strange procession left the park quickly amid a buzz of speculation. Percy leaned back against the large man behind him, too tired to worry about his dignity or the identity of his sister's escort. Damara crooned over the trembling dog in her arms, who for once in his life did not act up. Just behind her she could hear Simon's deep voice reassuring Percy.

"Well, they both seem to have survived their misadventure," Damara stated with relief as she entered the drawing room a short time later and gladly accepted a cup of tea from Evelyn.

"What has the young scamp been up to?" Evelyn inquired with an amused look of an experienced older sister. "I didn't think he still had the spirit left in him for such a journey."

"He didn't have time to explain while immersed in hot water," Damara returned easily, an affectionate smile curving her lips.

"That is your young brother, then?" Simon interrupted, finding that he wanted Damara to turn her dreamy smile upon him.

"Oh, dear." She flushed becomingly as she realized she had forgotten his limited acquaintance with her family, since it seemed she had known him longer than a few days. Her concern for Percy had overshadowed all else.

"Yes, that dirty bundle of rags is my brother, Percy," she returned quickly to cover her confusion, "and his companion is his faithful mongrel and part-time lap dog."

"Lap dog? An Irish Water Spaniel is quite an armful. I would hate to suffer sharing a chair."

"An Irish what?" Damara was momentarily diverted from her brother's antics at the legitimate-sounding name Emsley gave the disreputable Cretin. The brown, curly-haired hound with its rat tail and funny little peak of curls between his eyes had to be one of nature's mistakes.

"He looks to be the image of a dog one of the officers had at the academy, an Irish Water Spaniel," Emsley returned with a smile at both women's amazed expressions. "I've never seen another dog as . . . well—"

"Comical," Evelyn put in with a chuckle. "You don't need to worry about offending anyone, least of all Cretin. We have certainly called him worse. And now that that mystery is solved, how did our pedigreed hound and young Percy arrive in town?"

"Once he's eaten, he'll join us," Damara returned, still smiling over Cretin's suddenly respectable lineage.

"I'm here," announced an uncertain voice from the doorway with an unmistakable adolescent crackle. Percy was now a glowing pink from his recent scrubbing. The clothes he had worn were being boiled clean, so he was attired in the youngest footman's Sunday clothes. Although the sleeves were turned back and the stockings wrinkled around his ankles, the boy walked with erect pride to stand before his sister.

As Damara watched his earnest figure advance, she bit back a gasp of surprise. Percy was walking fairly easily without dragging his foot. There was almost no trace of his injury that had plagued him for the last year. She restrained her impulse to take the boy into her arms and express her joy. The overly dignified young man before her would not appreciate such a display before the impressive gentleman he was watching out of the corner of his eye. She contented herself with grasping Evelyn's hand.

"Please, dear, make your bow to Lord Emsley," she

instructed softly, and was glad her voice remained steady. "Then tell us what brings you from Tarrant's Mount."

Simon returned the boy's bow solemnly. He had noted the sudden tension between the two women at the boy's entrance. Something unexpected had occurred, and he was amazed that he was so attuned to Damara's change of mood. He was beginning to find there was a number of amazing things that had happened to his emotions since meeting Damara.

"We received a letter from Jasper at last." Percy allowed a triumphant grin to break through his grown-up facade before he forgot his pose altogether and dropped to his knees at his sister's feet. "I wanted to be the one to bring the news, but Ambruster said not."

"So I see," murmured his sister, trying to hold back a smile at his half-mutinous, half-imploring look.

"I waited until everyone was asleep and left out the library window," Percy continued, ignoring the quiet remark. "I walked to the village to catch the mail coach, but on the way down the drive I discovered Cretin had followed me. He sat baying in the road when I commanded him to stay."

"I'm surprised he didn't wake the entire countryside," Evelyn put in as Percy stopped for a much-needed breath.

"Oh, I fed him some tidbits from my bundle to quiet him and decided the only thing was to bring him along," the boy explained with a very heartfelt sigh. "I couldn't risk going back to the house."

"How did you ever manage the coach with that beast?" Simon asked impulsively, the picture of the animal climbing haphazardly over the helpless passengers clear in his mind.

"I couldn't take the coach with Cretin. I had to begin walking and begged a ride the next morning," Percy went on with a grimace at the memory. "All was fine until the next day. I took a ride with two men driving a wagon, and I fell asleep. When I woke up, I was laying by the side of the road with only poor Cretin, muzzled, next to me. All my money and my bundle were gone, so I had to walk the rest of the way."

"But what about Jasper's letter?" Evelyn shot out, all of

her earlier humor gone at the thought of the precious letter being lost.

"That was in the lining of my cap and quite safe. When I reached the city, I was misdirected a number of times and ended up in the park where Cretin decided he wanted to take a swim." The last came out in a rush as Percy brought forth a rather crumpled letter. He proudly presented it to his sister.

Damara could only stare at the long-awaited letter as it lay in her lap. She fought back tears of relief as she recognized the spidery handwriting. Finally Evelyn could not bear the suspense any longer. She jerked her friend's arm to bring her out of her dazed state. "Mara, get on with it."

"Oh, sorry," she murmured, broke what was left of the seal, and read the letter aloud.

"Dear Mara,
    I have just received your letter about Percy's injuries in the accident. You should have told me sooner, not waited until I was ready to return and be damned with the old goat's will. Now I worry about you at home more than ever. I'll sell out and return home on the next available transport and contact Wilkins as soon as I arrive in London.
    Regards to Percy and Evelyn. It will be a joy to see the green of Tarrant's Mount and be where it only rains half as much.

                                    With Love,
                                    Jasper"

"He's coming home at last. Hurrah!" Percy burst out and jumped to his feet to dance a little jig in the middle of the room.

"And with only one mention of the weather. Amazing," Evelyn murmured from behind her handkerchief, dabbing her misty eyes.

Damara was having similar difficulty with her own composure while Simon took in the entire scene. Whoever Jasper was—although he had a strong suspicion it was Tremonte—the man had quite an emotional impact on both the ladies. He wondered if Damara would be so pleased with her brother if she even suspected—as he did—who had engineered their engagement.

"Percy, be careful of—" Damara broke off her warning, not wanting to draw attention to his former infirmity which he seemed to have forgotten.

"My leg is fine, Mara," he assured her swiftly, but stopped his erratic dance. He looked down at his foot and shrugged almost philosophically. "I don't know what happened, but I noticed this morning it wasn't stiff anymore."

"I suppose the miles of walking could either cure it or damage it forever," his sister replied, equally mystified by the occurrence.

The matter was temporarily dismissed when she spied the young man attempting to hide a strenuous yawn. "Tomorrow we'll summon a doctor, but right now, my lord Percy, it's time for you to get some rest."

"Oh, Mara," he complained in disgust, although he knew when his sister called him by that erroneous title it was a losing argument.

"Where is he going to sleep?" Evelyn asked quickly, clearly trying to calculate where they had an empty room with her family in residence. "I could take young Lydia in with me, or perhaps we should air Jasper's room."

"Not Jasper's," his younger brother snapped in a voice that plainly said he would sleep in the attic before taking his brother's bed. "His room has to be ready when he arrives."

"If you hadn't grown so much last year, we could you put in the nursery," Damara commented, ignoring his outburst as well as the face he made at such ignoble banishment.

"Perhaps I might be of service," Simon put in quietly from his post near the fireplace, wondering if anyone still remembered he was present. He would need all the allies possible in the coming days when Jasper returned. "I've taken chambers at the Albany while Emsley House is being renovated. My man Bundy and I have room for another gentleman."

Damara opened her mouth to protest since she did not want to be obliged to her temporary fiancé; however, the delighted grin on her brother's face stopped her. Just less than a week past, she had acknowledged the absence of any male influence in Percy's life. Emsley appeared to be steadier than Jasper, whom she would not hesitate to have care for Percy. A friendship with another man would also help lessen the boy's overly possessive worship of his older brother. "That seems to be the best solution. Thank you, Simon, for your generous offer."

"Oh, thank you, Mara. Sir." Percy stood quivering in the middle of the room, torn between the desire to embrace his sister and the need to keep a semblance of dignity in front of the marquess. Then his elations turned into a disappointed frown. "What do I do about clothes? I only have what I arrived in."

"Tomorrow I'll take you around to my tailor and see what he can do for you," Simon offered before Damara could answer. He moved forward and clasped the boy companionably on the shoulder, giving him a purely masculine look of understanding. "We'll come 'round afterward and present your sister with the exorbitant bill."

"Too right," Percy agreed with his smile returning as a conspiratorial grin.

"Now we'll take our leave of the ladies and go meet Bundy. He was my sergeant-major in Portugal before I sold out." The news had Percy more animated than either Damara or Evelyn had seen him in months.

"Percy, fetch a strong lead for Cretin," Damara instructed, not looking at Emsley to see his reaction to an additional four-legged guest. He did not have time to protest before Percy took off at a run for the kitchen and the sound of voices announced the return of Lady Kath and her younger daughters from their shopping expedition.

— Chapter Six —

The shopping party's return speeded the departure of the gentlemen. Percy was anxious to escape the mothering of Lady Kath and equally annoying harassment of young Lydia. Damara followed Emsley and Percy to the street, giving her brother a sisterly lecture on the behavior of a guest, especially a guest with a pet like Cretin. As she turned back to the house with a final wave at the two figures on Nemesis's broad back, another visitor arrived by carriage.

The elegant figure of Lady Covering alighted, dressed in a jonquil carriage costume of spotted cambric, adorned with ruffles that Damara knew she herself could never wear. The lady gave the younger woman an abashed look from beneath the brim of her Gypsy straw as she stripped off her lemon-colored kid gloves.

"I've come to offer my apologies for not warning you of Simon's arrival." She began her explanation prettily, watching Damara's expression closely. When the younger woman smiled and took her arm for the short walk up the steps, Regina relaxed. "He made me swear not to tell. You'll also notice I waited a sufficient amount of time for your, er, surprise to have dissipated."

"My *surprise* has indeed had time to dissipate, so I readily accept your apology," Damara replied with a kind smile as they walked past the impassive figure of Hastings, who could have been mistaken for ornamental statuary. Damara had been on the receiving end of Emsley's persuasive manner and could well understand his godmother's dilemma. "Although there is one omission of yours that still has me a trifle piqued. You never told me what a pest he is, much like your Ajax."

"Ah, but an endearing pest," Regina returned, laughing

at Damara's charge against Simon. She had been dragged out on countless trips, going from shop to shop with her godson during the past few days in search of gifts for the young lady. His attentions, however, did not seem to discomfort the recipient very much.

Lady Covering's appearance in the sitting room soon had the other ladies chatting about their current purchases, and there was no other chance for a private conversation. Damara did divert their attention briefly with the news of Jasper's letter. Then she excused herself to change from her riding habit after agreeing to ride with Regina the next day.

"There you are. I see though Percy is back to his old self, you're taking up his invalid habits," Evelyn accused gently, and took a seat next to Damara on the stone bench in the small garden behind the house. "Lady Covering left over a half hour ago, and I've been trying to find you ever since."

"I should have known you would follow like one of Uncle Cedric's best dogs." Damara laughed softly at her friend's disgruntled look over the comparison as she leaned back on the trellis that formed a bow over the secluded seat. She had been sitting in solitude trying to sort out her thoughts about Simon.

"You know very well riding to the hounds makes me nauseated."

"Very true, but you're also as cunning as the wily fox and as tenacious as a hound who has the scent," Damara returned in hopes of prolonging the moment when Evie began asking questions that had no answers. "When you're anxious to know something, you stick to the trail of your prey, and now you have tracked me to earth. What has set you on the course?"

"We have any number of prime candidates for discussion. But from your tone I'd wager you're anticipating the worst," Evelyn began, her blue eyes twinkling and both dimples coming into play. She was using every amount of her persuasive manner to discover if her friend was as impressed with the strong and silent marquess as she thought. "Tell me what you think about Emsley, other than he is not bald."

"I see I'll never be allowed to forget that foolishness,"

was the laughing reply. Damara moved back further into the shadows of the bower and blessed the growing dusk of the approaching evening that hid her expression. Evelyn would immediately detect the wariness in her eyes.

"Never, my dear friend, and you aren't going to put me off this time. You have managed to avoid any personal comments about your fiancé since you met him." Evelyn tried to put as much dejection into her voice as possible to show her supposed hurt at not being her friend's confidante. Then she gave one more prod. "Something must be bothering you since you haven't even changed out of your habit."

"You don't fool me in the least, so don't pull out your handkerchief and enact a Cheltenham tragedy," Damara admonished, and clasped her friend's hand in a show of affection. "I haven't talked to you about Simon because I'm very confused and somewhat unsettled. Hardly a desirable state of mind for a responsible adult."

"Then it is just as well we burned your caps," the blonde put in, unable to suppress her sense of humor for long. "Clearly you aren't old enough for them."

"Evie, what did I ever do to be burdened with such a friend? Aunt Mathilde would be easier to discuss this with," she exclaimed in return. "If you won't be serious—"

"I promise, so you won't have to seek out the old dragon. Although now that she is mobile again, the woman is never at home," Evelyn observed with a perplexed frown. "She has been disappearing during the afternoons and has hardly complained about anything for days. In fact, last night I think I actually heard her humming."

"We should count ourselves fortunate and pray she continues to be so affable," her niece answered with a resigned sigh. She was ready to confide in her closest friend over her disturbing feelings toward Simon, but Evelyn was discussing the disagreeable Lady Mathilde. Before she lost her courage, Damara decided to meet the subject head on and in a manner that would ensure the other woman's undivided attention. "How do you feel when Jasper kisses you?"

"What?!" One word was all the dumbfounded Evelyn could manage. The handsome marquess with the delightful smile seemed quiet and reserved to her. Damara had not so much as hinted until now that he was not as dignified as his fiancée.

"You can see why I'm confused," Damara continued when her companion said nothing more. "I was the leading anecdote of one season, and now I'm very much pursued by a gentleman of the first stare. We *are* of similar height, and the gentleman *has* been away from feminine companionship while in the army, but can you explain any other reason for his determined interest?"

"How many times?" The words practically tripped over themselves as they rushed out of Evelyn's mouth.

"How many times what?" She was beginning to enjoy herself. Her friend's voice almost cracked in anxiety to know more. Instead of having to painfully bare her confused emotions, she was having fun teasing Evelyn about Simon's kisses. Damara knew it had been years since she had bested the petite blonde.

"How many times has Emsley kissed you?" Evelyn asked with great care, eyeing Damara's guileless face with suspicion as if she was not quite sure her friend had not gone soft in the head.

"Oh! Let me see, there was Justine's ball to start with," Damara returned in a slow drawl. Staring off into space, just beyond Evelyn's shoulder, she murmured under her breath and played at counting on her fingers. Abruptly she stopped, focusing on her friend to inquire, "Am I only counting kisses on the lips?"

Evelyn opened her mouth, but only high-pitched squeaking sounds came out. Hastily she cleared her throat and tried again. "Count all kisses."

Damara ducked her head to hide the smile—which was almost a smirk—that trembled on her lips at her friend's hesitant tone. Though the two had no secrets from each other, clearly Evelyn was dreading a disclosure of debauched behavior. "The night of Justine's ball there were four kisses all together. Two long ones and a short one on the lips and a rather interesting one on the side of my neck. You know, that tickled slightly as well as having the most curious effect on my toes."

"Your toes?" Evelyn echoed in a dazed undertone. Then

she shook her head as if to dismiss her chaotic thoughts. "Were there, er, did he kiss you any other times?"

"Oh, yes. The other day after Messrs. Wilkins, Palmer and Perkins left, Simon took exception to me being too formal. He has promised to kiss me whenever I forget to use his first name," Damara explained in a confiding tone that a society hostess used when imparting the secret of her latest beauty emulsion to a hated rival. "Simon was understanding and only kissed me a single time after he was done nibbling on my fingers. Has Jasper ever kissed your hands when you weren't wearing gloves?"

"Jasper has never kissed my hands, with or without gloves." The pronouncement was made in an unnecessarily loud voice.

"Evie, how many times has Jasper kissed you?" Damara could not keep back the words. She had assumed her ramshackle brother had stolen kisses when he and Evelyn went riding together or on long walks. From her friend's reaction, she was beginning to wonder if Evie was as sophisticated as she thought.

"Jasper has kissed me a number of times, but . . ." Evelyn's voice trailed off as she ducked her head to study her hands that she was nervously twisting in her lap. She took a deep breath and hurried on, "I wouldn't call them real kisses. They're like the ones he gives anyone under the mistletoe. Those quick, smacking schoolboy kisses. Certainly nothing like your Simon's, since Jasper's kisses never last long enough to curl my toes."

"But why?" She was truly mystified. Jasper had announced at Evie's eighteenth birthday party that he was going to marry her, though he intended to wait until he returned from university and also the military when the earl had insisted on his two years of service.

"Your brother isn't always playing the fool, although I'm not sure this is not another one of his starts." Evelyn began her explanation tartly and gave an exasperated sigh. "He refuses to kiss me as a grown woman until we're ready to wed. He doesn't trust himself to kiss me, except with the light-hearted touch of a schoolboy. Oh, Mara, what are adult kisses like?"

"Very nice," she admitted, without stopping to consider

how her response would be interpreted by her romantically minded friend. "That is to say, Simon seems most practiced. I really don't know if he is an expert."

"He can curl your toes, so he must be somewhat proficient," Evelyn put in quickly. Her usual daring returned to allow her to gently tease her friend. "Truthfully, Mara, is it exciting to actually be kissed by a gentleman?"

"Yes, it is, and very unsettling. Simon has a way of staring deeply into my eyes with an extremely disturbing expression in his sherry-colored eyes." Damara could not keep a wistful note from her voice. "I can tell when he is about to kiss me. Part of me wants to say no, but another is always tempted to see if this kiss will be as exciting as the last."

"I think we shall be having a wedding soon after all."

"Evelyn Townsend, you traitor. You think so little of me that I would marry a man simply because he knows how to kiss." Damara jumped to her feet, amazed that she had let her teasing get so out of hand.

"It's a start, and he seems to be an exceptionally nice man. Most marriages begin with less romantic reasons," Evelyn stated. She had never seen her friend in such a taking before this. Was there more about Emsley that Damara had been keeping to herself?

"The man is overbearing, arrogant, and has no manners whatsoever. He has never once asked me if I wanted him to kiss me, or if I even have an opinion in my head," Damara exclaimed as she began to pace back and forth in front of the stone bench, warming to her subject with each step. "Even my fool of a brother recognizes that I've a brain. Would you want to go through life with a man who dictated your every move and thought without a by-your-leave?"

"You make him sound like Napoleon," Evelyn put in when Damara paused for breath.

"That is exactly what I mean," Emsley's outraged fiancée stated, and emphasized her point by shaking her finger at her bewildered friend. "He is as diabolical as that little tyrant. I'm now convinced that Simon is the one who placed the announcement in the newspapers."

Evelyn could only gape at her friend in astonishment, wondering if Damara realized she continued to use Emsley's given name so naturally. "Mara, what reason could he possibly have for that? He has a title and his own fortune. What does he hope to gain?"

"Respectability, since the Fentner-Smythe name has been dragged through the mire for years." With a triumphant smile she placed her hands on her hips in a defiant pose as she nodded in satisfaction over her powers of deduction.

Evelyn's worried frown was suddenly replaced with a generous smile that blossomed into outright laughter. "That's the silliest thing I've ever heard. His connection with the Dempster family would give him suitable entree into society. Lady Covering is on the greatest terms with all the patronesses of Almack's, and she is received at court."

"I was hoping you wouldn't think of that," Damara murmured, her shoulders slumping in defeat as she took her place on the bench next to her friend once more. "I know he has to be responsible but haven't come up with a logical reason for it. I'm hampered by not being able to understand the male mind. It works so strangely at times."

She did not know how to explain her apprehension to Evelyn. Her friend had been planning to marry from the moment she could walk, it seemed, as all women were expected to do. Fortunately she had had a taste of freedom in making her own decisions, choosing her own course. And she was not going to be swayed by anyone, no matter how tall he was or how accomplished at kissing.

"You really haven't given the poor man much of a chance to be anything but overbearing, have you? You have known him less than a week," Evelyn reasoned, and received no immediate argument. "I say you should take your time and get to know more about Emsley while we wait for Jasper to return, since the solicitors seem to think that will be a momentous event. Then you can say farewell to His Lordship, knowing you have given him a fair hearing, or have been able to discover his purpose."

"Yes, I suppose that is the best course," Damara agreed with reluctance. She knew she would not change her mind and would return to her life at Tarrant's Mount. She would get to know Simon and then, if satisfied he had no ulterior motive, she and Evelyn would find him a nice young woman to marry. The last thought was not as agreeable as she would have liked, so Damara decided to change the subject. "We should go upstairs to change. What are we doing this evening, a rout? Or by some chance of good fortune, the theater?"

"Tonight is an evening of Handel at the Hanover Square Concert Room because Papa is still concerned about the disturbance over the ticket prices at Covent Garden since it reopened," Evelyn answered with little enthusiasm. Both young ladies found the restrictions of only Ancient Music at Hanover Square a bit wearing. They longed to hear the newest symphony by Herr Beethoven and begged to see John Kemble, but to no avail. Though nothing had occurred similar to the riots of the previous season, Sir Cedric refused all their pleas. So this evening they were destined to sit through a concert of music at least a quarter of a century old.

"There are visitors in the sitting room, milady," intoned Hastings the moment Damara stepped into the entry hall on her return from the lending library late the next morning. The man's expression did not give away whether or not he approved of the guests. In that moment Damara decided Evelyn was right. The Duke of Cumberland's horse, preserved in gilded iron, at the center of the square showed more emotion than the butler.

"Yes, Hastings?" she prompted for further enlightenment while placing the newly printed volumes of *Lady of the Lake* and her parasol on the japanned black and gilt pier table.

"Lord Emsley and your brother arrived ten minutes past," the man finally explained as Damara pulled off her York tan gloves. Then he assisted her in removing her sage green spencer that complemented her spotted green and cream raw muslin morning gown.

Damara quickly untied the green ribbons that secured her straw capote and handed the stiff-brimmed bonnet to Meg, who was waiting patiently to take her mistress's outdoor garments abovestairs. "Thank you, Hastings, that will be all. I'll ring if I need you."

She idly ruffled the curled fringe of her bangs and made a show of securing an errant hair while watching the humorless butler's departure in the three-sectioned gilt-framed mirror above the pier table. As she puffed out the short oversleeves of her dress, she peeked over her shoulder to make sure no one was in sight. Hastily she pinched her cheeks to give them added color and nibbled slightly on her lips to redden them. For a moment she practiced a gracious and winning smile in the mirror, but finally gave up the effort as hopeless.

She would have to face Simon as she was. There was no time to sneak up to her room for a more complete repair to her toilette. Due to her decision to become better acquainted with her fiancé, she had had her first sound night's sleep since their brief meeting at the Scarlet Lion. Today she was acting like a perfect ninnyhammer at the mention of his name. With an unladylike snort of self-disgust and straightening her shoulders, she walked sedately toward the sitting room, trying to ignore the rapid increase of her pulse.

"My dear, talk slower, please. I can't understand a word you've said," Damara instructed her brother as he tugged on her hand until she sat down beside Evelyn on the settee. After she was abruptly seated, she continued, "Now, start again."

Simon kept his lips from quirking into a smile when the boy gave her his account of their visit to the illustrious Weston's. Very soon, however, he had no reason to smile. Percy launched into reporting where else they had been during the morning.

"Jackson's Parlor?" Damara looked to her fiancé with a frown marring her pretty face. "Simon, you took Percy to a boxing establishment? I would think he's a little young."

"Oh, Mara, it was top drawer," Percy put in, but her accusing green gaze remained on the man who straightened from his relaxed position against the mantel.

"After we were fortunate enough to discover an already-made suit of clothing in Percy's size that had been forgotten at Weston's, we needed to occupy our time until it was a decent hour to call," Simon began, feeling as though he had been called to task by Wellington himself—or was it his nanny from earlier days? Whatever the memory, his neck-cloth was becoming excruciatingly tight.

"We had a bang-up morning, too. Before Jackson's we

went to the Guildhall Crypt to see Gog and Magog. Mara, did you know they are fifteen feet high?" Percy asked the question as if he were describing the seventh wonder of the world. "Then I finally got to see the mummy in the wall at St. James at Garlick Hill, just like Jasper said."

"You should be locked in your room on bread and water, my boy, not be entertained like royalty," Mathilde announced from the doorway, drawing the attention of everyone in the room.

Simon wanted to kiss the hem of the old harridan's violet dress. With her one scathing comment she had drawn Damara's anger from him. He had seen the gathering storm in her lovely face as Percy recounted their activities, surprised yet again how attuned he was becoming to her every mood.

When had he begun worrying about how to please her and wanting to see her smiling over whatever he did? He knew he should have asked her permission to take Percy about, but the visits seemed harmless enough in comparison to the boy's desire to climb to the top of St. Paul's to experience the whispering gallery and see the view of the city from the cupola. Jackson's had been a way to divert Percy from that high-flying adventure.

"Aunt Mathilde, I think locking Percy in his room would be very unjust," Damara answered while the woman crossed the room to perch on the chair across from her. "I'm sure he learned his lesson after being robbed along the road."

"Humph, that was just as he deserved. In my day, children were kept in the nursery until they were old enough to be allowed in civilized company." Her tone implied that no one in the room belonged in this category along with Percy, including Lady Kath.

"We did make an appointment to view Montague House," Simon put in, hoping this more elevating activity would regain the ground he had lost. He was beginning to wonder if Damara's earlier smile had not been just polite recognition that he had left off his sling. "We'll be able to pick up our tickets this afternoon, then tour the premises on the morrow."

"Really, how many tickets are there?" his fiancée asked,

her attention drawn away from her aunt's unpleasant countenance by the news. "During my first season ladies weren't allowed, but I understand that it no longer true."

"I was presumptuous enough to request three in hopes you would accompany us," he assured her, basking in her look of anticipation at being able to enter the hallowed doors of the museum. Facing a hostile enemy was by far easier than being confronted by a lady's displeasure. This part of being a peer was dashed difficult.

He could make a good showing with the bored noblemen he had met at White's and deal amiably with his fellow tenants at the Albany. He was able to order his solicitors with suitable aplomb, since it was very similar to giving orders to his troops. Unfortunately the one thing he wanted to do most in the world, impress Damara and stay in her good graces, was the hardest task of all.

"Girls, are you about ready to leave for Gina's luncheon?" Lady Kath's anxious question broke into Simon's troubled thoughts. "I've ordered the carriage for one o'clock."

"Mama, we have plenty of time," Evelyn stated in a calming voice from long years of practice. "We only need to call for our wraps. There's more than enough time before we must leave."

"You're actually keeping up a connection with Emsley's friends?" Mathilde demanded with her usual snort of derision, ignoring the fact the man was only a few feet from her.

"Lady Covering has kindly asked us to luncheon to meet Lady Sefton," Evelyn continued in her neverending role as placater.

"Well, you certainly won't see me toadying up to any of those ladies for vouchers to a very mundane evening's entertainment," the old woman returned, giving a decisive nod as though she had the opportunity, although she had not been included in the luncheon invitation. "It could be worse, I suppose. At least Maria Sefton is a lady—although a milksop—while Sally Jersey is a prattle-box as well as a woman of questionable morals."

"Then it it just as well you aren't accompanying us," Lady Kath replied cheerfully, not guarding her tongue in her excitement. "I wish we had something that would assure us favor. I would so like to attend Almack's, and this is the closest we have managed. Gina would decide to rusticate the season Evelyn came out."

"You do have something that could swing the tide, if I might be so bold," Simon volunteered. Here was a dragon he could fight for his lady and win her favor. "You have me. The patronesses are always anxious for more gentlemen, even if I'm no longer in need of a prospective bride."

"Yes, yes, that will do," Lady Kath agreed, clapping her hands in delight. "We'll send a note ahead that you're escorting us. How lovely."

"Simon, you really don't need to put yourself out for this," Damara rushed in to assure him, but he had made up his mind. She could not tell him in front of everyone else that the thought of Almack's petrified her—and more than likely she wouldn't tell him if they were alone.

"No trouble at all, my dear," he stated, unable to resist a beaming smile. Not only would he be helping to obtain the much-prized vouchers, he would be able to spend the afternoon with Damara. "Percy and Bundy can pick up our tickets for Montague House, and we'll take Lady Sefton by storm."

For reasons he could not understand, Damara's frown had returned. There was just no understanding women at all. He was putting himself forward to please her. A ladies' luncheon was not his idea of pleasure, but he would dedicate the time to his lady.

"Ohhhh, Lowd Emsley, that's so vewwy, vewwy bwave," gushed Letitia Templeton-Smythe for the dozenth time since Lady Covering's guests had been seated at the table.

Damara suppressed a shudder of distaste, hastily stuffing a portion of roll in her mouth as she looked across the table to see Evelyn rolling her eyes. Miss Templeton-Smythe had been holding forth from the moment she laid eyes on Emsley, the only male in the room. Her proud mama would nod in approval, jostling her triple chins whenever her darling managed once more to monopolize the marquess's attention. Presently the girl, who was almost buried in yards of insipid ruffles, was admiring the daring of his exploits on the Peninsula.

"Miss Templeton-Smythe, there really wasn't much bravery needed," Simon explained in a slow manner, enunciating every word carefully. He glanced beseechingly at Damara on his left, but she simply smiled and raised her eyebrows in question as if she, too, were waiting with bated breath for his reply. "The army has been at rest for the most part over the last six months. My troops spent a good portion of the time digging trenches in the rain and keeping the caissons from sinking in the mud."

"Oh, la, sir, such modesty," the imbecile reprimanded, and tapped his arm with her fan yet again. Damara was more than fascinated by the fact that the young person could eat, chatter inanely, and still manage her fan. Of course, she rationalized, since the girl did not have a brain it was mostly reflex action. If the Templeton-Smythe miss touched Simon one more time, however, she might find her fan broken, Damara decided as she twisted her napkin in her lap for practice.

"You mustn't worry, my dear. You won't be seeing her at our little assemblies," a soft voice assured Damara from her left.

Damara turned her head to meet the kind gaze of the lady, some ten years her senior, who was sitting next to her. Lady Sefton had not spoken unless directly addressed since her arrival just before luncheon for the twenty guests was announced. While the others chatted and exchanged gossip, she would nod occasionally and reward a few with her sweet maternal smile. Damara round herself tongue-tied, now that she was this close to one of the patronesses of the holiest of holies.

"Her father made his blunt in the mills and married his oldest girl Abigail to Sir Gareth Wilson, the quiet girl sitting next to her mother," Lady Sefton confided in a hushed tone no one else could hear. "Sefton and I are tolerant of others, including my own brother Craven, but the fact that this Smith person made his fortune at the expense of other's toil—then tried to hide his identity in a contrived name—cannot be condoned."

Damara began to relax under the soothing voice of her

companion. She knew that the Earl of Craven's marriage to
the well-known actress, Louisa Brunton, had caused a mild
sensation, but the lady was accepted by Craven's argumen-
tative family. "Yes, Lady Sefton, I agree. My dislike,
however, is from the strain on my nerves," she returned in
a whisper, her eyes matching the twinkle of amusement in
the older woman's glance. "I want to drag her up to the
schoolroom and give her elocution lessons."

"Weally?" the lady replied, widening her eyes in amazement, but her quivering mouth gave away her barely
suppressed amusement.

Damara had to look away or embarrass herself by
laughing out loud. She realized both Evelyn and Regina
were watching her avidly, straining to hear her conversation
with the revered lady. In the spirit of her companion's
amusement, she winked at her friends and surreptitiously
wiggled her fingers at the edge of the table in a semblance
of a wave. Then she turned back to her companion,
dropping her hand to her lap and brushing against Simon's
arms as she did so.

"I saw the countess perform Miranda in *The Tempest*
during my first season," Damara exclaimed, quickly breaking into speech to ignore the sudden tingling of her fingers
at the unexpected contact with her fiancé, wanting to leave
the distasteful subject of Miss Letitia. "She is a remarkable
lady; so lovely and believable."

"I'm sorry you missed her Lady Ann in *Richard III*,"
Lady Sefton returned with a genuine smile at the praise for
her sister-in-law. "They are at Combe Abbey now, little
William is almost a year old, and I've just learned they
are expecting another cousin for our boys before the end of
the year."

"Boys? How many?" Damara jumped and attempted to
act as if her sudden movement was surprise at the mention
of the boys, not the warmth of Simon's hand closing over
her own where it rested in her lap. "My brother is twelve
and has come to town with us. I'm not sure how to keep him
entertained for much longer."

"Ah, he comes between young Molyneux and George,
our two oldest of the four," Lady Sefton answered
quickly, seeming unconcerned that her young companion

was beginning to babble. "He must come for the boys' birthday party at the end of the month. They were actually born in July, but we have a celebration in town as well as a quiet gathering at home when we go north."

"Simon," Damara exclaimed loudly at the touch of his booted foot against her instep. Clearing her throat, she hoped her voice would come out in a normal tone and the telltale flush of her cheeks would not give away her confusion. "Simon has taken Percy around with him, but I cannot continue to impose."

"My dear Lady Damara, you seem to have found the perfect solution to keeping your fiancé out of trouble," Lady Sefton chuckled while giving her an approving nod. "I must remember to tell my other young friends your device of keeping Emsley from straying. Your brother's presence today might have improved most of the luncheon conversation, or should I say monologue?"

What she prayed was a knowing laugh was all Damara could muster. She hardly had any idea what Lady Sefton was saying. Simon had begun by trying to get her attention to rescue him from the importuning Letitia. When Damara had not come to his rescue, he seemed to change his tactics. His large hand no longer tugged at her slender fingers or squeezed them impatiently. Instead he cradled her small hand in his and stroked her sensitive skin with his thumb. The same was true of his foot.

He was not lightly tapping against her foot, but rubbing against her ankle and over the ribboned ties of her slipper. The action was making her tingle from head to toe in a pale imitation of how she felt when he kissed her. While still attempting to converse, she tried to capture his much larger foot under her own, knowing it was pointless to strike out at his leather-encased leg. She only succeeded in making the situation worse. Simon was now gently moving his knee against hers, seeming to set her entire leg ablaze.

"I look forward to introducing you to Lady Jersey and the others," Lady Sefton continued, seemingly unaware of Damara's distraction until she concluded her invitation. "Please, bring Lord Emsley. We have so few eligible partners, and he can hold your hand quite openly while you're dancing."

Damara could feel the heat of her mortification overcoming the strange feelings caused by Simon's touch. Lady Sefton's indulgent smile at the apparent love play did not lessen the mixture of embarrassment and anger she felt. He was taking blatant advantage of the situation, punishing her for not wrangling over him with the idiot Letitia. This was no different than his threatening to kiss her whenever she failed to call him by his first name. He arrogantly thought of what he wanted, never once considering how it would appear, or how she would feel about it.

She knew the perfect revenge. Let him be the one who was awkwardly placed through no action on his part, and see if he liked it as well. He had left off his sling and the bruises had already begun to fade, but Letitia would be enthralled by Simon's daring adventure. Damara might also discover exactly what had occurred, since the man had been so close-mouthed about it.

"Simon, have you told Lady Covering about your harrowing experience the other night?" Damara asked the question in a honeyed tone and accompanied her question with a nauseatingly adoring look she had seen Letitia use earlier.

"What is this? Has something happened you haven't told me?" As expected, his godmother joined in at the mention of anything adverse happening to Simon. "Has this something to do with the mishap to Nemesis's saddle?"

Simon knew it was probably futile to try to sidetrack the lady. Though he had been able to fob off her questions about the girth, there was no means of creating an innocent tale about the two men who had waylaid him. "Now, Aunt Gina, there really isn't a thing—"

"What happened to your saddle? Did this happen before the two ruffians accosted you?" Damara broke in, putting aside her anger for the moment in her concern. She vividly remembered her shock yesterday afternoon at the first sight of his battered face.

The questions from both his godmother and his fiancée drew the attention of everyone at the table. Simon knew his hopes of discussing the incident privately with Lady Covering were useless. "Both of you are becoming alarmed over nothing. An old piece of leather gave on my girth unexpectedly in the first instance," he explained in an even tone, failing to mention that the break had been too smooth. "And the second incident was merely a brief scuffle with two half-witted thieves with more drink in them than brains."

"Ohhh, Lowd Emsley, that's so tewwibly exciting."

"No, Miss Templeton-Smythe, it was damp and dirty when I was knocked down," he shot back, finally out of patience with the girl's childish talk. "I was wet through when I returned home and was forced to consign my favorite coat to the fire."

"Well, shall we withdraw to the drawing room?" his godmother said in a bright voice. She could sense her luncheon guests were on the point of squabbling like schoolchildren. Miss Templeton-Smythe was beginning to show signs of bursting into tears, Simon seemed on the verge of slapping her if she did, and Damara was biting her lower lip with her eyes clouded with concern. "Simon, dear boy, will you give me your arm?"

The other guests seemed relieved at the suggestion. They quickly left the remains of their repast behind for more comfortable chairs where the younger ladies would entertain them on the piano and harp. Regina purposely lagged behind, holding Simon in place.

"I want a full account of your mishap, young man," she ordered in a tone that brooked no argument. "I'm afraid your fiancée will have to return home without her escort. You can make up for that by taking Damara and Evelyn to Covent Garden tonight."

Her godson gave her an affectionate smile and shook his head. "Aunt Gina, have you ever considered a career in the military? Wellington could use a commander like you in the field."

An hour later Damara fumed all the way back to Layston Place. She and Evelyn had been bundled into the coach like naughty children while Simon stayed behind on the flimsiest of excuses—helping Regina decide on a birthday present for her son Bram—and undoubtedly telling her every detail of his misfortunes. It did not matter that his godmother had more right to know than his temporary betrothed. Damara was tired of being treated like an imbecile.

She also wanted to know if these incidents had anything to do with their engagement. Tonight she would have a few things to tell his lordship about the intelligence of a lady, and his promised treat of a performance at Covent Garden was not a sufficient bribe to keep her from questioning him.

— Chapter Seven —

Damara was out of sorts the next morning as she stood poised at the top of the stairs, hoping a late breakfast would dispel her disgruntled mood. The Marquess of Emsley was the cause of her sleepless night once again. Even the promised treat of seeing Mr. Kemble at Covent Garden tonight did not put Emsley back in her good graces, especially when he did not put in an appearance the previous evening.

She had been prepared to quiz him on the details that Lady Covering had undoubtedly wheedled out of him yesterday afternoon. There was also the matter of her suspicion that he knew more about the engagement announcement than he was telling her. The man was as slippery as an eel. When she did not want to see him, there he was; the minute she counted on his appearance, he was nowhere to be found.

The sound of voices from the hallway below disrupted her cataloging of Emsley's sins. Glancing down idly at a dark blue uniform sleeve with a gold epaulet at the shoulder, she cast aside all thoughts of her fiancée. Damara closed her eyes, thinking perhaps she imagined it, but when she opened them again the rounded leather helmet adorned with its distinctive bear skin strip that was tucked in the curve of the man's arm was very real. With a gasp of delight she flew down the stairs—not caring that she gave those standing below an immodest display of her shapely ankles—and hurled herself into the arms of the man in uniform.

"Jasper, you're home!" Her joyful cry more than expressed her happiness at his long overdue arrival and relief at finally having a shoulder to cry on—even her ramshackle brother's—after the frustration of the past weeks. The arms that lifted her completely off the parquet floor of the entry hall held her suspended in mid-air, tightening around her slender back.

Suddenly she did not want to raise her face from the cradle of his tanned neck, realizing her brother, who was no taller than she, could not possibly lift her in this manner.

"It seems that I shouldn't have sold out after all, if a uniform will precipitate such results," Simon murmured directly into her ear without relinquishing his hold, leaving no doubt about his identity.

Damara drew back as far as her arms would allow, bracing her palms against his broad chest while fruitlessly attempting to touch the floor with her questing toes. Her view of her fiancé was restricted to his face, which was exactly level with her own. Her anger at her own stupidity only increased at the sight of his smug grin, although the amusement was not reflected in his brown eyes.

"My dear, you must remember the name is Simon," he chided despite the presence of a disapproving Hastings, who had already turned his back on the couple in hopes of making their deplorable behavior invisible. "I think we have discussed this problem before. You were making excellent progress until this morning."

Damara was well aware of Hastings's rigid back and the gaping footman just entering the hall from below stairs. She was also remembering too clearly the results of her last conversation with Emsley on the subject of his name. She hesitated too long, however. His lips quickly came down before she could form one syllable of protest, and she was not prepared for the possessive kiss.

The delicately chiseled mouth that had fascinated her at their first meeting had a touch of iron. Pride would not allow her to struggle against his attack in front of the servants. As far as they were aware, this man was her fiancé and his display of affection—no matter how unorthodox— was not surprising. The name she had omitted to say a few minutes earlier came out in a gasp when his mouth finally released hers.

The mixture of confusion and accusation in Damara's emerald eyes cut deeply into Simon's heart as he ran his gaze quickly over her pale face and bruised lips. Suddenly all his protective instincts were aroused against himself. He was the person responsible for her pain and confusion. Once more he lowered his lips to hers, gently this time, to erase the memory of the punishment caused by his unreasonable surge of jealousy of her brother.

At first Damara did not respond; her lips were soft but did not answer his coaxing. Then he felt her slender hands grip the material of his uniform and her slim form relax against his. Drawing deep within himself for an ounce of restraint—and very conscious of the gawking servants—he raised his head.

"You really shouldn't have done that," Damara accused breathlessly, blinking at him owlishly as if dazed by what had just taken place.

"Forgive me, my darling, but I have discovered I am a very possessive man," he murmured as he set her on her feet. Giving her a tender smile, he smoothed back an errant wisp of auburn hair from her flushed cheek. He knew in that moment he would do anything to make her his wife. A few days before, he had rationally considered continuing their engagement to a convenient marriage; however, what he felt for her now eclipsed any other feeling he had ever experienced.

He wanted to protect her, make passionate love to her, and grow old with her. One minute she was worldly and regal, the next she was an innocent who had never been kissed in passion. If he had to steal her away and marry her across the anvil at Gretna Green, Lady Damara Tarrant was going to be his marchioness. He liked the idea of playing young Lochinvar and carrying his Damara away across his saddle bow like the fair Elaine.

Fleetingly he wondered if it would come to kidnapping his bride. Thus far he had not handled their relationship with much finesse. Now that he realized the importance of his goal, he would have to exercise even more restraint and patience.

"Simon?" Damara ventured when he remained silent for so long, his expression impossible to read as he stood looking down at her. For a moment she thought she detected sadness and regret, then suddenly his sherry-colored eyes darkened with an emotion she could not identify.

"Shall we go into the sitting room, sweetheart?" he said,

his smile only adding to her bemusement. "I think we have shocked Hastings enough for one day."

Damara felt her cheeks burn, realizing that once again he had put her in an awkward situation in her own home. Naturally the self-assured Emsley took her silence as assent and took action. He grasped her wrist and turned toward the sitting room.

"No, breakfast," she said hurriedly before he could take a step. She dug in her heels as she remembered her purpose in coming downstairs.

"Pardon?" Simon asked, now the one was almost speechless. He could not understand what brought on her comment, or how she could think of food at such an auspicious moment.

Since he was usually so self-confident, Damara could not contain a small smile at his dumbfounded look. Her mind was now cleared from his passionate greeting, and she was ready to assert her wishes in the matter. She must remember to tell Evelyn that he *was* most proficient and could do more than just curl her toes, even if he was the most overbearing gentleman of her acquaintance. When Jasper returned, she would encourage her friend to give him a stern lecture about his idea of kissing.

"I was coming down to have breakfast before I mistook your uniform for Jasper's," she explained, turning without another word to go into the dining room. Her confidence returned now that she had been able to confuse her overly tall, and usually irritatingly assured, fiancé. Buoyed by this, she looked forward to questioning him as she had anticipated the previous night. "You know your uniforms are remarkably alike, unless my memory is faulty, and I didn't expect to see you in yours."

"The Fourteenth Dragoons have the same basic kit as my own Royal Horse Artillery. Jasper has silver lacings where mine are gold," he explained with more calm than he felt. She could change like quicksilver; he never knew which facet of her personality would suddenly appear. He hoped she was distracted by making her breakfast selection at the sideboard and would not question how and why he knew Jasper's regiment. "I've been called to Whitehall to give a final report now that I have sold out. The old boys like us

to be on the up and up, so I'm wearing it for the last time,
I should think."

"That's a shame. It suits you so well," Damara replied,
then blushed at her impulsive words as she set down her
plate and took her seat.

"Thank you, my dear. You may take back the compliment, however, when you discover why I have come to call
this early," he stated, resisting the impulse to jump up from
the chair he had commandeered as close to her as possible
and take her in his arms again. "I have to delay our visit to
Montague House until the next viewing day, since I don't
know how long I'll be kept at Whitehall. They're still at
sixes and sevens since the Duke's resignation last year."

"Don't worry. I have had to wait four years, so I think I
can wait a few more days. Although I can't say the same for
Percy," she returned easily. Her disappointment was tem-
pered by the fact that she was not sure how the afternoon
would have gone with only her younger brother as a
chaperone.

"Percy has the heart of a rascal. He has decided that a
walk in Hyde Park with that beast of his will make him
forget his disappointment, though we have to put it off until
tomorrow."

"Oh dear, has Cretin been too much of a bother?" She
felt somewhat contrite at foisting her brother as well as the
undisciplined animal on Simon. There really had been no
other alternative with Layston Place crowded to the rafters
with the Townsend family and the unexpected addition of
herself and the temperamental Lady Mathilde.

"He did attempt to help me with my bath yesterday
morning," Simon informed her with a laugh.

"Oh," she remarked for lack of anything else. She could
feel the heat returning to her cheeks. Her discomfort at this
piece of news helped her come to a decision. Taking a deep
breath and staring fixedly at the morsel of ham she was
pushing around on her plate with her fork, she mumbled the
words before she lost her courage. "Simon, I think we
shouldn't wait any longer to end this false engagement,
once and for all."

"No," he said immediately, his tone dangerously low and
rough. He remained very still; Hastings could not have

made a better graven image. Then he slammed his fist on the table and rose to his feet. "No."

"Simon, please, this is best for your circumstance," she pressed on. Though she was flattered by his vehement denial, she knew this had to be said. "You need to find yourself a proper fiancée. You can't begin to pursue your own interests if you're playing nursemaid to Percy and his hound, or having your name coupled with mine. Jasper will be home any day, and he can unravel this puzzle without inconveniencing you any further."

She waited for his reply with her hands primly folded, resting against the edge of the table. For some unknown reason her hands were trembling, which she put down to nerves over finally having a rational discussion with Simon. Though she had given him a very logical explanation for recanting their engagement announcement, it left her feeling flat at the prospect of breaking off all contact with the infuriating but charming marquess. Perhaps she was experiencing a reaction to all the emotions she had felt since coming downstairs, running the gamut from extreme joy to disappointment and discomfiture.

Simon paced the narrow space between the table and the sideboard to work off his pent-up frustrations. Just when he knew how deeply he cared for Damara, she wanted to say farewell. He would not do it, not when he sensed she was beginning to care for him. There was so little time left before Tremonte came home. Damara must be tied to him irrevocably before she learned the truth.

He turned to face her at the head of the table, and what he saw gave him hope. She looked like a young girl waiting to be scolded for stealing a sweet without completing her lessons. She nervously nibbled on her lower lip while she held the rest of her body absolutely still, waiting for his decision. He placed his hands on his hips, keeping her in suspense for a few moments longer. The stance also kept him from going to her and taking her in his arms.

"My dear, I haven't been inconvenienced in the least," he began softly, walking toward her chair in measured steps. He stopped behind the chair he left so precipitously moments before and grasped the curved back. "This engagement has been very beneficial to me. I've gained immediate acceptance instead of being looked at as some oddity—a ham-handed major attempting to be a peer. And I like Percy. I've never had any brothers or sisters, so I've enjoyed spending time with the boy. He also gives Bundy someone to fuss over besides me."

"You aren't going to tell me you like Cretin also," Damara put in quickly. Although she tried to contain it, a smile curved her lips. "That I know would be complete fustian."

"Would you believe that I tolerate the hound?" Simon returned, knowing the silly grin on his face matched her delighted smile.

"Yes, that isn't too incredible," she conceded, allowing her laughter to ring out. Simon would not know it was from relief, rather than his dry comment. "For that bit of honesty, I'll grant you a reward. We're staying in tomorrow evening to celebrate Sir Cedric's birthday. Since he's always complaining of too many sauces and exotic town food, Mrs. Kasey has promised him a rack of lamb and her Yorkshire pudding for the occasion. Would you join us?"

"That would be a pleasure," he agreed readily just as the clock in the hall chimed the hour. "Now, I must be off and report to my superiors."

Damara was not sure how to react when he stepped forward to take her hand. Simon took an inordinate amount of time in kissing her hand, not on the back as she anticipated, but in the soft hollow of her palm. The touch of his lips danced up her arm to set her heart beating rapidly. She sat wide-eyed as he walked out the door without another word.

She did not move while the heels of his boots clicked across the entry floor and the front door closed behind him with an echoing thud. The sound brought her out of her daze, and she realized she was cupping her hand to her cheek. Her flustered gaze collided with that of Ned the footman, who entered the room with a fresh pot of tea. Hastily she jerked her hand down and placed it in her lap, cursing Simon.

The man was a menace. He had escaped again before she had a chance to learn more about his accidents, not to mention making her look foolish in front of the servants.

She was not experienced enough with flirtation to safeguard herself against his advances. If she were more practiced, she would not find herself going into a dewy daze whenever he touched her. This evening she would not be distracted from her course before she could speak her mind on a number of subjects. After all, she had done him the kindness to let their betrothal continue—for the time being—so he owed her the courtesy of hearing her opinion of what was happening.

With that decided, she balled up her napkin and tossed it on the table. Since Percy was at loose ends for the day, she would send a note around to the Albany requesting the pleasure of his company. She had hardly seen him since his unexpected arrival in town. Perhaps he would like a trip to Hookham's to peruse the shelves, or for pure entertainment a visit to Astley's Amphitheater. She would allow Percy to pick what he would like to do, and she would not think about her engagement, or the Marquess of Emsley, for the entire day.

"No, don't trouble to get out, Simon dear," Lady Covering ordered, and alighted from the coach with the assistance of the footman. "The play was lovely, my dears. Mr. Kemble is always such a joy, though I think he is a little long in the tooth these days for Romeo. Good night, all."

Damara wanted to jump from the coach herself and plead—on her knees if necessary—for Regina not to leave her alone with Simon. The man was trying to drive her stark, staring mad by paying her the most exaggerated courtesies all evening. And this after an afternoon of Percy prefacing every phrase with "Simon said" this and "Simon does" that. The man might as well as have accompanied them.

This evening, however, she would have welcomed Percy's prattling instead of the man himself. He seemed bent on exemplifying the perfect courtier. Whatever progress they had made earlier in the day was destroyed by his studious attentions that put her on edge.

First he presented her with a bouquet of perfectly formed white rosebuds, telling her he could not entrust their delivery to anyone but himself. Then he assisted her in everything she did; helping her down the steps and into the coach, refusing to let her walk a step into the theater without his aid, and finally, adjusting her chair three times before allowing her to sit down. He had maneuvered his chair so his shoulder brushed hers during the entire performance, even though there was ample room in the box with only his godmother accompanying them. When Damara had made a bid for freedom during the interval, Simon had secured her hand in the crook of his arm as they walked in the corridor.

She felt the play was appropriate. She knew exactly how poor Juliet felt with everyone ordering her about and not bothering to ask her opinion on what she wanted to do. It was ironic that they had similar problems of being ignored. While Juliet wanted to marry her Romeo, Damara wanted to break her engagement from a man who was treating her like a hot-house flower.

Simon cleared his throat from his place next to her and shifted slightly against the velvet-covered squabs. "Aunt Gina was right. The play was delightful. Is this your first trip to the theater since your arrival in town?"

"Yes." *And I barely remember anything that happened on stage*, Damara finished to herself, *especially the last act when you insisted on holding my hand*.

"Do you usually like going or, like my mother used to complain, hate the crush of the crowd?" he asked hopefully. Perhaps if he gave her a choice, she would give more than a monosyllabic answer. The only words he heard her utter all evening were yes or no, nothing more.

"Are you truly asking me to express my opinion?" Damara could not hold back the sharp question after fretting about it for so many days. Her slow-burning Tarrant temper was taking control in her disappointment over his behavior this evening. He had reverted to treating her like a mindless doll. "I prefer going to the theater, if you're really interested."

Simon was nonplussed by her question. What did she mean about asking her opinion? They could not hold a conversation if she did not express her opinion, or if she did not answer in more than a single word. He was mystified since he had just spent the evening seeing to her every need. Though still puzzled, he forged ahead in the hope of

discovering the mystery of the feminine mind. "Did you
think I wouldn't be interested in your opinion?"

"Well, you have never asked my opinion on anything
before this, so you took me by surprise. Thank you for the
compliment of recognizing I have the capacity to think."

Simon did not have time to answer as the coach came to
a halt, and the footman promptly opened the door. Simon
was sitting alone before he knew it. Scrambling out of the
coach, he discovered Damara was already at the steps.

"Damara, please wait," he called, catching her as she
reached the top step. The overly efficient Hastings opened
the front door before he finished speaking, allowing Damara to step inside. Simon slipped through before Hastings
had a chance to close the door in his face, but it was a near
thing. Ignoring the disapproving butler, he called to Damara
again. "Please wait."

She turned where she stood on the second step, her eyes
level with his when he came to stand in front of her. Simon
was confused even more when she batted her eyelashes at
him like that silly twit Letitia Temptleton-Smythe. "Why,
Simon, you've said please twice in the space of a few
minutes."

"Damara, would you please tell me what is going on
here?" Belatedly he remembered to remove his silk hat,
snatching it from his head.

She stood staring at him for a few minutes not knowing
what to say. Her unruly tongue had gotten her into the fix
that had Simon looking at her as if he was considering
consigning her to Bedlam. She knew she owed him some
explanation, but would he understand her feelings? "I'm
simply tired of being ignored."

"Ignored? When have I done that? I know our relationship has been slightly irregular, but I can't think when I
have neglected you during our short acquaintance."

"Oh, you've talked to me and look to my comfort, as you
did tonight, which may have been a touch overdone," she
admitted, giving him a tiny smile. "But until a few minutes
ago in the coach, you never acknowledged that I had a mind
of my own or an opinion of any value. Your solicitors and
mine have told me what to do, as well as my aunt and my
friends. Everyone has an opinion but me. You've never

once asked if I wanted you to kiss me. Instead you go right ahead."

"You want me to ask you if I can kiss you or not?" He could not be hearing her correctly. There were gaps in his education when it came to the niceties of society after so many years in the army; however, he was sure this was not a normal conversation.

"You shouldn't be kissing me at all," she continued with a frustrated sigh. Twisting her gloved fingers, Damara tried to think how she could make him understand. "The point is, Simon, you never gave me an opportunity to object. What if I did the same? What if, at this very minute, I decided to kiss you or slap you, without the least warning? Would you find it acceptable if I went ahead without asking which you preferred?"

"I think I would naturally prefer that you kiss me, but you said that we shouldn't do that," he answered with a crooked smile that changed the lady's earnest expression to a frown. "No, I would prefer that you ask my opinion."

"That is precisely my point, Your Lordship," Damara announced, giving him a smile of approval that took his breath away.

What she did next totally confounded him. She placed her slender hands on his shoulders and leaned forward. In an instant he knew her intent; she was going to kiss him. Startled, he turned his head and realized his mistake the instant her soft lips touched his. She had intended to kiss him on the cheek, but by moving he received her kiss on the lips.

She immediately pulled away, her green eyes tragic as she blinked back unshed tears. "You odious man, you don't understand at all."

She turned and ran up the stairs, not giving him a chance to defend himself. Simon never felt so helpless as he watched her disappear into the upper story of the house, or so alone. At the pivotal moment he was beginning to understand the workings of his betrothed's mind and emotions, he was condemned by an innocent movement of surprise.

Damara paced in front of the fireplace in her room, too angry and tense to sit still. He had to be the most infuriating man on the face of the earth, and she refused to even think his name. Her life had been in turmoil for what seemed like years from the first moment she had heard his name, though in reality it had only been a few weeks.

She longed for the tranquility of Tarrant's Mount where she never had to worry about a gentleman's kisses or if he thought she had a brain in her head. She was respected by the people there, even sought out to give advice. The thought of packing, leaving for home that night, was tempting; however, she was determined to show a certain gentleman that she was a lady with a mind of her own.

Tomorrow, come what may, she was going to discover what had been happening to Simon. He insisted that they were to continue their engagement, so she would establish her rights as his intended, temporary or not. Her decision helped to stop the angry tears that threatened since her innocent kiss had gone awry. At peace with herself once again, Damara prepared for a good night's sleep in anticipation of a momentous day on the morrow.

"Mara, my dear, you know I could have come alone— even sunk to bringing Ajax—and had a more lively conversation with my team," Lady Covering remarked amicably the next afternoon, keeping her eye on the prancing pair of matched bays that were pulling her high perch phaeton. The vehicle of white and royal blue was the despair of her husband. Damara had not uttered a word since they entered the park through the brick facade of the Cumberland Arch and began their progress around the famed Ring among the usual crush on the promenade.

"I thought you might want to concentrate on your driving," her companion answered at once, smiling at her friend's sniff of disdain. "I didn't know you directed your team with such . . . panache, shall we say, when I agreed to accompany you."

"You've been too much in the company of my godson, for you are beginning to sound exactly like him on the subject of my driving," Regina complained, but failed to look crushed by the younger woman's description. "From your faraway expression I also suspect that is the reason for your silence, not my skill with the ribbons. My Simon is responsible for your preoccupation."

"Spoken with the true objectivity of a discerning god-mama," Damara challenged, her chuckle masking the fact that Lady Regina had not been far off the mark. She shifted the angle of her amber-and-white-striped parasol so the shadow fell completely over her face to keep Regina's sharp eyes from reading her expression too closely. She did not want her friend to suspect her motive in coming to the park; Simon was somewhere about with Percy and Cretin.

"Since the poor boy's parents have gone to their reward, someone must take his part," Regina remarked in an offhand manner as she executed the bend in the gravel road as it followed the curve of the Serpentine.

"Then as his staunchest defender, I'm surprised you haven't spied him over near the water," Damara said dryly, looking beyond her friend to where the commanding figure of her fiancé seemed to stand out among the other pedestrians. "Although I shall admit my eyes were first drawn to my brother jumping up and down and moving his arms to get our attention."

She raised her hand to wave at the same moment Simon glanced over his shoulder. With Percy cavorting at his side, Simon had been giving a stern lecture to Cretin on how an aristocratic hound of his heritage should conduct himself while taking the air among his peers. Cretin was not impressed and seemed to prefer going wherever he wanted, even if it meant jerking and tugging to redirect the person on the other end of the leather strap that held him.

The sight of the two ladies, even in Lady Covering's phaeton, was a welcome sight to Simon. His tolerance for the animal, now attempting to pull his arm from its socket, had lowered considerably since he last spoke with Damara. Raising his free arm in response to Damara's wave, he turned, hoping his godmother would be able to stop her team within the next half mile.

Unfortunately Cretin was not prepared to leave his exploration at the water's edge. Suddenly Simon was pulled backward. He did not have a chance to catch his balance and gain a firm footing to bring the dog to heel. He knew what was going to happen, but he was powerless to stop it.

Cretin jumped forward, unconcerned that he would soon be leaving solid ground for the questionable waters of the Serpentine. Simon tried to plant his feet to stop the impetus that was carrying him rapidly forward, a great deal more alarmed than the heedless dog over being immersed in the brown waters.

"Oh, no!" Damara felt as if her heart had jumped straight into her throat when she realized what was happening. She winced as Simon barely missed a sapling on the edge of the clearing while Cretin continued his headlong run.

"Damara, sit down. These animals are skittish enough without you standing up," Regina snapped, keeping her eyes on the nervous horses in case they did indeed bolt.

"You don't understand! Cretin is running away and pulling Simon toward the water," she shouted, not caring that she turned heads with her unseemly behavior.

Regina pulled hard on the ribbons without stopping to worry about the horses' sensitive mouths. For once her team minded, coming to an immediate standstill that nearly tipped Damara out of the carriage, but Regina did not have time to remark on her accomplishment for her passenger was already scrambling down to the gravel road. Regina turned her head at the exact moment Simon's tall figure was catapulted into the air by the dead weight of Cretin's body hitting the water. She could not help but giggle when her godson had the presence of mind to toss aside his broad-brimmed beaver top hat while he executed an awkward somersault, going head over heels into the murky waters with a resounding splash.

She tossed the ribbons to a young man who stood gaping at the sight. "Here, sir, walk these horses until I return," she ordered over her shoulder as she scurried after Damara, already shouldering her way through the crowd forming in the clearing along the bank.

"Mara, what do we do? Cretin can't swim very well," rang out Percy's shrill voice over the murmurings of the spectators.

Damara was saved from an angry retort as a cheer went up from the crowd when both Simon and Cretin's heads surfaced from beneath the muddy water. The dog paddled happily in a circle around the man attempting to gain his feet in the chest-high water. Once he was able to stand, Simon made a grab for the cause of his mishap.

"Thank the Lord, he seems to be all right," Regina exclaimed, out of breath from her run. Then she wondered if she spoke too soon, for Cretin was not ready to return to dry ground and kept just out of Simon's reach.

"Five quid on the dog," called a voice from the ladies' right.

"Ten on the big buck. He looks mean enough to throttle the beast," challenged another man near the front of the crowd.

"Oh, capital. Can we place a bet, Mara?"

"Percy, not another word. Go fetch Simon's hat before someone steps on it," Damara hissed, but did not take her eyes off the sodden, muddy figure in the water. Her heart was racing and her hands unsteady and clammy while Percy wanted to play games.

Simon was in no better temper as he lunged for the numbskull dog a second time. He could hear the wagers being tossed back and forth among the crowd, making him very mindful he could not let free the oaths that were gathering in his throat. Eyeing his opponent, he knew it was not his imagination that the dog was laughing at him, taunting him. Standing very still, Simon took a deep breath. In his mind he pictured Cretin, so aptly named, in a cocked hat with cockade and drab gray cloak favored by Napolean, for he was sure the canine was as wily as the little corporal himself.

"What is the boy doing? He's just standing there letting that stupid mutt swim around him," Regina said with impatience. She did not relish being caught as part of this farce.

"I think he's waiting to pounce. Cretin is stupid enough to try and tease him by swimming too close," Damara answered, relaxing for the first time since she had seen the pair heading for the water. She was horrified to discover she was beginning to enjoy the battle of wits between the man and animal.

Just as she predicted, Cretin came within Simon's reach a moment later. He was grabbed by the curls at the scruff of his neck and dragged to the shore with his floppy ears floating like oars beside his head. The crowd gave a rousing cheer that drowned out the groans of the gamesters who had backed the canine. When Simon was close enough to the grass verge, water lapping at the top of what were once his best boots, he bowed deeply to his audience, all the while keeping a firm grip on his companion.

Percy ran forward, and with the help of another gentleman he took Cretin's lead from the scowling man in the water. Relieved of the hound's struggling body, Simon levered himself up onto the grass, only to be caught in the shower of Cretin shaking himself dry. The spectators quickly returned to their own pursuits now that the entertainment had ended.

"This isn't much, but it may help."

Running a weary hand over his face, Simon turned to find Damara kneeling beside him with his top hat in her lap. She held out a very small square of lace-trimmed linen. He took her handkerchief, trying to ignore the amusement sparkling in her emerald green eyes. For a moment he had the ungentlemanly—and adolescent—urge to run his grimy hand down the length of her stark white sleeve that contrasted with the amber material of her walking dress. Just the thought seemed to ease some of his frustration at playing the fool in front of her. He wiped what he could of the mire from his face, inhaling the fresh lavender scent of his fiancée from the bit of material. Then he cleaned his hands as best as he could on the grass.

"Simon, are you all right?" Damara asked anxiously when he did not speak, but sat staring across the Serpentine at the woodlands of Kensington Gardens. She could not mask the trace of laughter from her voice despite her concern as she gazed at his reclining form, propped up by his elbows. His usually commanding figure looked more like a bedraggled schoolboy. Patches of slimy mud clung to his blue superfine jacket, and his once white shirt and cream-colored waistcoat were dirty brown. His normally impeccably tied cravat was limp and hanging halfway down his shirt front.

"I have never been so humiliated in my entire life, even as a child when Bram put a newt down my shirt during vespers when we were at Winchester," he stated slowly in a monotone. "That stupid hound managed to play me the fool in front of absolute strangers as well as my fiancée, who even now is trying not to laugh."

"At least this time the headmaster won't give you ten lashes and write a very condescending note to your mama," his godmother announced briskly from behind Damara.

Simon gave the two men hovering over him a considering look. He noted with little humor that Percy was murmuring to his pet like a mother hen. He was pleased to see a tender expression on Damara's oval face, in spite of the amusement shining in her eyes. His godmother was not giving him the same consideration. She was giggling helplessly behind the shield of her handkerchief. When he met her glance, he could not continue his pose of martyr, and allowed his deep, rich laughter to escape.

"Do you know I had Cretin's lead because he might have been too strong for the boy to handle? We wanted to avoid another mishap in the park," he managed through his laughter after a few minutes. "I think we should frequent St. James in the future. No, there's the canal. Perhaps Green Park, but that has a pond. Aha, Kensington Gardens on the allowed Sundays. That should be— Damn, we're back to the Serpentine again."

"Simon, you are rambling. Did you swallow too much water when you went under?" Damara asked, allowing herself a chuckle at his antics. "We'll simply leave that undeserving animal at home and only take him for a morning amble around the square when most people are safely in their beds."

"You should count yourself fortunate that Brummel is away in the country and won't be back until next week," Regina stated, sobering at the thought of her godson being shunned by society because an unruly hound wanted to bathe.

"Too true, Aunt Gina," Simon murmured with the lack of concern of the untutored and got to his feet slowly, impeded by his sodden clothes. "Now perhaps we should make a quiet exit before the stupid beast decides to take another plunge. Percy, we'll be riding in Lady Covering's phaeton, so you'll have to be very, very brave."

"First, young man, you'll thank Lord Emsley for retriev-

ing that worthless animal of ours from the river," Damara
instructed as she accepted Simon's hand to rise to her feet.

"That's not necessary. I shouldn't have let myself be
distracted from my duty by two lovely ladies," Simon said
easily, patting the dejected boy's shoulder, unaware his
young friend had been more worried about his pet during
their misadventure. "So you see Percy, it is actually your
sister's fault."

Simon was rewarded by a delighted chortle from his
young friend and muttered comments from both Damara
and his godmother. Cretin even dared to join in with a bark.

"Ladies, shall we depart? I think our canine friend has
decided it is time to leave, and I know from experience that
the hound has a mind of his own," Simon observed, and
took the dog's lead from Percy as they walked toward the
white-and-blue phaeton waiting at the side of the carriage-
way. "I need to spend a few hours moving my souvenirs of
the Serpentine before I present myself at Layston Place for
dinner, or Hastings will bar the door."

"Yes, and now that the breeze has picked up again, my
dear, you must make sure to sit downwind on the ride
home," remarked Regina tartly before she swept forward to
reclaim her property from the bewildered young man, still
acting as a temporary hitching post.

As the ill-assorted party made their way out of the park,
Damara cast a sidelong look at her fiancé sitting closely at
her side and sighed in disappointment. The fates were
continuing to conspire against her as well as one thick-
skulled dog, who was now trotting happily along behind the
phaeton. She wondered if she would ever have a chance to
discuss the strange incidents that occurred over the past
week, and what Simon knew about their engagement.

Regina's invitation had seemed inspired. A chance meeting in the park and a few well-chosen words to Simon in
front of his garrulous godmother would have done the trick.
With real regret she studied Simon's bedraggled form as he
held Percy on his lap, laughing at one of the boy's
comments. He did not look much older than the boy, with
wet tendrils of black-brown hair plastered to his face and a
streak of dirt across his square jaw. She had never seen him
look so approachable during their acquaintance.

Unfortunately this was another missed opportunity. That left her tonight if she wanted to succeed. How she was going to question him in the midst of the Townsend clan, she did not know, but she would have to find a way.

— Chapter Eight —

"Don't turn around. Simply pretend the picture in front of you is a masterpiece," ordered a muffled voice to the veiled woman standing before a collection of amateurish landscapes placed in the darkest corner of Boydell's Gallery. "What did you want?"

"To see how much longer this farce will continue, you idiot," the woman hissed without turning around as instructed. "I haven't heard from you in days and thought your cohorts might have done you in by now."

"So you took a chance on being seen with me to allay your suspicions. What a perfect solution," the man snarled, and took a step closer when another patron—the only other person in the gallery—walked past.

"Cheapside at this time of day isn't heavily trafficked, my good man, and I've already established that none of my acquaintances are in town. Of course, you might have to worry, though no one would think you had enough taste or the inclination to visit a gallery."

"You'll get your share soon enough, you old banshee."

"The question is how soon. The brother should be home soon, and the end of the season is drawing near," she returned, moving on to the next painting, ignoring the growing menace in her companion's tone. "There will be no reason for anyone to stay in town. You said yourself it couldn't happen at Emsley Hall, and the opportunity was greater in London. As yet, nothing's gone right."

"Soon, soon, woman. A runner had been nosing around and asking some pointed questions about our friends." The man walked past, stopping at a painting further down the row. "The gentlemen had to recover from their injuries and stay out of sight."

"Ha! Two men who couldn't do away with a single target."

"We get what we can afford," he returned quickly. "Since our pockets are to let, we have to make do. They'll be able to strike again within the week."

"If they don't, I'll take matters into my hands," the woman snapped. "Now I must leave and return to the house before the others return. I've never seen women in such a buying frenzy."

"More like, you wish you had the wherewithal to spend twice as much, twice as fast." He gave a snickering laugh before snapping his hat onto his head. "The deed will take place, I assure you."

"Mara, are you going to play cards or stare at the doorway?" Percy asked his sister impatiently for the second time since they had set up the table after dinner.

Damara turned her glance away from the sitting room doorway to give her brother a dark look, relieved he had not caught her attention straying more than twice. Sir Cedric and Simon were taking forever over their port and cigars. She laid her cards down without much interest in the outcome of the game.

Although dinner had been a light-hearted affair with just the family, Damara had fidgeted the entire meal. Simon had arrived looking pale but otherwise none the worse for his unexpected swim. For some reason known only to Lady Kath, he was placed across the table from Damara, not next to her. Instead of finally being able to question him, she was forced to listen to Mathilde's muttering complaints about the food and her aching joints between the lively chatter of the others. She also could not ascertain if Simon was fully recovered from his plunge in the Serpentine.

Damara found the direct regard of his warm brown eyes very disconcerting whenever she chanced to look across the table, which was frequently. In spite of her confusion, she was sure she saw him shiver more than once during the four courses of the meal.

By the time the sweet was served, she was positive that Simon had also sniffled twice, then she chided herself for feeling overly guilty about foisting Percy and Cretin on her fiancé. It was an accident, and Simon seemed to be on the best of terms with her brother. Perhaps she was so watchful due to her overactive imagination that kept reminding her of *Maman's* chill that had turned into a fatal fever.

Damara almost jumped to her feet when she heard the sound of footsteps crossing the hall. To hide her agitation—and anticipation at the prospect of being able to talk to Simon—she turned to Evelyn, who was about to start a new deal of the cards. Lady Kath and Justine were occupied matching silks for new seat cushion covers, and Lady Mathilde had thankfully fallen asleep near the warmth of the fire.

"Evie, I think we should plan to visit Madame Lucretia tomorrow to get you outfitted properly for Jasper's return."

"Are you coming down with something, Mara? You're actually suggesting a shopping expedition?" Evelyn stopped dealing and studied her friend as if she had just grown another head. "You've been acting strange all evening."

"Really, Evie, you're being silly," she returned in a low tone, nodding her head in Percy's direction. He was following the conversation with rabid interest. "I'm perfectly fine."

"Simply worked into a frenzy because your fiancé is in the house, and you haven't been able to exchange more than three words," the blonde continued ruthlessly with a knowing smile, pointedly ignoring Damara's wish for caution around young ears. "What a shame you selected your periwinkle blue tunic dress to set off the fan Simon gave you, and he has been sitting with Papa all this time."

"Evie, will you—" Damara broke off when she saw the gentlemen were now entering the room. "I merely wished to apologize for his inconvenience this afternoon."

"Hark, he approaches," Evie whispered, and was rewarded with a sharp rap on her hand from Damara's fan.

"Does that mean we can play cards now?" Percy asked plaintively and gave a huge sigh of disgust for the foolishness of women. Neither his sister nor her friend were paying him the least mind.

"I tell you, Emsley, Prinny is planning to deface London the same way he did Brighton," Sir Cedric was expounding as the two men approached. "He already has plans drawn up by this Nash fellow. Plans to put in new thoroughfares, palaces, and God knows what else. All of it out of public funds no doubt."

"He can't do anything until the king dies, or at best becomes incurably ill again," Simon replied quietly, not nearly as affected as the older man by the paper plans to reconstruct the city. "The last time they had a Regent's bill drawn up, the king recovered."

"Mark my words, it will happen before we know it," Sir Cedric shot back immediately, pouring a glass of sherry for his gentleman guest and himself. Then he paused to offer a glass to the ladies which they declined. "Just yesterday I heard talk at the club about refurbishing there. Can you imagine a bow window at White's?"

Sir Cedric, however, was soon back in good humor when Justine presented him with birthday parcels from her older sister, Damara, and herself. The younger girls had had a special tea with their father in the afternoon and were now tucked away in their beds—a fact that gave Percy smug satisfaction as he sat up with the adults. While Sir Cedric exclaimed over his new slippers, an elegant watch fob, and monogrammed handkerchiefs, Justine displayed her talents at the pianoforte that had been the pride of the late Countess of Layston.

"Can we play another hand of *Bouillotte* now, Mara?" Percy asked almost the moment Sir Cedric unwrapped his last parcel.

"Percival, where have your manners gone?" his sister said sharply as Justine continued to play an adequate Bach minuet. "Have you made your apologies to Lord Emsley over this afternoon's mishap?"

"Percy has made a most sincere promise that Cretin won't act up again while they are in the city," Simon put in dryly, for the young boy was looking extremely abashed at the reprimand. "And Bundy assures me that we have our tickets for Montague House on Monday."

"Percy is worried I'll send him and his disgraceful pet back to Tarrant's Mount before he can view the mysterious treasures of the museum," Damara replied, but she gave her brother a smile, all the while knowing his humility would be shortlived, since Cretin never behaved in his life, "and before Jasper arrives."

"Mara, you wouldn't, would you?" Percy's voice cracked in the middle of his anxious query, his eyes round with apprehension.

He was saved from further teasing by the imperious entrance of Hastings. "The Countess of Covering and Baron Tearle."

Damara turned quickly toward the doorway. Hastings stood as rigid as a poker, staring straight ahead at the fireplace as if ignoring the family's pedestrian recreation. Behind him she saw Regina peek around the servant's rotund form and wiggle her fingers in greeting. Beside her was a tall man with light brown hair and a deep tan on his lean face whom Damara had never seen before.

"Bram!" Simon's delighted exclamation broke the tableau of the surprised occupants seated around the sitting room. Hastings made a dignified retreat, allowing Regina and her son to enter the room at last.

"Gina, you never said that Bramwell was coming home," Lady Kath accused as she crossed the room to greet her friend.

"I didn't know until he was standing on the doorstep," his mother explained, taking her friend's outstretched hands and offered her cheek for an affectionate kiss. "He says they made port for repairs from an unexpected storm off the French coast. I think he was languishing for home."

"Mama, an officer in the King's navy doesn't languish for anything," Bram reprimanded in an amused tenor voice and gave her a tolerant grin. He looked over Lady Kath's shoulder to the tall man standing behind her and the auburn-haired young woman at his side. "Although if I had such a lovely betrothed, I might consider it."

"I saw her first, you scoundrel," Simon challenged with an easy grin in return, and he went forward to clasp his old friend's hand. Everyone began talking at once until Sir Cedric announced it was downright silly to be standing in the doorway when there were plenty of comfortable chairs to be had.

The older ladies remembered their manners then and set about making proper introductions. Both Evelyn and Justine blushed prettily under Tearle's slanted smile and twinkling green eyes as he bowed solicitously over their hands. Damara regarded Simon's friend very seriously as she was presented. He was shorter than Simon by two or three inches, though he had the same wide breadth of shoulder and long, muscular legs. He was also very personable.

"So you're the young lady who has finally captured the Iron Heart? My compliments, m'lady," Tearle pronounced, taking her hand and actually brushing his lips over the back.

"And you're the one who put a newt down his back, I think," she returned with a teasing smile, at ease from the moment she recognized the wicked twinkle in his eyes that was so like her older brother's. She found it curious that she felt nothing at his flirtatious gesture. To share her amusement, she turned to Evelyn and was amazed to discover Simon was frowning fiercely at both Tearle and herself. For a moment she could not fathom his sudden change of mood.

Then he was at her side, securely tucking her hand in the crook of his arm. Damara noted with interest that his arm was rigid; in fact his whole body was tense, poker straight like Hastings. His words of the previous morning came back to her: *I find that I'm a very possessive man.* Surely he could not be angry at his oldest friend for the small attentions he paid her?

With very little coaxing, Justine was persuaded to join the card players—especially when Tearle requested her presence—and Regina settled into a comfortable cose with the Townsends. None of the shifts had the least effect on Lady Mathilde as she continued her nap by the fire with Cretin doing much the same at her feet. Neither were further disturbed as the card game became quite lively in teaching Justine and Tearle the game.

Seated between Simon and Tearle, Damara found herself in the middle of a competition. While Tearle complimented her and would tutor her play after he threw in his own cards, Simon would glower at his own cards until the hand was done. On the next deal, he would be the first to throw his hand down, insuring that he would be the person to oversee Damara's hand and leaving Tearle to flirt with Justine on his other side. Damara was vastly entertained by this novel experience and slightly guilty over their attentions, since she actively encouraged their wrangling.

"Simon, old man, I think these lovely ladies, especially Damara, deserve a special treat," Tearle announced after he had everyone's coins in neat stacks in front of him, "and Master Percy, of course. We should plan an excursion to the Tea Garden tomorrow, the one near Vauxhall that Mama is so fond of, I think. We can celebrate your engagement and my leave."

All three ladies agreed with enthusiasm, and Damara turned to Simon for his opinion. One look at his tense face made her forget her question and Tearle's amorous tricks. A fine sheen of sweat covered his brow, and he was trembling slightly, though he tried to suppress it.

"Simon, what is it?" she asked softly, laying her hand gently on his arm.

"I think my afternoon plunge is catching up with me," he murmured, "and I had best return home." Placing his hands flat on the gaming table, he pushed himself to his feet with an effort. He turned without another word, but swayed slightly as he took his first step.

"I don't think you'll make it more than a few feet, old boy," Tearle put in, his lean face deadly serious.

"No, it's nothing. Bundy will dose me with his noxious tonic, and I'll be right as—" He broke off as a tremor seized him.

"Quickly, Damara, we need to get him to sit down again before he falls flat on his face," Tearle instructed in a terse voice as they followed Simon's unsteady footsteps across the room. Damara came out of her fearful daze at Tearle's command. Simon's symptoms brought back chilling memories of her *Maman's* final illness.

Without hesitation she pointed Tearle toward the stairs. Though Simon allowed his friend to help him, he continued to claim he was not an invalid. Once he was settled, Damara sat down beside him and placed the back of her hand to his forehead. He was burning with fever. Calling to the nearest footman, she ordered him to summon Hastings.

"We need a doctor," she murmured, looking at Tearle for some answer to calm her fears.

"Bundy knows what to do," Simon managed to get out

between his chattering teeth, unable to stop the trembling. "Doctor won't do it right."

"Milady, has someone taken sick?" Hastings asked as he entered the hall from the kitchen entrance.

"Yes, Lord Emsley." She had trouble controlling her voice as she indicated the man beside her on the stairs. Simon continued to shiver uncontrollably, clutching his head in his hands. "Please open the master bedroom and send for His Lordship's man at the Albany."

Turning to Tearle, now sitting on Simon's other side, she asked, "What do we do about a doctor? Surely Simon doesn't know what he is saying."

"He had this before in India, and Bundy nursed him through it. It's malaria," Tearle finished softly, well aware that the word would alarm her. He frowned as he tried to remember the name of a physician who would be acceptable to his friend. "I have it! Dr. Horace Vaughan lives near Mama, and he spent a great deal of time in the West Indies. You just sit tight while I handle the matter."

The next few minutes were a blur of activity as Tearle took charge. Damara was too preoccupied with Simon to notice what was happening around her. She vaguely knew that someone had gone to fetch the doctor and that a message was being sent to Simon's quarters. She was brought out of her daze as Hastings and Tearle bent to help Simon to his feet. Sitting dejected on the step, she watched the two men half carry the sick man up the stairs. She was at a loss, not knowing what to do next.

Evelyn, with Percy clutching her hand, came to sit beside her at the same spot where Simon had lain as Lady Kath and Justine hovered close by. Lady Mathilde grew impatient with the dismal group. "I don't know why everyone is standing around. Either he will get well or not, and I want my tea before I retire," she declared, emphasizing her point by rapping her cane on the parquet floor. She turned and stomped back into the drawing room, not caring that the others were staring after her in open-mouthed amazement.

"I can't sit here any longer wringing my hands like some maiden in a Greek tragedy," Damara snapped and stood up, stretching her stiff muscles as the satinwood case clock in the library chimed the second quarter hour since Simon had been taken above stairs.

"Where are you going?" Evelyn asked with her eyes round in astonishment at her friend's angry tone while Percy stifled a yawn.

"To teach some gentlemen a little common courtesy," she answered, already starting up the stairs. "If they don't have the decency to tell me how Simon is, I'll go see for myself."

As she climbed the rest of the stairs, she forced herself to think calmly. She had to prepare her mind for what she would find in the master bedroom. Simon's collapse had been a shock, twice as terrifying as seeing him go headlong into the Serpentine. If the men decided not to return from the sickroom, there could very well be an excellent reason. The day Papa had died had been such a circumstance. She knew, however, that whatever condition Simon was in, it could not be any worse than her own imaginings.

She knocked softly on the door of her brother's room to announce her arrival but did not wait for an answer. Hastings turned from the patient as she entered. Only a single candle on the nighttable at the side of the canopied bed lit the room.

"I've no idea of what more to do, but he's asking for you," the butler informed her, his voice breaking in concern and showing more emotion than she had ever seen.

"I'll sit with him until the doctor arrives," she instructed with more assurance than she felt. Her temper subsided as she realized the two men had not been aware of the passage of time. "Fetch more blankets please, then bring the doctor and His Lordship's man here as soon as they arrive."

"I'll get the blankets, Damara," Tearle said and gave her shoulder a comforting squeeze. "Don't fret too much. We want old Simon to have something pretty to look at when he is better."

Damara smiled weakly at his attempt to lighten the atmosphere. With a satisfied nod he left to get the blankets. Taking a deep breath, she moved toward the bed. Simon's tall form looked so insignificant laying beneath the carved molding of the canopy, the size of the bed with its reed posts diminishing his usually robust body. He tossed restlessly, muttering incoherent words as he lay trembling under the blankets and quilt. Without hesitation she laid her hand against his damp forehead to brush back a lock of dark hair. His skin was hot and moist.

She dragged a lyre-back armchair from beneath the window and settled herself in it next to the bed. Simon's nightshirt was already damp as he threw back the covers. She pulled them back over his shoulders and tucked them securely in place. Keeping him warm was the only thing she could think to do. He seemed to notice her lingering hands and opened his feverish eyes. For a moment he recognized her, whispering her name as he groped for her hand.

Damara murmured reassuring phrases as she allowed her hand to remain in his painful clasp. She balanced awkwardly on the edge of her chair, stroking his forehead while she continued to whisper encouragement. She had no idea how long she remained bent over him, conscious of nothing but Simon until someone coughed to gain her attention.

Next to her stood a short, rotund man with the face of a prize fighter. "I be Bundy, ma'am. I came ta help ya look affer the major."

There was something in the little man's sad blue eyes that communicated his devotion to his major. Damara knew he would gladly suffer Simon's fever if he could. She started to rise from her chair, only to discover that Simon would not release her hand. To give Bundy room, she perched on the side of the high mattress.

The small man pulled back the bedclothes to examine his master. Without a word he turned to the small leather satchel he had put on the nighttable. He extracted a green bottle and spoon from the bag, then poured a measured quantity of liquid into the bowl of the spoon. Before Damara could protest, he turned back to the feverish man and held the spoon to his lips. Simon obediently swallowed the medicine without a murmur.

As the silent servant replaced the bottle in his satchel, Damara finally found her voice. "Bundy, what was that?" Her voice was shrill from surprise, and she flushed at his hurt expression.

"Jest a tonic, ma'am," he grumbled as he looked straight into her eyes, challenging her to reprimand him. "The medico in India give it ta the major, I mean His Lor'ship, when he first come down with fever."

"Is that the only time he has had the fever, Bundy?"

"No, ma'am, this be the third bout," the little man replied, relaxing under her gentle tone. "We needs ta keep him warm and dowse him with the tonic. I told him whot'd happen when he come in wet and bruised that night, leavin' on damp clothes whilest he talks ta that Bow Street bloke. Then dinnit he go get drippin' wet in the park."

"Is it the ague fever, malaria?" Damara asked to confirm Tearle's statement. She would question the man further about Simon's dealings with the runner later.

"Aye, ma'am, but doan ya fret 'bout this. His Lordship'll pull through," Bundy assured her, reading her fear in her expression when the patient began to murmur incoherently once more. "He wone be makin' sense most of the time till the fever breaks."

"Between the two of us, we should have him well again in no time at all," Damara stated softly, moving closer to Simon to relieve the ache in her arm and back as he continued to hold her hand.

"Aye, ma'am, that's so." He smiled at her show of confidence in him, displaying a number of gaps in his teeth.

The smile, however, disappeared quickly at the entrance of Hastings with another man behind him. "The doctor is here now, milady," the butler announced, giving the little man beside the bed a disapproving look.

"Oh, Doctor, I'm so sorry you had to come," Damara exclaimed while trying to loosen her hand from Simon's grip. "Mr. Bundy, His Lordship's man, has already given him the medicine he needs, having nursed him through the fever twice."

The thin, bespectacled man's eyes narrowed as he took in Damara's anxious expression and the manservant's stiff posture. "I understand you were in India with the army?" he queried as he moved to the patient's side. With a motion that told Damara she need not move, he performed the same examination that Bundy had, hemming and hawing as he did so. "Yes, this is a minor attack since the spleen is only slightly enlarged. May I see the medicine you gave him?"

"Aye, sir, it be a tonic the medico gave us in India," Bundy replied, his eyes wary of what the doctor intended, but he still retrieved the green bottle from his satchel.

The doctor took the bottle and removed the stopper. He sniffed at the opening, his forehead furrowed, then his face cleared as he recognized the odor. He poured a few drops in his palm and tasted it. Closing the bottle, he smiled. "Excellent, excellent, Mr. Bundy, cinchona and wine. You'll give him this every few hours?"

"Aye, sir," the little man answered, his wrinkled face bright with a huge smile.

"Lady Damara, your patient has the best care there is," Dr. Vaughan explained, his own smile matching Bundy's.

"There is nothing else to do but give him the tonic?" Damara asked, totally bewildered by the conversation that had just taken place. "Are you going to bleed him to purge the fever?"

"Milady, somehow Lord Emsley has obtained the most successful cure for malaria that I know," the doctor stated firmly, offering his hand to Bundy. "Sir, we must talk of this latter. I should like to observe His Lordship's treatment with your permission."

Bundy flushed with pleasure and looked at Damara for her approval. When she nodded, so did he.

"Good. I've been studying Talbor's treatment of Charles II and Louis XIV. This is an extraordinary opportunity since cinchona is so rare," Dr. Vaughan said more to himself than the others in the room. "But where did it come from? Ah, Mr. Bundy, were you stationed near a Portuguese settlement in India?"

"Aye, sir."

"Lady Damara, I'll call tomorrow in the early afternoon," the doctor stated, and signaled to Hastings, still hovering with his nose in the air, that he was ready to leave. He followed the disgruntled Hastings out, leaving two bewildered but satisfied people behind with the patient.

Damara tentatively broached the subject of Simon's care, knowing Bundy would be overly protective of his master. They argued in hushed voices over who would take the first watch, but Simon made the decision for them, refusing to relinquish his hold on Damara's hand. Once he fell into a fitful sleep, he relaxed his grip sufficiently to allow her to move from her awkward position.

She was forced to straighten her body slowly in order to stand upright, her movements awakening Bundy from his nap on the carved, gilt sofa before the fireplace. He came to her rescue by massaging her arms and feet to restore her circulation. Once her body was sufficiently recovered for her to move, Damara went to her room.

She automatically went through her nightly ritual of preparing for bed, then flushed to her hairline as she studied the picture she presented in the mirror. How could she appear in Simon's room clad only in this ridiculous diaphanous material?

Stifling a yawn, she promised herself a few choice words with Miss Evelyn Townsend on the morrow.

— Chapter Nine —

The sound of rattling china awoke Damara with a start. She lay staring up at the morning sun's mottled design on the gathered white silk on the underside of her canopy, attempting to recall the cause of her feelings of expectancy. She absently watched Meg picking up her haphazardly discarded clothes from the previous evening. Suddenly her tired brain recalled Simon's flushed face and feverish eyes.

Meg was startled as her mistress flung back the bed-clothes and began pulling fresh garments from the clothes press, all the while talking to herself under her breath. Damara quickly donned a pale yellow muslin morning dress without the maid's assistance. She rushed from the room, belatedly calling over her shoulder that her breakfast would be taken in the sickroom.

A few steps into the hall she heard raised voices coming from Jasper's room and immediately recognized Lady Mathilde's strident voice.

When Damara stepped into the sickroom, she froze in place. Lady Mathilde was gesturing wildly with her cane at an almost snarling Bundy, who stood before the bed with his arms stretched wide as if to bar the old woman's approach from any direction. At her aunt's feet was a tray with broken crockery scattered on its surface in a pool of liquid. Tess, the youngest and most timid maid, was kneeling and trying to clean up the mess while avoiding being hit by the waving cane.

"What is happening here? This is a sickroom, not a cheap theatrical," Damara hissed, almost running to place herself between the two combatants after a worried look at the sleeping patient.

"This impertinent idiot tells me I'm not allowed in here. I brought Emsley some broth to help build up his strength,"

Lady Mathilde accused without bothering to lower her voice, so they could undoubtedly hear her in the kitchen. "Then he tells me that no one has bled the man."

"That is true, and no one will, unless the doctor and Bundy say differently," Damara returned with heat, placing her hands on her hips. Once and for all she was going to have the last word on her irritating aunt's interference. "Simon must have quiet. Though it was kind of you to offer your help, Bundy and I can manage his care."

"Well, I never," the old woman snapped, her eyes narrowing in a malevolent manner. With a last smoldering look she spun on her heels and narrowly missed tripping over the hapless Tess and showed her final displeasure by slamming the door behind her.

"That one be a right term'gent," Bundy murmured and let out a deep breath as he lowered his hands to his sides. "I doan trust her like with them mean eyes. Beggin' yer pardon, ma'am . . . Yer Ladyship."

"You did the right thing, Mr. Bundy." She was having trouble keeping back her smile at his earnest expression. "No one has permission to be in this room unless you approve of them. And you may also call me Miss Mara as they do at home."

"Thank ya, Miss Mara, and I be just Bundy," he returned with his almost toothless smile and ducked his head as a flush rose to his round face.

"Well, then, except for our unexpected drama, how is our patient?" she asked, resisting the urge to hug the little man. Instead she walked to the side of the bed to take a closer look at Simon.

"He be awake before the dragon come in and asked where he were. Then he dropped off onest he tooks his medicine."

"Very good, Bundy." Damara sat in one of the chairs near the bed. He was still flushed, but to her mind did not seem so feverish. This would be the perfect opportunity to question Bundy about Simon's mishap with the two cut-throats. She waited until Tess picked up the tray and carried the broken crockery from the room before patting the chair next to her. "Bundy, sit down while we wait for my breakfast tray," she invited, giving him a gentle smile.

When he took the offered chair, she began. "Tell me about what Simon discussed with the man from Bow Street."

"Miss Mara, I doan rightly know—"

"Bundy, I'm His Lordship's fiancée, and we don't know how soon he'll be well enough to take care of this business," she said in an authoritative manner that she hoped would convince Bundy she really did have the right to know Simon's business dealings.

"He come home with the Bow Street bloke after them two thieves twere set on him," Bundy explained hesitantly with an uneasy glance at his master's slumbering form. "His Lordship hired the bloke ta look inta why summun'd hire them two ta rob him."

"Someone hired them? What does this have to do with his fall from his horse?" Damara was amazed at what she was hearing.

"Tweren't an accident neither. That saddle was fairly new an' ther girth were cut too clean to be a break, specially with a nail unner ther saddle," Bundy continued, his pudgy hands doubling into fists at the thought.

"But why would anyone want to hurt Simon?" Damara frowned. Looking at Simon's handsome face relaxed in sleep, she wanted to gather him in her arms to protect him and keep him safe, even though it was silly to think she could protect a man of Simon's proportions. "Bundy, what was the man's name that Simon hired? We must contact him at once to see what he has learned."

"Aye, Miss Mara. Affer I catch a bit of sleep that's wot I'll do, go an' see ta this bloke," Bundy replied, still not telling her the man's name. He was going to protect his lordship's lady, just as he did Emsley. Now that he was sure Miss Mara cared for his major the same as he did, Bundy would give his life for her as well.

Silently entering the sickroom during the night, Damara found poor Bundy using the two armchairs as a makeshift bed, just as she suspected. For the past two days he had barely left his master, unless given a direct order. He woke at the sound of the door clicking shut.

"M'lady?" His voice was slurred with sleep as he rubbed his eyes with his fist and stumbled to his feet.

"Manfred Bundy, I'll not have another patient on my hands as soon as His Lordship is better," she whispered, making sure there was a hint of iron in her voice, as if she was scolding Percy.

"Aye, Miss Mara." He was too tired to argue with her determination to see that he took care of himself.

"Hastings prepared a room for you off the kitchen, which you have not seen fit to use. His Lordship is much better now, and from what the doctor said this afternoon, our patient will be a handful once the fever is gone."

"Aye, that be true. Affer the fever gits past, he won't stay down." Bundy gave a drowsy chuckle and went along to his bed.

Damara rearranged the chairs, snuggling into one with her bare feet tucked under her and laying her head against the padded side panel. During his illness she found herself fascinated watching Simon's face relaxed in sleep. How a man who was so irritating in full health could look so innocent in sleep, she did not know. He appeared to be Percy's age, guileless and defenseless, nothing like the persistent male who plagued her life. When he regained his strength, they would be at loggerheads again, of that she was certain. Foolishly she almost missed their battling wits, and knew that Tarrant's Mount would be flat without having to worry about what order the marquess would give her next.

Finally her heavy eyelids closed, and she fell into a light sleep. She was not aware of how long she slept, but Simon's mutterings brought her quickly awake. Moving to sit on the bed, she stroked his face in an effort to quiet him. He was more violent in his delirium than she had seen since the first night of his illness. She began murmuring nonsensical assurances along with endearments, which seemed to slow his movements, but the shivering continued. The chime of the bracket clock on the mantel told her it was time for his medicine. She quickly reached for the bottle and measured the tonic into the spoon. More luck then skill allowed her to give Simon the dose he needed.

Since he would not keep the bedclothes around him, she went to stoke up the dwindling fire. Momentarily wondering if she had sent Bundy away too soon, she decided she would persevere. She perched on the side of the bed and trapped the bedclothes between their bodies. Unexpectedly this seemed to calm him. Damara knew, however, she could not stay in this position for long without developing a cramp in her back.

With a fleeting thought to the impropriety of her position, she lay down and was able to anchor the blankets securely around Simon. After a few minutes his breathing deepened, signaling he was falling into a refreshing sleep again. In relief, she laid her head on his chest, the steady rise and fall and the rhythmic beat of his heart giving her renewed confidence. A weary smile formed on her lips as she closed her eyes to give a prayer of thanks.

The noise of carriage wheels sounded in Damara's ears, and she determinedly burrowed further under the bed-clothes. The morning had arrived too soon. Then her body tensed. Her rooms overlooked the garden at the back of the house, away from the sounds of carts and vendors' cries in the street below.

As this thought crystalized, something moved against her side. Her gasp of surprise was cut short by a heavy weight closing around her waist. Slowly she opened her eyes to gaze directly at the fireplace against the far wall. She looked upward to gaze at the indigo bedhangings that confirmed her worst fears. She was in Simon's bed.

The movement behind her began again, and she slowly turned to look over her shoulder. With a groan of despair she closed her eyes, then quickly opened them again. Unfortunately the amused—and alert—face of Marquess of Emsley was still mere inches from her own.

"Good morning?" she barely managed to choke out as she tried to remember what had led her to this embarrassing circumstance. As usual, her befuddled brain was most uncooperative.

"Good morning, my love," Simon murmured, giving her a slight smile before he bent his head to drop a light kiss on the curve of her shoulder.

Damara jumped at his intimate touch but became still as the realization that his skin was dry against her own sank in. Her surprise overruled rational thought as she turned in his arms and reached up to trace her fingers over his forehead. "You aren't feverish," she said in a wondering tone as her hand lingered, brushing back his tousled hair from habit.

"When I awoke last night with so charming, though unexpected, a companion beside me, I thought I was dreaming," he returned, carefully choosing his words. Could she really not remember? The idea that had come to him when he first came to his senses and found her sleeping next to him began to look like it might be possible. He was tempted to cross his fingers, almost amazed at his luck. "But I assure you, I wasn't delirious. You were somewhat, shall we say, bewildered during our . . . er, conversation."

As he spoke, Damara began to take in her surroundings. She was under the bedclothes, though the last thing she could recall was leaning over Simon to keep the blankets in place. The bedclothes, however, were not the only change that was disquieting. Simon's chest was warm against her hands; the only barrier between their bodies was the gauzy material of her nightdress.

She almost did not dare voice her thoughts, but she knew she must do something. Taking a deep, controlling breath, she reluctantly posed a question, amazed that her voice did not come out in a hysterical scream. "What conversation?"

"Well, you were very pleased with my recovery, *very* pleased," he explained as his smile widened into what he hoped was a reminiscent grin, not a leer.

"Wha—What happened to your nightshirt?" She snatched desperately at any subject to counteract her awareness of his slightest move.

"The nightshirt was damp and uncomfortable. So I removed it." He continued his fabrication smoothly, controlling his voice. He was a desperate man. Although this trick was unfair, almost cruel, he had to grasp at the opportunity before Jasper returned. "You needn't worry. You managed admirably to keep me most sufficiently warm."

"I see," Damara murmured weakly, although she did not. Staring fixedly at his collarbone, she refused to meet his gaze. This must still be a dream; it had to be. Since it was a dream, she did not have to fully understand what he was trying to imply, because otherwise it made no sense to her at all.

"I must go tell Bundy you're awake and much better. He has been so worried about you," she said in a rush. By trying to leave the bed she would truly wake up, and everything would be fine. She began to slide away from the solid figure of her fiancé and retain her dignity. After all, she reasoned, one must preserve appearance even when dreaming. He would allow her to go since he was only a figment of her imagination, not solid, living, breathing flesh.

But Simon was real, his arm closing around her waist and drawing her close to him again. His free hand came up to brush aside the disordered curls that hid her face from his view.

"I've been wanting to do that for days. I would be burning with fever and for one brief, rational moment I would feel your cool hand on my face and hair." His tone was full of wonder while his brown eyes searched her averted face. The tender words brought her troubled gaze upward. "Damara, we must talk. The maid has already been in to check the fire."

"I don't see the need for any further discussion," she returned with a false, childish confidence. If she pretended nothing out of place had occurred, they could simply go on as they intended. This was something ladies and gentlemen did not talk about, and she had never been told what did happen in the bedroom. "Simon, we'll simply go on as before. In fact, I'll send a note to Mr. Wilkins today to discover what he has learned to stop this ridiculous charade," she continued, ignoring her shortness of breath.

"What will happen a few months from now if Lady Damara Tarrant goes into seclusion with a mysterious malady? Will you also claim that you took Princess Sophia's miraculous *beef cure*, and put about that the young child in your household is the poor, orphaned offspring of a dear, departed friend?" Simon's voice was dangerously quiet. He was beginning to feel guilty over his pretense, but he knew he must continue, or chance losing Damara when Jasper returned.

"I certainly can't foresee myself coming down with some

mysterious ailment. I am never sick," she began heatedly,
warming to her anger now that she was coming fully awake.
Then her next words stuck in her throat as she understood
his meaning at last.

The gossips of her first season still whispered that
Princess Sophia had a child out of wedlock, for only three
of the King's six daughters had married, the Princesses
Charlotte, Augusta and Mary. While his sister was the
subject of much speculation, the Duke of Clarence seemed
to have another child by Mrs. Jordon every few years
without anyone batting an eye. There were now eight or
nine FitzClarences to the one child insinuated to be Princess
Sophia's.

Hastily Damara tried again to recall the past night but
could only put together fragments of her restless and
meaningless dreams. The single clear memory was lying at
Simon's side to secure the bedding over his thrashing body.
She knew it was almost useless to refute his words, even if
she did remember. *Maman* had died too soon to tell her
daughter of the ways between men and women, and Papa
certainly never took time to enlighten his innocent daughter,
who only experienced her first kiss a mere two weeks ago.

"I think, my love, our best plan would be to procure a
special license at the earliest opportunity to avoid any more
speculation on our marriage. We've already caused enough
gossip without the tattlemongers counting on their fingers if
the need should arise." Simon pressed on, knowing from
the stunned look on her face that Damara now understood
what he was saying. He gently stroked her cheek to help
comfort her.

"Surely you're jesting?" she finally managed in an
attempt to rally. The fever must have affected the man's
brain, or perhaps hers, which was ridiculous since she had
not been ill. She had been averse to marrying from the
moment the announcement appeared, and she was as bound
and determined now that she would not be forced into
marriage due to the consequences of a single night that she
could not remember.

She was ignorant of how babies were conceived, but
certainly what he implied could not have occurred without
her knowledge. For now she would remain silent and allow

Simon to think he had convinced her, for whatever his reasons. There would, however, be no wedding ceremony until she either recalled the past night or learned more about human conception.

"Here is your wrapper. I suggest we present a less compromising picture before anyone else descends upon us."

Damara stared at the sheer material draped over his hand, and snatched the garment from him before she scrambled out of the large bed. With her back turned toward him she pulled it on and secured the sash under her bosom. When she turned to face him, Simon was studying her with a strange expression on his face. Only her angry determination kept her from turning and running from the room.

"Perhaps you should borrow my dressing gown, now that I've had a chance to reconsider," he suggested without moving, though his eyes lingered over her figure.

She could feel her entire body flush bright red as she grabbed the garment from where it lay at the end of the bed. Fleetingly she mused that even Evelyn could not fault the quality of the blue brocade accented with mustard-colored trim at the cuffs and lapels.

"Send Bundy to me, please," Simon asked as he adjusted his pillows to his satisfaction once she was shrouded in his dressing gown. "Then I'll pursue the matter we discussed, my sweet."

He smiled contentedly at the sound of the door slamming, then had to choke back a laugh at the sound of voices in the hallway. His amusement was not long-lived. Another resounding slam further down the hall quickly sobered him. He did not know if he could carry on with his lie, though it was only a lie by implication and innuendo.

This was not the resolution he had hoped for, but it would have to suffice. During his fever he had sensed Damara's care and sometimes heard her call him love, although he was not sure if that was reality or delirium. He was waging a campaign of subterfuge that could fall apart at any moment; the moment his love remembered that nothing happened last night. He could simply hope she did not discover the truth until after the knot was tied and he confessed contritely but lovingly.

* * *

"I see you managed to find a replacement for Jasper's ratty cast-off," Evelyn observed with interest the moment her friend entered the room rather dramatically, punctuating her entrance by slamming the heavy paneled door as hard as she could. "Although I fear it is a trifle early for all this agitation. Meg has just brought the chocolate, and I see she was able to find you."

"Yes, I met her in the hall. I hope you don't have other plans for this morning. We're going to Madame Lucretia's as soon as the shops open," Damara announced, standing belligerently in front of the other woman with her hands on her hips as if daring her friend to cry off. "It seems I'm missing some necessary items from my wardrobe."

"What is that?" Evelyn called as Damara stalked into the bedroom. The blonde leaned forward on the sofa, but Damara was obscured by the door of the clothes press with only her arm appearing as she tossed dress after dress onto her bed.

"A wedding dress," Damara stated flatly as she stripped off Emsley's dressing gown and had the satisfaction of dropping it on the floor and stepping on it. Irrationally she decided that if she still retained her former mode of night apparel, this situation would have been averted.

There was no response from the sitting room. For once Evelyn was speechless. Damara changed into a fresh chemise and pulled on a pair of pink stockings, wondering what she would say to her friend about the sudden wedding. Still at a loss, she searched for a suitable gown among those she had tossed onto the bed. She studiously avoided her reflection in the large glass to her right, unable to confront her image there with her new knowledge, however foolish it seemed.

Finally selecting a cambric walking dress with sky blue and white stripes and a solid blue spencer to match, she dressed and went to join Evelyn. She had no idea what she should say to her friend. How could she explain this? From their conversation that evening in the garden, Damara knew her friend's sophistication was only a thin veneer. Evelyn had never really been kissed, so how could she explain how babies were conceived?

"Shall we send a message around to Regina to see if she would like to join us?" Evelyn asked to break the silence that was becoming oppressive. Something strange was afoot, and perhaps the older woman would be able to wheedle the story from Damara, who sat down to frown at her cup of chocolate as though it was something repellant.

Damara stared at Evenly for a long moment, then smiled benignly. Regina was exactly the person she needed to consult on this matter. "Evelyn, have I ever told you how glad I am that you're my friend?"

Damara felt much more like herself when she returned from the modiste later that morning. Madame Lucretia's florid praise while selecting the right pattern and material for a wedding dress—which could easily be converted to an evening gown—was a balm to Damara's lagging spirits. She had also arranged to have a quiet coze with Regina the next morning.

"I really don't think I can afford to remain in town much longer," Evelyn remarked as they removed their outer garments and passed them to Meg. "Neither my pocket nor my stamina can stand much more shopping, so it is— Emsley!"

Damara whirled away from the mirror where she had been straightening her hair after removing her beehive bonnet. Emsley stood in the doorway of the drawing room looking as if he had never been sick a day in his life. Dressed in a chestnut brown morning coat over dun-colored pantaloons and tasseled Hessians, he returned her startled look with an unsmiling, level gaze.

He knew he was still in bad odor as Damara rose to her full height, her back becoming a match for Hastings's. In spite of the fact he had sent a note to Tearle to bring Percy and Cretin around as reinforcements, he knew it would take more than the pair's nonsense to bring her out of her sulks. Just as he stepped forward to break the awkward silence— almost ready to confess—the door knocker echoed through the silent entry hall.

Damara was relieved at the interruption, no matter who was at the door. She had not expected Emsley to be on his feet quite yet, though Dr. Vaughan and Bundy had warned her the patient would not be content to lie in bed. She had counted on him being bedridden a few more days.

A familiar whoofle from the front door announced the arrival of Cretin, which meant Percy was not far behind. She tuned to greet the new arrivals, the perfect shield against a private conversation with her fiancé. There were, however, two adult figures framed in the doorway behind the boy and dog.

At the sight of Emsley, restored to health, Percy ran forward with Cretin in tow. Tearle smiled in greeting, then followed Damara's gaze, looking quizzically over his shoulder at the man just behind him on the front steps before strolling into the entry. The slighter man stood alone, silhouetted in the door with the sun behind him obscuring his features. Still somewhat distracted, Damara noted that the man was in uniform.

Then her breath caught in her throat as he moved forward. His dark blue uniform did have silver lacing, as Emsley had explained. Tears started in her eyes as he stood there giving her a lopsided grin as Hastings closed the front door. She could not believe what she was seeing, closing her eyes to give a prayer of thanksgiving, and quickly opening them again to make sure he was actually standing there.

"Jasper!" she cried out, bringing the new arrival to everyone's attention. Her feet found life at the same moment as her tongue, and she ran to welcome him. She heard his helmet hit the floor the precise moment his arms closed around her trembling body. Murmuring his name over and over, she hugged him fiercely. Once she had broken the spell of astonishment, everyone began talking at the same time. Cretin joined in with excited barks when Percy hurled himself at his brother and sister.

Though Damara was aware of Tearle questioning Emsley, she could not take her eyes off Jasper's face. He was older, bearing the marks of his service. She cupped his tanned face in her unsteady hands, still trying to assure herself he was really there. There were new lines on his face, carved by hard living and exposure to the elements, but his emerald green eyes—almost identical to her own—still gleamed with the wicked light she remembered.

"I believe you missed me, Mara," he teased, as if he had simply taken a brief sojourn, but the sheen of moisture in his twinkling eyes belied his offhand tone. "And who is this person that is clutching my legs? This can't be Percival-pup. He is a scrawny little boy with a runny nose."

"Oh, Jasper, nub it," his brother complained, stepping back while fisting his eyes that were suspiciously wet. To add to his lack of dignity, his voice cracked at the end of his complaint about Jasper's use of his nickname.

"Mara, my dear, I think we're setting a bad example for the servants," Jasper commented, looking over her head. "There's a large piece of statuary dressed like a butler giving us the evil eye."

"You fool, that *is* the butler." Damara giggled and reminded herself that she must tell him of Hastings's resemblance to the statue in the square. "Hastings, this is my brother, the Earl of Layston, the master of the house."

"If you insist, milady," the man replied without moving a muscle as he spoke. "Once you and your guests retire to the drawing room, I'll instruct Mrs. Kasey to serve refreshments."

"Oh, my dear, where did we find him?" Jasper asked as the man made a perfect about turn and walked with his nose in the air to carry out his duties. "And who are all these other people? Mind you, the gentlemen are of little interest, but I must make the acquaintance of the delightful blonde standing there clutching her parasol and biting her lower lip, if you promise not to tell Evie."

"I think it is too late, scamp," Damara answered with a chuckle as Evelyn stamped her foot and tossed back her ringlets. Without a word she walked over to Tearle, took his arm, and led him into the drawing room. "Now I know you're truly here. Only in the house for five minutes and you've already caused Evie to pout. Not that you don't deserve it, but I'll speak to you about that later. We best follow Hastings's orders, or we'll not get anything to eat."

"But who are our other guests, sister dear?" Jasper asked, ignoring her scolding as he always did, but cherishing it also. He looked at the large man who was waiting patiently to be introduced and almost missed a step at the moment he recognized him. He gave Damara a sharp look, but she merely smiled up at him, revealing nothing except her happiness at having him safely at home. She did not know, he realized with guilty relief; however, the man did. Jasper could see it in the fellow's look.

"That's Simon. Mara is going to marry him," Percy put in to be helpful, beaming at his knowledge. "I'm staying with him at the Albany like a real gentleman, though Tearle came to stay while Simon was ill."

"Jasper, this is the Marquess of Emsley." Damara performed the introduction in a prim voice, clutching Jasper's arm like a lifeline. "Emsley, my brother, the Earl of Layston."

"I believe we've met," Simon responded, momentarily enjoying the younger man's start of surprise. The rascal deserved to sweat a bit before he told him that his secret was safe. He was the last person in the world to tell Damara that her brother was responsible for their engagement.

"Really, I don't seem to recall the occasion," Jasper replied, recovering quickly from his surprise. "I had no idea Mara was thinking of marriage."

"Yes, it happened suddenly, but we'll discuss that later." Damara rushed into speech to keep the subject of marriage at bay. "We'll all sit down and bring everyone up-to-date. You have yet to meet Baron Tearle, Emsley's friend who has been invaluable over the past few days."

"Yes, I think I should meet him if he is the bloke Evie walked off with," Jasper commented. He nodded at Emsley, signaling him that they would talk later, though it appeared to the others he was simply motioning the man to proceed the Tarrant family through the door. "I always say, it's best to know the man before you challenge him to a duel."

"Oh, Jasper, it's so good to have you home," his sister said as they moved to join the others. She gave him a watery smile as tears threatened to overwhelm her again. Then her Tarrant blood came to the fore, and she stood on tip-toe to whisper in his ear. "I have it on good authority that if you knew how to kiss properly, you wouldn't be plagued by rivals."

— *Chapter Ten* —

"You have outdone yourself, young jackanapes," the woman snapped the instant her companion sidled up to her where she waited in the shadow of the charred ruin of Lanthorn Tower. "Even those stupid black birds could guess you're ready for the sheriff's bracelets, about to be hobbled and led to the noose. Why the Tower of London? Why not make a complete hash of it and meet in the drawing room of Layston Place?"

"Snubble it, you old bawd. You're all jaw like a sheep's head with your whining," the man growled, yet he pulled her deeper into the shadows. "No one will notice two more gaping hicks touring the grounds on public day."

"Well, what half-nab idea have you devised this time for Emsley? Though if I see more than a half guinea from the enterprise, it will truly be a miracle."

"How did my father withstand your complaints for so long?" The man shuddered, eyeing the crone as if she was a slab of beef gone bad. "If you were a celebrated highflyer in your day, men must have been blind and deaf."

"Insults won't improve your luck. Emsley didn't turn up his toes from the ague, so you'll need to hire those two brainless snafflers again," the dame ordered, dabbing her nose with her lavender-scented handkerchief as the wind blew from the direction of the Menagerie. "He is dressed and been going about since early afternoon. Something is amiss as well. The brother has returned, and there is talk of a wedding, possibly within the week."

"Then we'll need our friends to create another tragedy in the Emsley line very soon," he muttered, ducking his head when a passing warder turned to study the pair lurking near the half-burned tower.

"Just make sure they aren't noddy-headed from gin in

some gutter, or we'll be all a heap." The woman made a
close study of the nearest wall's masonry after spotting the
warder changing his route to walk in their direction. She
hissed under her breath before the man was within hearing,
"I've no desire to end the rest of my days in accommoda-
tions like the Dungeon of the Little Ease as that fool Guy
Fawkes did after failing at murder."

"Evenin', madame, sir. We'll be closin' early today due
to the ceremony," the warder stated as he approached the
mismatched couple. "The gates are about ready to close."

"What ceremony is that, my good man?" the woman
asked, taking her companion's arm. She gave the warder a
condescending nod to assure him he was dealing with
Quality, hoping to offset the surly expression in her companion's watery gray eyes.

"The anniversary of King Henry VI's murder, ma'am,"
she was informed before the warder nodded solemnly and
turned on his heels.

"Perchance it's an omen for this harum-scarum affair,"
she exclaimed with a cackle of laughter as they passed a
gathering of men carrying lilies and white roses near the
entrance to Wakefield Tower. "They're celebrating the
murder of an insane king, and we're plotting the untimely
death of a peer, though I believe the madness is on the side
of the conspirators in this instance."

"Don't push me too far, you harpy," her companion
challenged with his usual sneer. "Take a good look at where
the block stood. Your scrawny neck would only need a
sharp blade, not the heavy axe of the executioner."

"Just set the tray there, Meg, then go on to bed," Evelyn
instructed with an airy wave just as the ormolu clock on
Damara's mantel struck the hour of midnight. Crossing the
room, she flung herself onto the Grecian sofa while Meg,
eyeing the decanter of amber liquid and two glasses on the
silver tray, silently placed them in the center of the
Pembroke table and scurried out of the room.

Damara watched her friend artfully arrange herself on the
sofa. After drawing up her feet to recline full length, Evelyn
arranged the flowing skirt of her Nile green negligee, then
leaned languidly against the curved end of the sofa. Satis-

fied with her position, she stared with rounded blue eyes at her friend, a wicked smile on her face showing both dimples. "Do you think a slow poison, or a Lancer's sword through the heart, or perhaps a pistol shot between the eyes?"

"Am I to assume you're plotting the death of my dear, sweet, older brother after he has survived the rigors of war only to be wantonly slain by a woman's ire?" Damara parried dramatically as she sat back in the armchair directly across from her friend. "You seem to be planning to find your courage for the deed in what appears to be your father's best sherry."

"I always, always said you were an extremely bright girl when we were cutting our teeth on chap books," Evelyn responded with a nod. Then her bravado left her, and she folded her hands on the arm of the couch, resting her chin on her knuckles. "He seemed to enjoy his liquor so much that he is now asleep in a chair by the fire. I think your Aunt Mathilde consumed as much wine, and is snoring louder than he."

"You could have tried talking to him. He was only teasing in the hallway," Damara reprimanded gently, and gave her friend a coaxing smile to bring her out of her doldrums. "He knew it was you and was simply nervous about greeting you in front of strangers."

"Mara, Jasper has been gone for two years and does look a bit older, but you can't convince me he has become shy and nervous," Evelyn stated in a reproving tone, her eyes mournful. She sighed heavily as if resigning herself to the fate of an old maid who keeps cats for companionship. Whatever her thoughts were, they did not agree with her. She leaned over to pull the stopper from the decanter.

"Flirting and laughing with Tearle and Emsley all evening certainly didn't give him the impression he was welcome to pursue his interest." Damara accepted the glass Evelyn offered her and shuddered as the blonde tossed back the entire contents of her own glass in one swallow. Damara could not contain her amusement a moment later when her friend ended the amazing feat with a half-hiccup, half-cough.

"Go ahead and laugh, but I didn't see you going out of

your way to charm your own betrothed," Evelyn challenged, defiantly refilling her glass.

Hastily Damara tasted her sherry, lowering her lashes to cloak her expression. She could not let Evelyn see how perceptive her comment was. The subject of Emsley was an uncomfortable one. Until she was able to talk to Regina, she did not want to explain what had occurred this morning, if anything, in the sickroom.

"I refuse to see you so downcast. Jasper can be odious when he is in a teasing mood, but you know that as well as I do," his sister stated, renewing her argument with more heat than was warranted. The longer she had stared into her glass, the more she remembered Emsley's eyes at the moment before he would kiss her; something that was only fleeting memory now. "You were simply hoping he would sweep you into his arms, press you to his manly bosom, and *finally* kiss you as a grown woman should be."

"You've been borrowing too many of Justine's novels," Evelyn accused accurately, giving a shudder at the thought, though she read them every time she could sneak one away from her younger sister.

"Yes, I have, and you're acting like one of those die-away ninnies." Satisfied that her ramblings were finally giving her a point to make, Damara reached to refill her own glass. "The Evie I know and love, as does my idiotic brother, wouldn't be sitting here whining and wringing her hands. She would make sure she found out what it was like to be kissed as an adult. You're nothing if not resourceful."

With a triumphant smile Damara sat back in her chair and waited. She had never seen Evelyn so listless. If practically calling her a coward did not do the trick, she had no earthly idea which way to turn next. Sipping her wine, Damara wondered if she had gone too far.

The musical sound of Evelyn's laughter quickly told Damara that she had succeeded. "I don't know why everyone says Jasper is the devious one in your family, Mara."

"Because he has a decided talent for being caught out with his schemes, while I enjoy cunning and an innocent countenance."

"All right, I'll do it. I don't know how or when, but the

Earl of Layston may find that he had a much easier time of
it in the rains of Portugal," she said decisively, and filled
her glass once more, then held the decanter up in question
to Damara, who reluctantly held out her glass. "We'll toast
the campaign of the Joking Earl."

"Evie, perhaps we should simply go to bed. We've more
than sufficient wine to see us through for one evening,"
Damara hastened to say when Evelyn ended her pronouncement with a high-pitched giggle. "We had wine at dinner
and sherry while playing cards, and now this."

"Mara, Mara, Mara, how do you expect to win the overly
tall marquess if you continually allow your scruples to
dampen your adventuresome spirit?" Evelyn waved her
arms in a grand arch and managed not to spill a drop of
liquid from her full glass. "Besides, I'm not so sure I'll be
as confident in the morning. I'll need a reminder of this
evening to stiffen my resolve. A painful head will be just the
incentive I need to remind me of my noble sacrifice this
evening . . . er, morning for love."

"Oh, why did I ever let Evelyn in my room last night?"
Damara muttered, clutching her pounding head with one
hand while groping for the bannister with the other as
she cautiously made her way down the stairs the next
morning.

The two women had polished off the first decanter,
then—with the wisdom only known to the intoxicated—
decided to forage below stairs to replenish their supply.
Never again would she allow her friend to lead her into such
debauchery. Even her morning chocolate had not seemed
appetizing, though Meg brought it two hours later than
usual.

"At last I've learned to stay abed to the fashionable hour
of eleven, but at what price?" she asked aloud as she finally
reached the bottom of the stairs. Her descent had taken
twice the normal time, carefully moving from step to step to
keep from jarring her throbbing brain. "Perhaps some dry
toast and weak tea will help."

Turning to the dining room to see if breakfast was still
laid out, she hoped against hope that this one morning Cook
had not prepared Sir Cedric's favorite kippers. Before she

took a single step, an exclamation from the back of the hallway caught her attention.

"Evelyn Danielle Townsend, what are you about?"

Damara grasped the smooth surface of the curved mahogany newel cap and peered around the staircase to see where Jasper and Evelyn were. The door of the library was partway open, and there was no sign of the pair anywhere else.

"I want to be assured that I have you full attention for this discussion, so I am sitting on your lap." Evelyn's laughing words confirmed that she and Jasper were indeed in the library.

Damara tiptoed forward, looking guiltily over her shoulder to make sure none of the servants were about, to close the door so the couple would not be disturbed. Though the Townsends allowed their oldest daughter more freedom than other unattached women of her age, Damara was sure they would be taken aback to discover their child in such an intriguing position. It could possibly seal her brother's fate, but she thought the pair should be permitted to come to some accord without parental interference. She knew only too well the lowering effect of being forced to marry due to a compromising situation.

"Evelyn, this isn't proper," Jasper blustered as his sister reached the door.

"Jasper Sedgewick Cedric George Tarrant, you aren't seriously going to preach at me like a starched-up Calvinist about what's proper? I really can't give it much credence, since you're the man who put a sow and her newborn litter in my father's study on All Fool's Day."

"Now, Evie, that was—"

"Jasper Tarrant, either you kiss me like an adult woman should be kissed, or I'll marry the next man who asks to pay his addresses to Papa." Evelyn's voice was not coaxing or the least bit loving as she demanded her due.

Damara knew she should not be eavesdropping, but she could not resist waiting to discover if her dearest friend would succeed. There was no one else who was more ideal for her troublesome brother. Evelyn's spirited and determined nature was the perfect balance for tempering Jasper's impish sense of humor when it got out of hand. His sister stealthily wrapped her hand around the brass doorknob in preparation for a hasty retreat once Evelyn accomplished her goal.

"Evelyn! What do you know about adult kisses?" Jasper sputtered, sounding almost like Percy as his voice cracked in his amazement.

"Damara has informed me that Emsley is most proficient. He can curl her toes," she explained with painstaking clarity, enunciating each word as though talking to a small child. "I want to discover if we're compatible also. If not, mayhap I'll still have Papa accept the next offer for my hand."

"The next? How many have there been, young lady?" Jasper's voice lowered again with anger. "Have any of them curled your toes?"

"I'll tell you if you would shut up and kiss me, you fool," she exclaimed after a loud sigh that signaled her exasperation with the man.

"And just what is Mara thinking of to allow this Emsley—"

Jasper's heated words were suddenly cut off. Damara knew that Evelyn's limited patience had finally run its course, and she had taken the matter into her own hands. With the stealth of a practiced robber, she closed the door and managed to secure the latch without a sound. The last thing she heard was Evelyn's breathless, "Ohhh, Jasper."

Feeling much better than she had since waking that morning, Damara headed once more for the dining room, knowing she had a silly smile on her face. The sound of the front door knocker told her she was not destined to break her fast any time soon, or perhaps not at all. Since Hastings did not seem to be lurking about, she decided to answer the door herself, immediately regretting her breach of proper etiquette the moment she opened the door.

"Simon." Her surprise was so great she uttered his given name naturally, as if she had not purposely used his title since the moment she had awakened in his bed.

"Good morning. I know it's a trifle early, but your brother sent word he wished to see me," he stated, not taking a step forward. His stiff tone was the only indication of his discomfort at seeing Damara before he confronted Jasper.

Oh, dear, not now. Damara quickly looked over her shoulder, then back at Simon, his confused expression making her wonder if she had spoken aloud. "Jasper is rather . . . ah, busy at the moment. Perhaps you can wait until his . . . ah, business associate leaves."

"Of course. May I come in?" Simon wondered if her agitation was caused by something more than his unexpected appearance. It was clear that her brother had not mentioned his forthcoming meeting.

"Oh, yes, yes, of course," Damara managed in a rush, backing away to allow him to enter, knowing she was babbling like a half-wit. Simon looked magnificent—as he always did—dressed in dark brown morning coat, buff pantaloons, and top boots. She stared at the top button of his waistcoat, at a loss over what to do next.

"Milady, did I hear someone at the door?" Hastings asked from behind her. When he noticed Emsley's hat and cane, the servant's nose went up in the air to show his disapproval of the lady's poor behavior.

"Yes, Hastings, the Marquess of Emsley is here to see my brother, but His Lordship is occupied at the moment. I was just going to see if there was any breakfast to be had." She felt as if she were in the nursery again, being reprimanded by her nanny, and dared not meet Simon's gaze. Still looking at his waistcoat to keep from bursting into laughter, she asked primly, "Shall we, Simon?"

"By all means, my dear," he responded readily in relief at escaping Hastings's disapproving stare so easily. Following quickly at Damara's heels, he wondered what they were going to discuss once they were alone. Though she was talking to him now, his betrothed had not addressed one word to him last evening.

Damara was wondering much the same thing as she sat in the shield-backed chair at the head of the table and rang the bell. She refused to rehash their conversation in Simon's bed until she had an opportunity to talk with his godmother. Though she still could not remember what had taken place during the night, Regina would be able to enlighten her concerning Simon's claim.

"Would you care for tea or coffee?" she asked when the footman brought the tray with a fresh pot of each beverage, breaking the silence that stretched between them. After pouring tea for them both, the footman withdrew. Damara decided she could not stand the strain of waiting for Simon to start the conversation. With deadly calm she determined to broach the subject that had been uppermost in her mind in recent weeks.

"Simon, we have to discuss our marriage," she began in one breathless rush of words before her nerve failed. "No matter what the consequences, I'll not go through with the ceremony unless we have an understanding beforehand."

"What is it, Mara?" He did not trust himself to say anything further. His guilty conscience had been working overtime during the night, and Damara's wary expression this morning did not help. He had, however, set his course and must see it through.

She hesitated a half-second, thrown into confusion by the husky sound of her more intimate nickname. But she pressed on. "I must insist that our marriage be a partnership, not the usual one-sided affair. I've been accustomed to making my own decisions and choosing what I wish to do, something that has been sadly lacking in my life recently. Do you understand what I am saying?"

"You touched on this the other night after the theater, I believe. You haven't been consulted about your opinion," he answered, not having to give it a moment's consideration. She wanted his assurance that he would never make a decision without asking her opinion first, which presented him with a singular problem. No matter what he promised her after the wedding, their marriage would be based on a lie.

He stalled for more time to think. "We are in accord on your wishes?"

"Yes, you've stated the situation correctly," she conceded, giving an emphatic nod. "Is that agreeable to you? Having a wife who will speak her mind, and at times cause you to compromise on an issue?"

Compromise. That was exactly what the situation needed. He was creating a need for their marriage, because he was positive it was right, more right than anything else in his life. The wedding could take place because in this instance he knew what was best. Damara would see it that way when he confessed after their wedding. In a way it was a compromise, after a fashion. He would be asking her opinion later. Since he was older and more experienced, the decision to marry should be his.

"No, I've no objection to a wife who knows her own mind," he said easily, rising to his feet and crossing to her side. Solemnly he raised her hand to his lips. "I swear to you at this moment that during our marriage I'll always seek out your opinion on every aspect of our life together."

Damara rewarded him with a smile of approval, finding she was having some difficulty in meeting the warm regard in his sherry-colored eyes—as well as with her breathing. To overcome her unease, she decided to put her betrothed's promise to the test. "Bundy tells me someone is attempting to injure you."

She allowed herself a small smile at his start of surprise before his eyes narrowed in displeasure. Apparently he had not realized she would be making good on his promise before the wedding. The practice would be good for the man, rather than having to make a sudden adjustment when they were married.

"Bundy can be as troublesome as an old woman at times," Simon answered when he recovered himself, taking his seat again. The little sergeant-major had become very fond of his Miss Mara during Simon's illness, so it was to be expected the man would confide his worries to her. This compromising was going to take some getting used to.

"Who could possibly want to do you harm? Is there someone in your past who wants to settle an old debt?" Damara warmed to the subject, heartened that at last they were going to have a rational conversation on the matter. Men were not really as complex as she had once thought; it merely took a little reasoning with them.

"There's no one. I've never made any enemies, except for the Frogs, of course, but that is war," he returned, giving a shrug to show his bewilderment. "All my relatives are dead. I am the last of my family. We'll discover the culprits given a little more time, I hope," he stated to ease her mind. Nothing else had occurred since his unexpected scuffle returning from White's. Perhaps they had mistaken him for someone else, and perhaps the girth had actually broken.

"But, Simon—"

"Oh, we have company. How nice," Evelyn announced breathlessly from the doorway. Her hair was slightly disarrayed—though no more than was fashionable—and there was a special happiness gleaming in her blue eyes. "How is everyone this fine morning?"

Despite her frustration at the untimely interruption, Damara could hardly keep from laughing when her friend literally floated into the room with a fatuous grin on her face. She could not resist teasing. "I'm feeling fine. However, this morning my feet were a bit sore from those new slippers I wore yesterday. They had a slight tendency to curl my toes. Did you find that was true of the pair you purchased?"

Evelyn gave her a dazzling smile, then began giggling helplessly as she poured herself a cup of tea at the sideboard. "Yes, that's exactly the same feeling I had. How wonderful."

Looking back and forth between the two grinning women, Simon knew that he would never understand women if he lived to be a hundred. They were delighted that their shoes pinched? He was rescued from this puzzlement by the appearance of Hastings, announcing the earl was ready to see him.

Almost relieved to make his escape before the women could confound him further, Simon jumped to his feet. Before taking his leave, he had one more question to pose in light of his recent promise. He took Damara's slim hand in his and raised it to his lips. "I'll be visiting the Exchange this afternoon to purchase an engagement ring at a jeweler Bram recommended. I can't offer you any family jewels, since my uncle and cousin sold everything of value. Do you have a preference?"

Damara's smile evaporated at the mention of an engagement ring. Staring up into Simon's intense brown gaze, she was unable to speak and simply shook her head.

"In that case I'll select an emerald as planned, to match your lovely eyes," he murmured, kissing her hand once more, then turned on his heels and left without another word.

"And good-bye to you, Emsley. So nice we had this chat," Evelyn remarked with a chuckle. "I'm not sure the man knew I was in the room, or cared for that matter."

Her friend's teasing brought Damara out of her daze. With a shake of her head she threw off Simon's spell, chastising herself for being so foolish. She really had to find a means of staying rational whenever he kissed her. Ruthlessly dismissing her fiancé's disturbing image, she turned a calculating eye on Evelyn. "Never mind about me. What exactly have you and my brother been doing in the library for the past half hour while Simon was cooling his heels in here?"

Evelyn's fair skin turned a brilliant shade of red from the moderate decolletage of her blue jacconet gown to her hairline. Demurely she lowered her lashes but could not keep a chuckle from escaping her reddened lips. Batting her lashes, she exclaimed, "Ohhh, Mara."

Jasper attempted to bring some order to his tousled hair by combing his fingers through it, wishing he had time to run above stairs for the ministrations of Sir Cedric's man and make repairs to his crushed cravat. He also had to concentrate on wiping a silly grin from his face before Emsley came through the door. Much as he enjoyed—and fully intended to continue—making up with Evelyn, he had to remember the size of the marquess-major, twice his own lean frame. He was surprised the man had not flattened him on sight the day before.

From what Evelyn said, however, the man seemed to be taking advantage of the situation. That erased the smile from Jasper's face. He was ashamed to admit that he had forgotten about the engagement notice within a week of penning the letter. The sight of the tall man standing in the entry hall yesterday had immediately brought back the night in the barn with great clarity. This scheme was probably his most cork-brained notion, and when his sister discovered his part, there would be hell to pay. He hoped Emsley could see his way clear by keeping the instigator of the announcement a mystery.

"The Marquess of Emsley," Hastings announced like the voice of doom heralding an execution, the name seeming to bounce off the book-lined walls.

"Ah, Emsley, so good of you to come," Jasper managed with creditable calm as he walked from behind the walnut desk to greet the oversized marquess. The ominous look on his caller's face dashed all hope of a compromise.

"I thought it best to see if my debt was now paid in full," Simon replied once he took a seat in the green leather armchair that Jasper indicated near the fireplace. It was an effort to keep his foreboding expression in place. From the looks of Jasper—who was as disheveled as Evelyn a few minutes before—the conversation of the two women was beginning to make sense, though he still could not comprehend the reference to curled toes. Then Simon returned to his purpose. Propping his elbows on the arms of the chair, he steepled his fingers and crossed one ankle over his thigh, then waited.

Jasper paced nervously back and forth in the limited space in front of the fireplace, not knowing where to begin. Taking surreptitious looks at the gentleman seated before him, he almost groaned in despair. He knew that look, for he had seen it countless times on his father's implacable face for most of his life. Emsley was not going to make this easier.

"I suppose I should start by apologizing for determining the payment without your knowledge," he finally managed, turning to face Emsley with his hands clasped behind his back, more to keep them steady than any other reason.

"On the contrary, I should thank you for such a delightful solution. When I returned to England, there were so many estate matters to see to, I don't think I would have time to look around for a suitable wife for many months." Simon answered, making sure to keep his voice neutral. He was not ready to let his future brother-in-law know he actually wanted to jump up and shake his hand, slapping him on the back for such a perfect match. "I need a wife who is used to living quietly in the country, and your sister comes from excellent stock, so she should be a good breeder. We'll have the seven children in no time."

Jasper felt as if he had been landed a facer. The man was

talking about Damara as if she were prime livestock being
sold to the highest bidder at Tattersall's. He wondered if the
fool had checked her teeth as well. His sister was a proud,
intelligent woman with a lively sense of humor. What had
he done?

"Look, Emsley, there's no reason for you to continue this
farce. It was merely an idle bet that we can both forget. I've
long since lost the note." Jasper looked anxiously at his
companion for some sign of agreement and was disturbed to
see the man frowning. "You can simply cry off—as I am
sure the pair of you have already decided—and Mara will
never know the difference."

"But there's no need to call off the engagement. In fact,
we can't. I'm procuring a special license to allow us to
marry within the week because "—Simon paused purposely
to keep Jasper guessing or perhaps to come up with a reason
of his own—"you see—How can I put this delicately. I was
sick and your sister nursed me. The maid came in one
morning before she left my bed, so we need to—"

"Out with it, man! What does this have to do with a
special license?" Jasper broke in impatiently, his feverish
brain not comprehending a word the man was saying.

"You see, I was delirious half the time, and Damara was
half asleep." Simon continued with his nattering explanation, enjoying the deep scarlet color that was flooding
Jasper's face. "Dash it—to be blunt, your sister could be
expecting."

"Expecting what?" Jasper asked, though he knew the
answer, but wanted to prolong discovering the truth. This
could not be happening. This cold fish was going to marry
his sister, keeping her in the country—maybe under lock
and key—and constantly with child, all because he had a
drunken inspiration after a card game. It was not supposed
to be this way. Damara was supposed to be happy, no longer
at her family's beck and call, not a slave to this ogre.

"My child."

The words hung in the air, the two men staring at each
other in a battle of wills to see who would drop his gaze
first. Finally Jasper could not stand the oppressive silence a
minute more. He flung himself into the chair directly
opposite Emsley. Covering his face with his hands, he

groaned out his frustration, wanting to run the man through, but then what would happen if his dear sister was increasing?

"I do love her very much, and I believe she is growing fond of me as well."

Emsley's quiet, emotional words broke through Jasper's misery. Jerking his head up, he met the warm brown eyes of his companion. What he saw there was a reversal of the grim, harsh-faced expression of minutes earlier. This was the man he remembered from their meeting in that rainy barn; this was the stalwart major who was spoken of highly by everyone. Jasper could not find words, his mouth gaping open.

Simon did not bother to suppress his amusement. The scamp had been more than paid back for his harebrained scheme that could have been a disaster for his sister. Jasper had no way of knowing that Simon was any better than his repulsive cousin Chauncey when he sent the announcement. Simon still did not plan to tell him Damara was not in the family way. He would confess that to her at the appropriate time, but Jasper could continue to suffer.

"You were bamming me this whole time," the other man said in wonder, then burst into relieved laughter. He slapped his knee in enjoyment of the joke. "Emsley, you're a complete hand. No one has ever bested me, and so convincingly. You had me going there, believing you were going to lock Mara away and that she is—"

"Oh, that part is true. When I was recovering from the malaria, we weren't able to resist . . ." Simon allowed his words to die away, hoping the man would not learn how recent Damara's nursing duties were just yet, hopefully not until after the wedding. Jasper might become suspicious. "You and Evelyn are in love, so surely you understand."

"Yes, yes," Jasper muttered absently in a daze. He was an experienced man, but this was his sister they were discussing. "You *do* love her?"

"With all my heart, and in honor of your contribution to our romance, if it's a boy we'll call him Jasper." Simon got to his feet with a complacent smile. He walked past his stunned friend, slapping him companionably on the back. Softly whistling to himself, he left to pursue his duties for the day, which included purchasing an emerald to match his love's eyes.

Damara twisted her dove-colored gloves in her lap as she waited for Regina a few hours later. She was tempted to run from the room before her hostess even arrived. What had seemed to be an excellent notion in consulting Emsley's godmother now was completely impossible.

She was ready to get to her feet at the precise moment Regina swept into the room wearing a smoke-colored morning gown with a scalloped hem. The older woman gave her friend a welcoming smile, then arranged herself elegantly on the blue-and-cream striped settee. "Now what is this nonsense about Simon procuring a special license? I'm bound it has something to do with this rather clandestine meeting we are having. Otherwise why would you ask to be put in my private parlor where we won't be interrupted?"

"I don't know where to begin,"Damara admitted, swallowing nervously while trying to gather her scattered thoughts. Then she looked into her friend's concerned eyes and began to relax a little. Without hesitation she launched into her prepared speech. "Simon has implied that we did something . . . that is, *something* happened the last night he was ill. Since this, ah, occurred we need to be married as soon as possible, hence the special license."

"My dear, are you making sense? Could you be a tad more specific about this something?" Regina's usually smooth brow was furrowed as she tried to make heads or tails of the matter.

"You see, *Maman* died before she could tell me what actually happens between a man and a woman when they . . . well, when they are in bed together." Damara continued to mangle her gloves, refusing to look the other woman in the eye. She chewed on her lower lip, trying to decide what to say next. Finally she threw all caution asisde and blurted out, "Please, Gina, how is a baby conceived?"

"Good heavens. You and Simon . . . You think that . . . Oh, my," was all she finally managed. She had not been prepared for the amazing question. This was something she had never had to deal with, being the mother of a boy who went to his father for advice of this nature. What did one do?

"That is what Simon says."

"Wait, Simon has said you're . . . that you—Oh, this is ridiculous," the older woman exclaimed impatiently at her own uncooperative tongue. "Damara, tell me as quickly and concisely as possible what happened, and what Simon told you."

"You see that is my problem. I don't remember what happened," she answered, sighing in resignation before rapidly telling Regina the events that led to this awkward interview. She was not prepared for the other woman's response.

Regina could not believe what she was hearing. Any minute she would wake up in her own chambers and think about what an extraordinary dream she had had. The more she listened, the more she realized this was not a dream, but a comedy of manners being played out before her very eyes. Until now she would have never guessed Simon had it in him. He must be desperate to tie Damara to him, but why so suddenly?

Unfortunately she could not keep from bursting into laughter. Once she started, there was no controlling her mirth. When she caught sight of Damara's startled look, she laughed even harder. Her side was beginning to hurt and tears were streaming down her face when she managed to bring herself under marginal control.

"Oh, dear, I'm so sorry, but I couldn't help myself," she murmured as she dabbed her eyes with her handkerchief. "For some unknown reason, my godson has invented this flummery. He's playing on your innocence to hurry the date of your wedding."

"You mean that if what he said happened, then I would have remembered?" Damara was still dazed by her hostess's reaction to her dilemma. Laughter was the last reaction she had expected during this interview.

"I'm more than sure you would. Contrary to the old wives' tales, a woman can enjoy lovemaking," Regina answered her with a dreamy smile, then shook her head to return to the matter at hand. "The mystery here is why Simon suddenly felt the need for haste. There's something we don't know that is causing him to insure you'll marry him."

"But why? I'm more confused than ever." Damara propped her chin in her palm, giving her companion an imploring look. Just a few hours before Simon had promised to consult her on all their decisions. "He couldn't possibly be fabricating this tale. He has promised me—"

"Ah, there's always danger when a man promises something. Men only swear to something if they think it's to their advantage," Regina interrupted, a slight smile curving her lips. "When a man promises, you should be the most suspicious. What did he promise?

"He promised that he would always seek my opinion on every aspect of our lives during our marriage. There, you see, he couldn't—" She broke off as Regina's polite smile turned to smug satisfaction and the import of her own words became clear. He made his promise for *after* the wedding. It was possible that he was lying to her now. Could it be that he had been the one to put the notice in the newspapers after all? She had begun to trust him, and now this. Damara was at a loss and gave Regina a pleading look.

"I think the boy is getting rather desperate. Your brother was coming home, and you weren't being exactly cooperative," his godmother chided, but with a gentle smile. "With Jasper home as the official head of your family, you could have cried off immediately and gone home without ever seeing him again."

"Are you saying that he truly wants to marry me?" Damara felt her heart begin to pound at a rapid pace. Anxiously she waited for the reply, unsure why she wanted to know the answer so urgently.

"I would like to take the pair of you and knock your heads together to make you both see some sense," Regina stated and made a clicking noise with her tongue. "You're both besotted with each other and have too much pride to admit it. If he had any sense—which men seldom do when they are in love—he wouldn't be weaving fairy tales. Instead he would take you in his arms and tell you he loves you."

"Oh, Gina, are you absolutely sure?" Damara asked breathlessly, knowing she sounded like one of the heroines from Justine's novels. She was just as idiotic as one of those die-away girls. For all her talk of maturity and knowing her own mind, she had not realized that she had fallen hopelessly in love with the aggravating man.

He made her laugh and made her angry. She could not wait to be with him again, just moments after he walked out of the room. Since they had met, she kept denying that she liked his attentions, when deep inside she longed for him to overcome her resistance and take her in his arms once more. Simon made her feel more alive than she had felt in her entire life.

The thought of returning to her peaceful life at Tarrant's Mount had become more depressing with each day she knew Simon, and, fool that she was, she thought it was the excitement of town life. The realization stunned her. She was in love with her overbearing, obnoxious, and sometimes rag-mannered fiancé, who was also endearing, gentle, and very confusing.

"I'm as sure about Simon's love for you as I am that you love the rascal to distraction. Otherwise you would be furious at what he had done, not that I didn't suspect before this," the older woman stated firmly, breaking into Damara's chaotic thoughts. For a minute she had to think about what her question had been.

"Gina, what shall we do about this tangle of Simon's? How long can he keep up this fiction that I might be *enceinte*?"

"I feel sure he planned to confess once you were married. After all, by then you would have known how a child is conceived—realizing, of course, you wouldn't have forgotten—and you also would not be increasing in size," Regina answered with a knowing laugh. "Even Simon can't think you'll remain innocent forever."

"First, I would like you to tell me what I need to know about . . . what I should know. Since I've done *it* in my sleep before, I don't want to spoil my wedding night," Damara said, giggling as her companion flushed to a becoming rose color. "Then we'll discuss how to bring him around before the ceremony."

"Oh, dear, why did your mother have to depart this world without telling you? You wouldn't consider asking Kath?

No, of course not." Regina thought of her sweet but sometimes addlepated friend trying to explain this delicate matter, and it stiffened her resolve. She was the only person Damara had to turn to. Taking a deep breath, she began.

Damara did not say a word during the entire disclosure. It was all she could do to keep from staring in open-mouthed amazement. No wonder Regina was convinced that she would have remembered what had occurred. What Regina was telling her would certainly do more than just curl her toes.

"Bram, old man, you never cease to confound me," Simon admitted as the two gentlemen left the smoky interior of the Boar's Head Inn to be jostled among the crowds on the Cheapside streets. "I mistakenly thought when I became a peer that I would be rubbing elbows with a better class of people."

"Just a few weeks a marquess and already you're a snob," his friend chided and elbowed his way through the throng, calling back over his shoulder. "This way we had a refreshing pint and shall be assured our horses haven't been stolen after we make your purchase. The boy we paid so handsomely will keep a sharp eye out for felons in hopes of an added reward."

"I admit a fondness for the West End after my last expedition here to the Guildhall with young Percy," Simon yelled back above the din of the humanity around them. "Army life is beginning to become a golden memory. We were crowded at times, but never like this."

Tearle shouldered his way onto the street so that they were finally walking abreast. "I don't see why you're worrying. As I said before, you're going to be murdered by your bride the moment you confess."

"Ah, that's a distinct possibility. I'm hoping, however, that Damara will be so angry at her brother's manipulations that my little act of deception shall be overlooked," he confided with a grin of masculine satisfaction. Then he narrowed his eyes as he spotted a figure slumped in the seat of a wagon that was making its way down the far end of the street at a rapid rate. There was something familiar about the man, even at this distance.

"I'm already preparing your eulogy and shall be more than willing to comfort the grieving widow," Tearle returned cheerfully, giving his friend a slap on the back.

"Just consider yourself fortunate I was taken ill when you first met Damara. You wouldn't have survived the evening. If you value your freedom, you had best keep your attentions on little Justine," Simon advised, turning to glare at his lifelong friend, who always enjoyed getting a rise out of him.

"Little Justine could prove to be dangerous. That young lady has marriage on her mind, and I don't—My God! Look out, Simon, that fool has lost control and is heading straight for us."

Simon looked in the direction of Tearle's horrified gaze. The wagon he had seen moments before was indeed being driven straight at them. The man slapping the reins against the angry horses' backs was none other than his old friend Jem. Though his hat was pulled low over his face, the wide brim had been pushed back by the wind.

That was Simon's last thought as he was jerked to the side abruptly. Tearle pulled him out of his distraction over recognizing the driver. Voices rang out, shouting at the reckless driver as the two men slammed against the wall of a tenement house.

The incident was over as quickly as it had started. The wagon careened down the street to be swallowed by the protesting crowd. The two men brushed themselves down, removing the dust thrown up by the rush of the wagon wheels.

"I take back everything I said. I may never leave the West End again—no, make that the sea," Tearle exclaimed, and wiped the dirt from his face. "We don't have grit at sea."

"That was no accident."

"What?"

"The driver was one of my assailants in that little impromptu boxing match in St. James," Simon explained, his face closed and his eyes mere slits as he gazed down the street. "I had hoped it was a case of mistaken identity until now."

"I would say once we complete your errand, we should pay a call on your hired runner," Tearle observed as they continued toward the Royal Exchange and the jeweler's shop. "Someone besides your lovely intended is out for your hide. Layston, perhaps?"

"No, he wants me to marry his sister, now more than ever," Simon stated emphatically. A likely person came to mind, but he quickly dismissed the thought since the man was dead.

"Ah, you haven't told him that he'll have to wait a while to be an uncle, then?"

"Why should he know before his sister? Then she would have a real motive to take a knife to me," he replied with an absent smile as he recalled Damara when she was in temper. "What worries me is she has too much in common with your mother. So I think I need to purchase a rather special token for our engagement."

Tearle gave him a compassionate smile after years of living with Lady Covering. "Have you *really* given this marriage some serious thought?"

— Chapter Eleven —

"Do you think the celebration should be just family, or perhaps a small rout with card playing and dancing? It is Jasper's first birthday back at home," Lady Kath said at lunch the next day. The men were all out for the day, so she grabbed the opportunity to plan the party without Sir Cedric's usual grumblings.

"Mama, we could keep it very select and simply invite a few friends. I'm sure Mara would want Simon to be there, as well as Lady Covering," Justine put in eagerly as she always did when it came to anything festive.

"And naturally we just couldn't have Emsley or Lady Covering without inviting Baron Tearle, now could we?" Evelyn drawled with a sweet smile that immediately had her sister blushing. "The poor man—all six feet plus of him—gets so *vewwy, vewwy* lonely at sea."

"Please," Damara groaned from her place beside Evelyn, "one afternoon with Letitia putting me off my food was more than sufficient."

"Well, I think you are both horrible," Justine stated, an attractive pout on her young face.

"Mara, I can't believe how accomplished Justine has become in such a short time." She leaned toward her friend, holding her hand at the side of her mouth, but not bothering to lower her voice.

"Evieeeee," Justine exclaimed, then regressed to her salad days by sticking out her tongue.

"Girls, girls, this isn't achieving anything toward Jasper's party," Lady Kath said with a sigh that was reserved for those truly familiar with martyrdom. "The only added distraction would be Lady Mathilde here disapproving of everything in sight."

"That is strange, since she usually doesn't miss a meal,"

177

Evelyn stated, frowning over the matter. "Mara, have you seen the old—her today?"

"No, I think Meg said something about Aunt doing some shopping this morning. I really didn't pay much attention since she goes out on her own so often," Damara returned readily. It was not Lady Mathilde that she wanted to see. Simon, however, was proving to be as elusive as the old woman. He had not called last evening as she expected after his announcement that he would be purchasing her engagement ring. Though Percy had arrived for dinner with the family, the marquess did not put in an appearance.

Perhaps Regina had let slip about her visit yesterday, and both women were wrong. Simon was not in love with her. If she could, Damara would march over to the Albany and demand to see him, but there were some things a lady did not do, especially when preserving her pride and dignity.

The rap of the door knocker made her catch her breath, but the sound of Lady Covering's voice dashed her hopes.

"Hello, everyone," Regina called as she practically danced into the room after dismissing Hastings. "Isn't this a lovely day? I have such news."

She stripped off her gloves and took an empty chair next to Justine. "I have just come from Emsley House, and the carpenters have finished the repairs. Mara, dear, we'll be able to go shopping for new drapes and furnishings once you see the house. Then we only lack a butler, for I have taken care of all the other servants."

"Now all we need to do is find Simon," his fiancée said dryly. She was beginning to lose all patience with the man. If he was supposed to be in love with her, where was he?

"What is this? You haven't seen him? How strange," Lady Regina murmured, then waited while the footman served her tea. "He was closeted with Bram in the study last night until quite late."

"Gina, we have just been trying to decide what sort of celebration to have for Jasper's birthday. He'll be five and twenty on Sunday," Lady Kath interpolated, a hint of steel in her voice, determined to stick to her purpose.

"Then, dearest Kath, it will have to be something small for just the family. There really isn't time for anything more ambitious, is there?" Brushing aside her friend's concern with a wave of her hand, she addressed Damara's more interesting problem. "He hasn't called?"

"Not since yesterday morning," Damara returned, then broke off as Hastings entered the room carrying a note on a silver tray. He looked terribly disapproving, which made her wonder what could possibly have set him off with the only family members at home gathered around the table.

"A person of dubious origins delivered this to the kitchen door, milady. The urchin insisted it be given to you or His Lordship at once," the man intoned, giving a sniff that conveyed it was her fault the miscreant appeared at all.

Damara took the soiled paper, simply nodding to dismiss the disgruntled butler. With a curious frown, she opened the paper that did not have a seal, then gasped as she read the printed letters aloud.

"If ya Want ta see the boy Percy agan. Cum ta the Spread Eagle in Gracechurch Street by Six o'clock. Only Marquess Emsley and Lady Damara twill get futther Instructions. Brang no one else or ya'll Never see the boy Agan."

"Why would someone want to take Percy? Only you and Simon are to go to this place?" Of the stunned women around the table, Regina was the first to speak.

Damara threw down her napkin and jumped to her feet, calling for Hastings. She almost ran into his plump figure at the doorway. "Hastings, I'll need two footmen at once to take messages to the Albany and to White's. Have them come to the drawing room in a few minutes, ready to leave."

She did not bother to see if he followed her instructions. Still clutching the note, she ran across the hall for her writing materials in the secretary. With more haste than coherence, she penned notes to Sir Cedric and Simon, for she had no idea where to locate her brother. Sir Cedric always left word at his club, and Bundy would know where his master was.

There was nothing to do but wait. The others joined her in the drawing room. Regina sent a note of her own to Hanover Square on the chance Bram and Simon would stop at home. She sat on the settee next to Damara, trying to offer comfort along with Evelyn seated on Damara's other

side. No one spoke. The only sound was the ticking of
the clock on the mantel. Occasionally Hastings would
wander into the room, hover for a few moments, then leave
again.

What seemed like an eternity passed, but was only a half
hour when Damara glanced at the clock, as the door
knocker finally sounded. She was on her feet in a second,
then was brought up short by the familiar woofle of Cretin
just before he bounded into the room. He loped over to
Damara, who went down on her knees to gather him into
her arms. Tears sprang to her eyes, though she did not have
time to shed them, for Bundy was standing in the doorway,
his eyes downcast as his shoulders slumped in defeat.

"Bundy?" She rose to her feet, holding her hands out to
the little man.

"Ow, Miss Mara, I be so shamed. The boy, he say he
gots a errand ta run. So I lets him go and doan think nothin'
bout it," he muttered, not meeting her eyes as his hand
remained limp in hers.

"Bundy, it's all right. We'll get Percy back, never you
mind. You sit here with us while we wait for Simon to
arrive."

"Aye, I sent him a message at Bow Street where he and
Mr. Bram be," Bundy said, then he realized what she was
asking. "Ow, Miss Mara, I best go down ta the kitchen."

"No, you'll wait right here and watch over Cretin.
Hastings will bring us some refreshments, since we can't
continue to sit here with long faces."

The tea cart arrived at the same time Jasper came bursting
into the room with Simon and Tearle at his heels. Behind
them was a tough-looking individual whom no one recognized. "What's this about Percy? I met Simon and Bram on
the steps, but they didn't have time to explain."

Damara handed him the note and started to dispense tea.
Her hands were shaking so badly that Regina had to take
over the task. Everyone's eyes were trained on the four men
as they passed around the note. As soon as he read the note,
Simon looked to Damara. He did not say a word but
extended his hand, his face eloquent in his understanding.
Without even considering her actions she was on her feet,
running into his outstretched arms.

"It will be all right, love. We'll get Percy back," he murmured into her curls, echoing her earlier words of comfort. Stroking her back for a moment, he hoped to ease her distress in some small way. Then he placed his hands on her shoulders and, holding her at arm's length, demanded, "Tell me everything that has taken place."

With an unnatural calm, she told him what little she knew about Percy's kidnapping.

"What do you think, Mr. Peal?" Simon asked the man who was standing near Bundy, scratching Cretin behind the ears.

" 'Pears yor man 'as cum inta the op'n, gov'ner," the rotund man replied with a nod.

"So it would seem. Gentlemen, we need to plot our strategy before Mara and I step into the lion's den," Simon instructed giving Damara's shoulder a squeeze. "My love, you go up and change into that fetching habit of yours. You'll need to be warm for our adventure. We'll have a council of war while you change."

She started to protest, but he forestalled her by placing a finger over her lips. Giving her a tender smile, he raised her hand to his mouth and murmured, "I promise to fill you in on every detail when you return."

Simon turned to the others once she left the room. "All right, we need to deploy ourselves so our friend doesn't know there is anyone on the trail. Only Damara, Cretin, and myself can be visible. We don't know how many we are up against, though I doubt it is more than one. He is attempting to be clever by spacing out the instructions, but that should be his downfall."

"We'll divide and surprise him on his flank then," Jasper commented thoughtfully. "I do wish he had taken the dog. It might make him want to regret this whole caper."

"Well I know it," Simon agreed. Like Jasper he was feeling the excitement of battle. After a fruitless evening and morning with Peal, trying to go over his "accidents," the chance to do something at last was a balm to his spirit. "My guess is he has the boy outside the city. We'll set a watch post at the ruin of the watch tower near the Charter-house on Barbican. We're sure to travel north or west. If we're watched, the route won't be suspicious. We'll pass it on our way out of the city proper."

"How will you get us word of your direction?" Tearle put in, accepting a glass of wine from his mother and going to lean against the mantel.

"I'll take a pouch and place the new instructions there. It will be a simple matter to toss it out the carriage window, even if we are accompanied, which I doubt," Simon explained, pacing as he thought out the plan. "You should work in pairs—two at the watch tower, and two following us on horseback."

"You'll need arms. I think Papa's old pistols are in the library," Jasper stated, turning to retrieve them.

"Major, er, m'lord, I tooks the liberty o' fetchin' yer ol' pistols when I cum with Cretin," Bundy stated, speaking for the first time since the arrival of the other men.

"Good. Bundy old man, you're a treasure," Simon answered with a grin, walking over to take the two service pistols the man pulled from under his coat. "You stay with Mr. Bram at the watch tower, then ride for more runners. Mr. Peal and Layston will follow the carriage. Aunt Gina, do you still have that ancient vehicle with no marking on the side panels?"

"Yes, and it isn't that ancient. Bram, go back to house and tell John the coachman to ready your grandmother's old coach."

When Damara returned, she found the drawing room had been transformed into the headquarters of a general planning a battle. The men were clustered together by the fireplace, gesturing and commenting on various plans. Regina and Evelyn watched in fascination, sipping their tea while Lady Kath and Justine sat apart still separating silks for the embroidered seat cushions.

It was another hour before they were ready to depart. By that time Damara had worked herself into a nervous state. The men seemed to be treating the venture as a lark. When she looked into Simon's eyes just before leaving the house, however, she saw his concern. He settled her into the coach, giving last minute instructions to Tearle and her brother as he climbed in himself.

Without a word he settled beside her and drew her into his

arms. They rode the distance to the Spread Eagle drawing comfort and warmth from each other. Too soon, they arrived at their destination.

"Please stay here, love. If anything untoward happens, Hastings has instructions to spring the horses. Peal and Jasper will come to my aid," he said firmly before giving her a quick kiss. "I want to know you're safe with only Percy and my unknown enemy to worry about. I feel like he has taken my own little brother. Please?"

"Yes, Simon. Though are you sure Hastings knows what he is about?" Damara asked, trying to keep him with her for a few precious minutes, tracing the side of his face with her hand in the dim gray light of the coach's interior.

She felt him smile against her hand at her subterfuge, warmed by her concern, then he turned his head to place a tender kiss in her gloved palm. "I was as surprised as everyone else when he demanded to come along. He apparently started service as a coachman, and he could probably scare off any opposition with nothing more than his forbidding stare."

Then he was gone. She stuffed her hands into her sealskin muff, gripping her fingers tightly together. She began reciting nursery rhymes to keep from thinking about what Simon was doing and what could possibly have happened to Percy in the time he had been gone. They had arrived at the inn within a half hour of the dictated time. Cretin whined from where he was tied to the other banquette of the coach. She spoke to him soothingly and waited.

Simon was back long before she expected him. She could see his smile before he closed the coach door and blocked out the dim light of the gathering dusk. Abruptly he took her in his arms and gave her a smacking kiss.

"We're set, my sweet. We're off to Kilburn and the ruins of the Abbey Farm," he exclaimed as the coach lurched forward. "The innkeeper says a slight man wearing a loo mask gave him the instructions. He didn't mind giving me the information, since the fellow was nasty and barely paid him for the service."

Since Simon was assured they were not being followed by anyone but their own allies, the coach stopped at the watch tower. He jumped out to talk with Tearle and Bundy, allowing Peal and Jasper to overtake them. Once the revised plan was settled, Simon gave Hastings the directions to travel northwest on the Hampton road.

"Now, my love, we'll discuss domestic matters to wile away the miles until Percy's rescue," Simon stated, taking his place beside Damara. He moved to take her in his arms again, only to be brought up short by a hard object pressing into his hip. "What is this?"

Before she could explain, he reached down and extracted her pistol from the pocket of her habit. "Papa gave me that on my sixteenth birthday for protection when riding around Tarrant's Mount," she said softly, not sure how he could react to her initiative.

"Do you know how to use it?" His voice was tinged with amusement and surprise.

"Yes, quite well. Jasper taught me to shoot the center from an ace at fifty paces." She could not keep the smugness from her voice, daring him to say more.

He did not. Instead he held out the firearm, butt first for her to take back. "Would you put it in your muff? It will be easier to get from there, if needed. That way you won't be hampered by your skirts. Now, back to our other business."

While she placed the pistol inside her muff, Damara felt him move restlessly beside her. The darkness of the closed coach gave the evening a sense of unreality. She could feel the warmth of Simon's body next to her, enfolding her into his embrace once more. The remaining daylight filtered through the drawn curtains so she could only see the barest outline of his profile. An added touch was an occasional whine from Cretin in his corner where he was being ignored.

"Give me your hand, love," Simon murmured into her ear, his breath disturbing the curls at her temple.

She obeyed without thinking of doing otherwise. He removed her glove, and a cool circlet was slipped onto her third finger. She barely realized he had placed a ring on her finger before he lowered his head to kiss it in place.

"Though you can't see it, that is an emerald which was the closest I could come to matching your eyes when you're in a temper, or just after I kiss you, which I am about to do."

His hand came up to catch her chin between his thumb and forefinger, tilting her face up to his. Warm lips settled on her own, coaxing them apart as his arms pulled her tightly against him. Her slender fingers gripped the material of his cloak hoping in some way that would keep the world from tilting off its axis.

"Oh, my love, it's a good thing I have applied for a special license. I find I'm very impatient for you to be mine," Simon said hoarsely against her lips. Then he tucked her head into the cradle of his shoulder. "Much as I would like to continue, that is our last kiss until we have Percy safe and sound. If I allowed myself to be lost in your soft arms, I would forget everything else."

She nestled contentedly against him, tempted to tell him what she had learned from his godmother. She knew, however, it was not the right time. She wanted all of Simon's attention when she declared her love. Confident that Simon would rescue Percy, she closed her eyes. Soon she drifted into a light sleep as they covered the miles to face Simon's enemy.

"Love, wake up. We are here," Simon called gently as he moved Damara to sit upright.

She blinked to clear the sleep from her eyes, then realized she could not see because of the darkness. Simon opened the door and jumped down as she stretched, but the tension did not leave her body. The confidence she felt earlier was quickly replaced by apprehension as Simon helped her down. She looked around the overgrown vegetation of the yard as Simon untied Cretin's leash and led the dog from the coach.

"I'm going to remove his muzzle and have you take his lead," he explained close to her ear. Though no one seemed to be about, he kept his voice low. "Hastings will wait for the others at the start of the lane. You'll stay close to me and behind me."

Slowly they made their way up the remains of the stone path to the house. The upper portion of the house had been mortar and timber under a thatched roof at one time. Only a corner of the upper story remained, the rest sagging drunkenly over the lower half that was built of stone. The

paneled door at the entrance was open with a dim light
glowing in the hallway beyond.

Simon entered the house first, signaling Damara to step
carefully behind him. Though a single candle burned on the
broken-down stairway, no one was in sight. There was no
furniture, and the cobwebs and layers of dust told them the
farm house had not been inhabited for years.

"Come into the room to your right," a ghostly voice
instructed, echoing throughout the house. The disembodied
voice was followed by a laugh that could only come from a
madman.

Cretin whimpered in response, pulling on his leash to go
back out the door. Damara held fast so she would stay
within reach of Simon as he followed the directions of the
voice. She grabbed for the back of his cloak and held tight.

The room they entered apparently had been the dining
area at one time. A long, planked table dominated the room,
though it tilted toward them with two of its thick legs now
laying on the floor. To their right was a massive stone
fireplace with some of its appointments still in place.
There was a small fire burning that threw shadows of
grotesque forms on the decaying walls.

"Welcome to my humble abode," announced the same
voice that called to them from the entrance. It did not sound
as ominous at close range.

Damara peered into the gloom, having to bend slightly to
the side to see around Simon. She could make out the slight
figure of a man seated at the end of the table that remained
upright. His face was still obscured by the shadows. Simon
continued walking forward with sure steps, clearly not
intimidated by the man. When they took a few more steps,
she gasped in surprise as the firelight reflected off the man's
face.

"Well, cousin, how nice of you to drop by to introduce
your fiancée," Chauncey Fentner-Smythe said with a sneer
on his narrow face. He was holding a pistol level with the
table, but Damara could see that it was cocked and aimed at
Simon's heart.

"I always said you were in league with the devil, cousin.
However, I never knew you were accomplished enough to
rise from the dead," Simon stated without a tremor of

emotion. He stopped walking, making sure Damara was behind him and there was nothing between them and the solid protection of the fireplace.

"Yes, you were always the one with talent in the family. Of course, you came from the side of the family with money," Chauncey returned, managing to sound petulant rather than menacing. He rose to his feet a little unsteadily but kept the pistol pointed at Simon "'Tis easy to have talent when you have money."

"Ah, which brings us to the point of this exercise. Is it ransom that you have in mind or something more ambitious?" Simon made his question sound casual, though he was sure he knew the scheme, now that he identified the author of his "accidents." Chauncey was not planning to leave any witnesses to his resurrection. No one must know Chauncey was alive and ready to inherit, or re-inherit, his title until Simon was disposed of.

"Oh, something much more ambitious, cousin. Since we're the last of the line, we should go out in style," the slender man continued, and walked toward them. "I *am* remiss, though. I haven't complimented you on your choice of a bride. Damara, dear, how charming for you to be part of our little family. You should never have slapped me that time when Jasper was sent down, you know. It doesn't bode well to be on the outs with your intended's family."

Simon had always thought his cousin resembled a weasel, and now his features were uncannily like the small mammal. The fire's glow highlighted the younger man's long pointed nose and beady dark eyes as he moved closer to the pair. Simon noted his cousin's hand was not quite steady, and he walked with the careful step of a man who had imbibed a good deal of wine. From what he remembered of the wastrel's character, courage was never a strong part of it. Chauncey had been turning to the bottle for the backbone he lacked.

"If you wanted money, you could have asked," Simon stated, turning slightly to keep facing the other man as he moved toward them.

"Ha, that's amazing, cousin. I tried that once with your father and was laughed at for my pains," Chauncey snarled, his thin upper lip curling at the memory. "This way I don't have to beg then return for another loan. It will be mine."

"I don't understand what either of you is talking about,"
Damara put in with the hope of prolonging the conversation
until the others arrived. Where were Jasper and the runner?
She had an inkling of what Chauncey was about, which
meant she and Simon would come to harm.

" 'Tis really very simple, my dear. Simon had money, but
he had no title, being perfectly content as an officer in His
Majesty's army," Chauncey explained in a tone that showed
he thought she had no more brains than the whining dog
cowering in her skirts. "On the other hand, I had a title
which needs money to maintain in a style I would like to be
accustomed to in no time. The problem was, how did I get
the money I needed? Unfortunately most of society didn't
approve of the pleasures that Papa and I enjoyed that also
took our money. I couldn't marry money, though I did try
on numerous occasions, but wasn't permitted to select a
bride of proper lineage for the Emsley line."

"Kidnapping two girls, one directly from the schoolroom, isn't a good means of selection," Damara interrupted, thinking of Evelyn's cousin, now safely married to
the younger son of a duke.

"Very true, so that limited my opportunities, and the
creditors would become restive after Papa kicked up his
heels. Therefore I had to get my hands on the ready without
alienating anyone further, which included the law." He
gave them a negligent shrug as if to say what else could
he do. "Here is my cousin and heir with all that money he
didn't seem to care about, and there I was in great need. I
considered the problem from every angle. It was quite
simple actually. Simon would inherit the title and bring all
that lovely money into the family, just waiting for someone
to inherit. There was no one else, no cousins, no anyone."

"But I made a will, cousin," Simon reminded him,
growing impatient with the man's posturing.

"There was that. However, you only stipulated that the
money should go to the Royal Academy for all those
sniveling boys learning to be soldiers, if you had no heir."
Chauncey's feral smile widened in triumph at his own
brilliance. "I did have a few problems to work out in any
event. Bribing the clerk in your solicitor's office was almost

too easy for the start. I wasn't directly named as your heir but was your only living relation. You also had the uncanny ability not to be blown to small pieces on the battlefield, so what could I do to make sure your death was timely?"

"You were responsible for the girth being cut and hiring the two men who attacked him." Damara was not asking for confirmation, merely stating her thought aloud. She had been following his twisted logic step by step to its horrible conclusion. The man was clearly mad, not just a fool as everyone supposed. Why else would he be carefully explaining his intricate plan—relishing every word—when she was sure he meant to kill both Simon and herself?

"Exactly, my dear. Unhappily, my cohorts in executing this part of the plan were, shall we say, rather incompetent, but that takes me ahead of my story," Chauncey exclaimed, clicking his tongue in a chastening manner as if reprimanding a child. It was apparent he felt superior in intellect to his two hostages. "The creditors were actually dinning me for payment by this time—even before Pater had crossed the river Styx—and I needed Simon close at hand so I was assured of my inheritance. I was able to take care of both matters in one fell swoop. I died in a brawl in the Indies, or so everyone thought."

"No creditors, and I would be in England untangling estate matters," Simon supplied, hoping for just a moment in this diatribe when his cousin would let down his guard. His only worry was Percy's location, and if Chauncey had an accomplice who would harm the boy. He knew, however, that his cousin would tell him about Percy in his own good time. Now he was recounting his strategy like a soldier retelling his exploits in battle.

"Precisely, old boy. I'd really taken the packet to Ireland, and the news of my death was spread when I sent a forged letter to an old friend. Left him my watch, which I thought was a nice touch." Chauncey had stopped a few feet from them, teetering back and forth on his feet, but the pistol remained level. "The only hitch came when you did something unexpected and became engaged. Those bumbling fools botched each job, and you proved stubborn again by refusing to die of the fever. Now I have to dispose of you myself as well as your lovely fiancée who unfortunately, it seems, could be carrying your heir. This has proven to be most troublesome. Though, after tonight, I simply wait a few weeks following this tragedy and return from the dead as originally planned."

"Where is the boy?" Simon demanded, ready to move, but could not with Percy still missing. He felt Damara's hand on his arm exerting pressure at his question. Though he dared not turn his head, he inched forward a step.

"Ah, yes, the reason you're here," Chauncey replied, giving the same mad laugh as he had when they first entered. "Georgette, dear, would you bring out the brat? Our guests are getting a bit restless."

There were scuffling noises from the dark regions beyond the fireplace. A shrill voice could be heard, and suddenly two figures appeared out of the darkness, though they must have come through a door that was hidden in the shadows. One was unmistakably Percy, his hands bound and a gag in his mouth. He did not seem to be harmed except for a tear in his coat. He struggled in the grasp of a taller figure that had him by the scruff of his neck.

When the pair stepped closer to Chauncey, Damara did not recognize the other person at first. She was dressed in the height of fashion, wearing a stone-colored habit trimmed in swansdown. Her hair was hidden by a Prussian helmet, so only a few curls of sandy blond hair were arranged around her thin face. It was not just the elegance of her garb in comparison to the shabby surroundings that caught Damara off guard, but the fact the woman was the last person she expected to see.

"Aunt Mathilde?"

"May I present Georgette Rogers, late of the London stage about thirty-odd years ago," Chauncey said, performing the introduction with great panache by waving his free hand. "She found her talents were more suited to the boudoir—my father's among them—but of late has served as the slave of one Lady Mathilde Lambert."

"But what about my aunt?" Damara stammered, amazed at the hoax that had been played on them. She felt her temper building as she realized an imposter had had the effrontery to burn her clothes. She knew she had to keep her feelings in check until they were all safely away from this place. She noticed that Percy was wiggling his head to loosen his gag, so perhaps he could keep the old woman occupied while Simon dealt with Chauncey. Cretin was certainly no help where he cowered at her feet, and Jasper and Peal seemed to have disappeared into the night.

"The old witch is safe and sound at home, ordering her servants about like she was old Bess reincarnated," Georgette informed them, making a rude noise. "Why do you think I had to take to my bed for days? The one time I was able to rub elbows with the posh, and I couldn't chance running into any of her cronies. Luckily the old bat's acquaintances are mostly dead, or bedridden like herself, and her last trip to town was years go."

"Well, that seems to take care of our old business, so we needs must proceed with the new business at hand. How do we dispose of the fifth marquess so the fourth marquess can become the sixth marquess, or do they regress to my former number?" Chauncey was now grinning from ear to ear, which only emphasized the madness gleaming in his eyes. " 'Tis a bit confusing, but I'm sure the House of Lords will have no trouble straightening out the matter most satisfactorily. Now, cousin, I must ask for those pistols I see peeking out from beneath your cloak."

Later Damara was never sure what happened first. A sense of fatalistic dread had come over her at Mathil—no, Georgette's disclosure. If this woman was in league with Chauncey, what about Hastings? He had been hired by Lady Kath at the beginning of the season. What did they know about the man? He could be another imposter and have waylaid Jasper and Peal on the road until Chauncey accomplished his grim deed. Then the shouting began from both ends of the room at once.

"Mara, who is that man? What does he want?" Percy's shrill voice rang out as he finally loosened his gag and let it fall over his chin. In response, Cretin came to life at Damara's feet, barking furiously. Startled by raised voices behind her, Damara let go of his leash.

" 'Alt in the name of the law," Peal's gravelly voice rang out, followed by Jasper's demand, "Where's Percy? Mara, are you all right?"

Damara started to turn, but was knocked off balance

when Cretin bounded toward the beloved sound of Percy's voice still questioning and complaining. As she was thrown against Simon, she saw her younger brother kick back at the old woman who was trying to restrain him. Then all she saw was the material of Simon's cloak. He kept his balance and enfolded her in his arms, so she would not tumble to the filthy floor.

Muffled in the folds of his cloak, she could hear angry voices, then the loud report of a pistol. Something hit the floor, but she was still blinded by Simon's embrace. Suddenly there was silence. Simon stood absolutely still, holding her tightly against his chest. His heart was beating rapidly, and his arms never loosened their crushing hold on her. She knew he had not been shot, but what of the others?

She struggled to stand upright again without his support. Almost reluctantly he released her, making her fearful of what she would find. She blinked, wondering why the room was brighter, then she saw the lanterns that had been placed on the table. There was a body stretched out on the floor before the fireplace and Peal was bending over it.

"Mara?"

Turning in relief, she found Jasper behind her. Without a word, she flung herself into his arms, hugging him as fiercely as the day he walked in the front door so unexpectedly.

"Well, gov'ner, ya doan 'ave ta worry none 'about this 'ere bloke no longer," the runner announced from where he knelt by the body.

"Is he dead then, Peal?" Simon asked the question in a flat voice. He was standing rigidly at attention, his hands hanging at his sides, staring without blinking at his cousin's lifeless form.

"Yep. Looks like 'e musta 'it 'is 'ead on this piece of iron 'ere at ther edge o' ther fireplace," Peal determined. "Yer 'ound knocked 'im down afore 'e knew wot 'appened."

Sounds of scuffling came from the far end of the room and Tearle came into the light, pushing Georgette in front of him with her arms bent behind her back. "Lord, she's a fiesty one for her age." His sigh of exasperation at almost being bested by an old woman and his grin of accomplishment eased the tension, bringing a weak laugh from everyone, including a bark from Cretin a few feet away where Percy was hugging him.

"It looks like I owe that mangy dog Cretin my life," Simon declared, giving the animal a disgruntled glance. The dog looked up in expectation at his name, his tongue lolling out the side of his mouth.

"Yes, it's very lowering, my love, but we do have to thank the beast for once," Damara murmured with a giggle, wrapping both arms around one of his. She tilted her head up to reward him with a smile. "This may be the only time that stupid dog has ever done anything right."

"But I never even got to draw my pistol," Simon replied, more to himself than the others. They were all giddy with relief at being alive, but he could still remember those horrifying minutes when Damara's life was threatened and he seemed helpless.

"Oh, pistols. What has happened to my muff?" Damara looked around, discovering the object had rolled near the end of the table and was covered in dust.

"Mara, you didn't bring that pop gun of yours?" Jasper asked in disgust before Peal called him away to help look for a conveyance to take Chauncey's body and Georgette back to town.

"Milady, would you care to wait in the coach until everything is settled?" Hastings asked at Damara's elbow. He sounded almost human, though unlike everyone else who had seemed to collect a few smudges, the man's black suit of clothing was immaculate. She felt a twinge of remorse over her earlier thoughts.

"Simon?" She turned to her fiancé where he now stood by Chauncey's body. "Do you think we can leave soon?"

"What? Oh, yes," he replied, coming out of his distraction. "I'll have a few words with Peal, then we can be off."

Calling to Percy and Cretin, she accepted Hastings's escort to the coach. She was still curious about what had taken the others so long to find them. "Hastings, what happened to my brother and Mr. Peal? I expected them much sooner."

"Mr. Peal's horse threw a shoe, and they changed mounts at the nearest inn but were misdirected," he answered with a semblance of a smile. "They took the wrong turn and had to double back."

"I see. Thank you, Hastings. Percy, get Cretin settled down before we put him in the coach, or we'll have to muzzle him again," Damara called to the boy as he threw a stick for his companion.

"Oh, Mara, could we ride up in the box with Hastings, please?"

"Hastings? I'm not sure you know what you're getting into if you agree," she said with a smile, still trying to salve her conscience.

"They can ride up top, milady. This may not be the proper time to ask, but I couldn't help overhearing Lady Covering say you don't have a butler for your new establishment," the man stated in his usual rigidly polite tone.

"Why, no, Hastings. Do you know of someone who is looking for a post who would be suitable?" Damara widened her eyes in disbelief. He could not be asking what she thought. It was too impossible.

"If I might be so bold, I would deem it an honor to serve you and His Lordship." He actually clicked his heels and gave her a slight bow, which consisted of a bob of his head.

Damara looked anxiously over her shoulder to see if Simon was at least in sight. What was she to say? "I'll mention it to the marquess."

"Thank you, milady." Hastings seemed to have a grateful look in his eyes. "Sir Cedric's household wasn't nearly so exciting until you came to visit. It makes for a much more interesting occupation."

With that he assisted an astounded Damara into the coach and called for Percy to bring Cretin to heel. She was still sitting in stunned silence when Simon joined her a few minutes later.

"Damara, are you all right?" Simon asked at the arrested expression on her face the minute he settled beside her.

She turned to stare at him for a moment. Since Hastings had pulled back the curtains, the gray light of dawn made Simon's features discernable, so she nodded. Suddenly she was shy with him, forgetting all the plotting she and Regina had done. "It seems Hastings wants to be our butler. He says we make his life more enjoyable."

Simon had had more than enough surprises for one

evening and was not moved by this piece of news. Nor did
he comment when his fiancée collapsed against him in a fit
of giggles that bordered on hysteria as the coach lurched
forward. He simply sat holding her until her mirth subsided
while he rehearsed what he had to say.

After everything that had taken place, the most important
being the threat to Damara's and Percy's lives, he knew he
had to tell the truth about everything. He would make a
clean breast of it all from the card game to his own
fabrication of their night together. His tricks had placed her
and her loved ones in danger. Like her brother, he had only
thought of his own needs.

Chauncey would never have threatened her or Percy if he
had not learned the servants' gossip from the woman
impersonating Mathilde that Damara had spent the night in
Simon's bed. He owed her the truth, even if he had not
promised to consult her on all matters.

"Simon, what is it? I know I should feel more remorse at
Chauncey's death, but somehow it seems so hypocritical,"
Damara said softly, tilting her face up from where she rested
against his shoulder.

"Damara, you don't have to marry me. Nothing happened the night you fell asleep in my bed," he responded in
an attempt to get over rough ground as quickly as possible.

"Yes, I know. You're not thinking of rejoining the army,
are you? Please say you're not going back." She sat up,
bracing herself against the swaying of the coach over
the rutted road. Grasping the edges of his cloak to keep her
balance, she turned pleading eyes up to his.

"No, I can't do that. You saw what kind of man my
cousin was. The people on the estate need me. You should
have seen the state of their houses—" He broke off as he
recalled exactly what she had said. "What do you mean,
you know?"

Damara smiled up at him, adoring his look of absolute
confusion. She savored the moment, doubting that there
would be many times that she would be able to confound
him. "I couldn't remember what had happened, and even if
I did, I wouldn't know if that is how a child is made. I was
woefully ignorant about what happens between a man and a
woman."

"Were?" Simon was slightly dazed from her admission, and now she was telling him she had had to learn about lovemaking. From whom?

"There was only one person who could help. Gina," Damara almost whispered, lowering her eyelashes, suddenly embarrassed at her admission.

"Good Lord, what did she say?" He was continually amazed at the workings of the female mind, especially this particular female. It would have been worth a fortune to overhear her interview with his godmother.

"She was able to confirm that if it had happened, I would certainly have remembered," Damara stated firmly, beginning to wonder what would shake him out of this strange state he had been in ever since climbing into the coach. "There was, however, one thing that has us puzzled. Why were you so anxious to make sure I married you? Gina says there is some reason that must have forced you to lie."

Simon could only groan. Though she had not been angry that he lied, what would she do when she discovered her brother's manipulations? He took a deep breath, knowing he may as well get it all out in the open. "The person responsible for our engagement is your own brother. Jasper and I were in a card game in Portugal not long before I learned about my inheritance. I confess what I did was foolish, but he was beginning to get on my nerves."

"Yes, he can be wearing," his sister agreed with a sigh, laying her head on his shoulder once again. The explanation looked as though it was going to take time, and she wanted to be comfortable.

"We had been playing all day and drinking a little to relieve the boredom. I bet myself, to end the game quickly," he continued as though she had not spoken. Absently he settled her in the cradle of his arm. "Your brother decided you had been buried in the country too long, so he determined the payment of my bet by sending the notice to the papers.

"I forgot the incident until dinner with Sir Cedric one night. No one ever noticed that the announcement never named which Earl of Layston. I had to make sure that you had no way to back out of the engagement when Jasper returned and the truth came out."

He waited for her response, more nervous than he had ever been in his life. She did not say a word, merely played with the cord that secured his cloak. Absently he watched her slender fingers twisting the cording without any idea of what she was thinking.

"Now I know why he has been avoiding talking to me alone since his return. Well, I suppose if you won't marry me willingly, I can bring suit for breach of our betrothal," she murmured, not looking up from her task.

Simon was stunned. He could not believe he was hearing correctly. Given her freedom, she was threatening to take him to court to force their marriage. He had to be dreaming. Perhaps he had fallen asleep the minute he relaxed in his seat.

"Why?" He managed to croak out the question, sounding like Percy, who never knew when his voice would turn on him.

"Why did you want me to believe I was going have your child?" she challenged in return. Although she was being brash enough to refuse his offer of freedom, a lady liked to be told she was loved before brazenly declaring her own love. She and Regina had determined that loving her could be his only reason for lying.

"I'll tell you, if you tell me something first," he replied with his own small challenge. He knew he had an idiotic grin on his face, and he wanted to cherish the heady expectancy of the moment before they declared their love. "What was that nonsense you and Evelyn were talking about curled toes the other morning?"

Damara laughed out loud in delight at his foolishness and glanced up at him through the veil of her lashes. "It's really rather silly. Evelyn had never been kissed properly by Jasper. She asked me what adult kisses were like, so I told her how you make my toes curl whenever you kiss me. Now, why did you make up that nonsense about a baby?"

"Because I love you, and I didn't want you to disappear from my life when you learned how our engagement came about," he explained simply, then waited for her reply, holding his breath in case he had somehow misread her intentions.

"Oh, Simon, I'm so glad, for I love you so very much,"

Damara exclaimed, finally lifting her lashes to meet his gaze. "I would have hated having Mr. Wilkins take you to court, or whatever he would have had to do."

"Mr. Wilkins would have run in the other direction the moment I said boo to him," Simon declared, running his finger down the elegant line of her nose, laughing when she wrinkled it like a small child. "Happy, my love?"

"Very, although I did think that you would want to kiss me after we confessed our true feelings."

Simon smiled down into her hopeful face, wondering for the hundredth time what he had done to deserve such a delightful creature. "Do you love me enough to take Hastings on as a butler? I'm sure we can teach him to unbend just a little, and think of all the unwanted guests he will turn away."

"Yes, fine. Now, are you going to kiss me?" Though she was enjoying his teasing, Damara was growing impatient. She stuck out her lower lip in imitation of Justine's pout to see if it had any effect. It only made Simon laugh. Then she had a wicked idea; the man needed an incentive now that he was sure of her.

"Mara, I'm trying to have a serious discussion. I did mean what I said when I promised to consult your wishes on everything when we were married." Simon regarded her very solemnly as he made his speech.

"But you won't, and it was rather presumptuous of me to make you promise," she returned without rancor, smiling at his startled expression. "Of course, I won't consult your opinion on every little matter, either. Imagine if I had to check with you on every single garment I wore or purchased. We'll talk over important matters, like raising children for instance."

Simon smiled sheepishly at her example and nodded, but he still made no move to seal their true engagement with a kiss. Damara pushed back from the circle of his arms and began to unbutton the top of her habit very slowly. As she released the first button, she looked at Simon in anticipation. He stopped her after the second button, though his eyes seemed to be riveted to the shadowy cleavage she had uncovered thus far.

"What are you doing?" he asked in a choked voice with his large hand holding both of hers still.

"Well, Regina said that a gentleman didn't always limit himself to kissing on the lips," she explained very patiently, wondering how she dared. "So I thought it might be awkward later on if you—"

"Come here," Simon snarled and pulled her against his chest. Before she could say another word, his chiseled mouth came down to claim her parted lips. Damara could feel her toes curling at the first touch of his mouth. After that she forgot everything that Regina had told her, deciding that experiencing it was much nicer than just being told about it.

All too soon she was brought back down to earth as the coach came to a stop. Percy's excited voice could be heard mingling with Cretin's barks.

"You would have to spend most of the time talking," Damara sighed against Simon's mouth, unwilling to move though she knew she must.

"Young lady, it's past time someone took you in hand," Simon declared, kissing her quickly one last time while deftly rebuttoning her habit. "By this time next week, we'll not have interruptions."

"Promises, promises," she murmured for his ears alone as he lifted her out of the coach. Lady Kath, Sir Cedric, and Regina spilled out of the house without causing Hastings to blink. He simply nodded to Damara and climbed back up into the driver's box to take the empty coach back to Hanover Square.

"Thank heaven, you'll all unharmed," Regina exclaimed, managing to hug Simon and Damara at the same time. "You won't believe what has happened. No one will know a thing about your little venture because it's already all over the city that the Duke of Cumberland murdered his valet last night. Can you imagine? They say it was over the man's wife."

"Aunt Gina, Damara is going upstairs to rest from our little venture as you call it," Simon ordered, giving his fiancée a chaste kiss on the forehead before turning back to his godmother. "And before another minute passes, I'm going to find out exactly what you have been telling her about kissing."

— Epilogue —

England, October 1810

Damara made her way down the ornate oak staircase, absently patting the Emsley panthers carved into each newel post as she passed. The staircase that descended into the octagonal, oak-paneled entry was one of the two architectural features of the original Elizabethan structure they had been able to salvage at Emsley Hall. All the other rooms, except the Great Chamber that Simon claimed for his library, had been gutted and converted into light, airy rooms. The large case clock at the foot of the stairs boomed out the hour of midnight as she came down the last step.

She hardly missed the pink brick and stone-faced walls of Tarrant's Mount now that she was settled in her new home. Being a marchioness was agreeing with her nicely, although she wondered where her husband had disappeared for the past few hours. In honor of the house being ready for company, they had done what was expected and invited their friends and family to celebrate the occasion. The newly appointed rooms were filled to overflowing with the Earl and Countess of Layston, young Percy and Cretin, who had managed to discover the reflecting pool in the garden within minutes of his arrival, Sir Cedric and Lady Kath, and of course, the Earl and Countess of Covering. Lord Covering proved to be the ideal mate for his outspoken wife, an older version of his son in appearance.

While the ladies spent most of the first day going from room to room, the gentlemen took themselves out of doors away from the trappings of domestic life. They had all met again at dinner, recounting their adventures while in London in the spring. Simon announced he would take Damara again next year, if she promised the trip would be uneventful. The gentlemen then disappeared for the rest of the evening.

Damara had a fair idea where they had gone and exactly how they were occupying their time, especially if it kept Simon from bed this late. She felt herself flush at the thought, though no one was about, for her husband often commented how he enjoyed country hours when he carried her off to their bedchamber.

Shielding her candle from a sudden draft, she opened the oak-paneled door that lead to the private rooms of the house. When she saw the light coming from beneath the library door, she smiled. She had run them to ground and would soon see if her other guess was correct. Quietly she opened the door and peeked into the room.

The gaming table was set up in the middle of the room. The men were oblivious to the intricately carved panels of religious motifs while they smoked their cigars and concentrated on their cards. Only one man stood up when she entered the room, and she waved Hastings back in his seat. She approached her husband, laying a gentle hand on his shoulder, which he immediately covered with his own.

"Dare I ask what you are playing?" she inquired, studying her husband's cards over his shoulder, then eyeing the money in the center of the table.

"Dealer's choice, so as the dealer I naturally requested *Poque*," her brother announced without looking up from his hand.

"Dashed complicated game," Covering muttered.

"Who is winning?" Damara continued her questioning, knowing who usually came out ahead.

"Hastings, of course," Simon grumbled, watching the butler bet with a jaundiced eye. Hastings merely smiled at his mistress, who winked in return. "And it's my bet, before you ask."

Damara sighed, knowing that if she did not do something, they would be at it all night. The news she had been waiting to tell her husband privately could not be put off, in her opinion. "Well, my dear, you should hold onto your money and save it for Hastings's wages. I have something else you can use instead."

"What would I use in place of money?" Simon asked,

finally looking up from his cards. He frowned when he noticed his wife's manner of dress. She was wearing a cloak over her nightdress. From the ice blue material that peeked from beneath the hem, he knew exactly what nightdress and hoped the cloak remained closed.

"Since you have a history of betting unusual collateral, I thought you could bet your firstborn child. I doubt, however, any of the gentlemen will be willing to wait the needed six months for payment."

"Six months?" Simon echoed, looking at his wife as though she had gone daft, then he went white as her meaning sank in. "Damara! You could have waited to tell me."

"When?" she challenged in return with a triumphant smile.

"She has you there. Congratulations, sister dear," Jasper called across the table, raising his glass and waited for the others to follow suit in a toast to the news.

"Gentlemen, it seems I must leave you in the hands of my butler and retire to discuss this with my wife," Simon stated when he placed his glass back on the table. He grabbed Damara's hand and walked rapidly toward the door with Damara skipping to keep up with his long-legged strides.

"I would have taken the bet," Jasper called just before they reached the door.

"It would have to be made first. I have learned my lesson, though the outcome the first time was exceptional," Simon called back over his shoulder. "I only bet money in games of chance."